THE
SPECIALIST

NEW YORK TIMES AND USA TODAY BESTSELLING AUTHOR

MELANIE MORELAND

MEN OF
HIDDEN JUSTICE

Dear Reader,

Thank you for selecting The Specialist to read. Be sure to sign up for my newsletter for up to date information on new releases, exclusive content and sales. You can find the form here: https://bit.ly/MMorelandNewsletter

Before you sign up, add melanie@melaniemoreland.com to your contacts to make sure the email comes right to your inbox! **Always fun - never spam!**

My books are available in paperback and audiobook! You can see all my books available and upcoming preorders at my website.

The Perfect Recipe For **LOVE**
xoxo,
Melanie

THE SPECIALIST by Melanie Moreland
Copyright © 2022 Moreland Books Inc.
Copyright #1197532
ISBN Ebook 978-1-990803-20-8
Paperback 978-1-990803 -22-2
All rights reserved

MORELAND
BOOKS INC.

Edited by Lisa Hollett of Silently Correcting Your Grammar
Proofing by Sisters Get Lit.erary Services
Cover design by Karen Hulseman, Feed Your Dreams Designs
Cover Photography by Eric D Battershell, O'Snap Media
Cover Model Christian Petrovich
Cover content is for illustrative purposes only and any person depicted
on the cover is a model.

of fiction, which have been used without permission. The publication/use of these trademarks is not authorized, associated with, or sponsored by the trademark owners.

Readers with concerns about content or subjects depicted can check out the content advisory on my website: https://melaniemoreland.com/extras/fan-suggestions/content-advisory/

DEDICATION

For all the fans who went along for the ride,
Love you!

A special thanks to Maria Mititelu for all your assistance with this
book. I appreciate your valuable explanations to honor Egan's
heritage.

And to my Matthew.
Always.

CHAPTER ONE

Egan

The hallway was dim, the walls crumbling. Dusty from years of unuse. The mold and decay were all around me. I traced the miles of cable, checking and rechecking every inch. Ensuring the charges were in the correct place, the amount of dynamite exactly as needed to bring down the building in a perfect synchronization of an inward sequence.

As always, I felt the thrill of anticipation. The high knowing all the work, the planning, and the intricate details would soon pay off. Soon, where a tall building once stood, only a pile of rubble would remain.

Hours passed as I did the final inspection. Everything was perfect. I had overseen every detail, calculated and recalculated the explosives.

The building would fall faultlessly.

Outside, I headed to the control area. I was alone, which seemed odd, but I continued. I did one final sweep of the building, finding zero heat sources. I hoped no small animals wandered in at the last moment seeking shelter, but I knew it happened at times. The haven they sought became their final resting place, but better them than a homeless person or a curious onlooker. That had never happened, thank God.

I checked all the cameras, pleased to see them working. The implosion would be captured as the building went down, both inside and outside. I would use it to study, seeing if I could have changed something, if something needed fixing next time, or God forbid, it didn't explode the way it should have today. But I was confident. Ready.

I looked around as dawn broke. The building would collapse as the sun rose. One life ending as another day began. I felt as if there were some sort of poetic justice.

I flicked open all the controls. Checked the area. Began the countdown over the loudspeakers, that was followed by the warnings. Had the thumbs-up and okays from all the people connected to the project. We were all clear. Far from the building on the edge of the site, some people gathered to watch it come down. They were distant enough to be safe but had a great view as the building collapsed. For some, it was a hobby, watching structures being demolished —their fascination endless. Security kept them from getting too close. I frowned as I looked around, wondering why no one else was on-site with me. Usually, a few people watched from behind the controls, but today, it seemed I was alone. Once I had the final all clear, I pressed the button, the one-minute timer beginning to count down to one.

Something niggled at me, growing in my mind. I felt a sudden swell of anxiety, then one of pure fear, blossom in my chest. I stumbled back from the controls, gasping for air, unsure what was happening. A small light came on, indicating a heat source in the building. Ignoring the crippling agony in my chest, I checked the cameras, shocked to see a person in the building. I zoomed in, terror dripping from my throat as I focused on the face of the woman sitting in a chair in the middle of an empty building.

Sofia.

My Sofia.

How had she gotten there? What was going on?

I pressed the kill switch, horrified when nothing happened. "Get out!" I shouted, pressing it again. "Sofia, my love, get out!"

She stared at the camera, shaking her head. I saw she was tied to the chair, helpless.

She was trapped high in the building, and I couldn't get to her.

I began to scream her name, desperately hitting the control keys, trying sequence after sequence to stop the explosives from detonating. She looked at me, her lips moving.

"I love you," she said.

Another voice whispered somewhere around me. *"Stop this, Egan. You have to stop this. Only you can prevent this from happening."*

I knew that voice. Quavery and soft, I knew it. But it was impossible.

Then the explosions started, and the screen went black. I fell backward, the pain of the moment overwhelming and intense. It felt as if I had been blown apart in that building with her.

I woke up screaming, drenched in sweat, panic-stricken, and on the floor.

My gasping breaths were ragged and filled with fear. I looked around the room, trying to get myself under control.

I was in my apartment. The light in the corner was dim but offered me the security I needed at the moment. I was safe. I was home.

I bolted to my feet.

Sofia.

I grabbed my cell phone, pressing her name, the rings far too long. But she picked up, her voice filled with curiosity. I never called her at work.

"Egan?"

"Sofia," I gasped out, clutching my hair and pulling on it. "My love, are you all right?"

She sounded impatient. "Of course, I'm all right. I'm at work. What is it? Why are you calling?"

When I didn't respond, she dropped her voice. "Egan? What's wrong?"

I lifted my head, brushing away the dampness under my eyes. "I had a dream. I had to check on you."

"I'm fine. What was the dream about?"

"You—you were in trouble, and I could not get to you," was all I could say. I couldn't tell her the truth.

Her voice softened more. "It was just a dream. I'm fine," she assured me.

"I will pick you up in the morning."

"Egan, I have my car."

"Breakfast, then. I will cook for you."

"Waffles?" she asked teasingly.

"Yes. And decent coffee."

"Dark water, you mean."

It was our thing. As a doctor, Sofia was used to the tar they drank in the on-call room. I made good coffee that tasted the way it should, rich and full—not like burned rubber. She teased me all the time. I needed her humor right now.

"You love it, woman."

"Good God, stop with the caveman shit, Egan. My love, *woman*," she snorted. "You know it drives me crazy. I have told you a hundred times, we are friends. Just friends."

She was wrong there, but I didn't argue with her.

"I will be waiting."

"Okay," she agreed. "Try to go back to sleep. Can you do that?" she asked, a note of worry in her voice.

I smiled at the sound of it. Regardless of what she claimed, she cared.

And soon, I would make her admit to it.

"Yes. I will see you shortly."

I hung up, looking around my bedroom. I had lied— I doubted I would go back to sleep now. The dream had been so real. I had felt the wires under my fingers. Smelled the decay of the building. Felt the almost sexual pull of knowing the rubble my work would produce. It was always a rush.

I had also felt the terror. Hers and mine. Watched helplessly as she died.

I shook my head, reminding myself it was nothing

but a dream. One I didn't understand, but that was all it was.

I ignored the sudden flash of memory of my grandmother back in the old country, who used to dream of things that made no sense. She would pick apart a dream and warn you of things to come. People came from miles around to seek her opinion. She always said I had the same talent. She used to boast to people, because we shared the same birth date, that I had gotten that "gift" from her. She looked forward to watching it develop. She died before we left Romania.

Yet…I had heard her soft voice in my dream.

Hadn't I?

I stood, dismissing the thoughts. That was all folklore and bullshit, and I had no idea why I'd suddenly remembered it. She had been a sweet old lady who liked to make up stories to entertain herself. I hadn't thought about it in years. I didn't believe her then, and I didn't believe her now.

I lived in the real world. And the mumblings and warnings of my late grandmother had no place here.

I refused to admit it was her voice I had heard in my dream.

I decided to get up and do some paperwork. With all my businesses, there was always paperwork.

It would help pass the time until Sofia showed up.

I wouldn't rest until I saw her face.

CHAPTER TWO

Sofia

I leaned my head on the hard metal wall of the elevator, grateful to be home. I had worked extra to cover a shift for a fellow doctor, and he was returning the favor by covering for me tomorrow night. So I only had to get through one more night and I could sleep as much as I wanted.

"One more night," I whispered. "Just one more night."

I huffed a laugh to myself. My body was so used to the lack of sleep, I doubted I would sleep much anyway. I glanced at my watch, noting it was three o'clock. I had seven hours until I had to be back at the hospital for the shift. I would sleep for a while, eat, then head back in.

Egan would understand my canceling dinner plans. He always understood, his patience seemingly endless. He was understanding when I'd texted him earlier, putting off breakfast since I had to cover the shift. He assured me he would make us dinner instead.

I sighed and rubbed my eyes.

Egan.

I had no idea what to do about him. The man of many sides. Dark and light rolled into one. Deadly when he needed to be. I had seen him in action. He was lethal. Then in the blink of an eye, he would turn into the sweetest man I had ever met. He was a great neighbor. Helpful, kind, protective. Damien, my cousin, thought the world of him. Egan was an amazing friend who would do anything for me.

But he wanted so much more.

More than I could give.

I had made that clear to him more than once, and he always nodded, never reacting badly, quietly continuing on with his quest for us to be together, no matter how I tried to discourage him.

With my past, I couldn't be with him. I didn't want to be with anyone. My heart couldn't bear another loss.

So, we had to stay friends.

The elevator door opened, and the man I had been thinking about stood there. My breath caught, simply looking at him.

Friend or not, he was an incredible specimen of a man.

Tall and lean, with muscles in all the right places, he was extremely sexy. Solid. His biceps were impressive, his torso taut. I was average height for a woman, but at 6'5", he towered over me, making me feel small. The scruff he was wearing these days dusted his jaw, highlighting his lean, hawklike face. His profile was chiseled and sharp. His hair was swept high off his forehead, one dark brown lock hanging to the left. His eyes were a rich green with flecks of deep coffee in them. Set under heavy brows, they were expressive and intense. I had a thing for hands, and Egan's were incredible. Large, with long, tapered fingers capable of building a bomb that could wipe out a block of houses in a moment or touching me with the gentlest of caresses.

His gaze met mine, and not for the first time, I glimpsed his desire. It smoldered and beckoned in his gaze. I saw something else in his stare today. Something I couldn't place. He held out his hand, his voice low and raspy.

"Sofia," he murmured. *"Iubirea mea."*

I didn't know what the words meant, although I had a feeling I wouldn't be happy if I did. The way he said them was saturated in emotion. It stirred something in me I tried to ignore.

"Egan," I replied.

I let him take my hand, refusing to admit how right it felt when his long fingers closed around mine. He drew me close, wrapping me in his arms.

"You are okay?" he asked.

I let the moment surround me the way his body was. Warmth, safety, and something else filled my chest. Something I didn't want to name.

"I'm fine," I replied.

I felt the press of his lips on my head, and he drew back, studying me.

"You are tired."

"I am."

He tugged on my hand. "Come with me."

"Egan, I need to sleep."

He frowned. "I know this. I have it all ready."

I let him take me into his apartment. "Have what all ready?"

"A bath. Food. Then you sleep. I drive you to hospital after."

I opened my mouth to object, but the aroma of whatever he was cooking stopped me. My stomach grumbled at the appetizing scent.

"I have a bathtub," I protested weakly. It was the truth, but Egan's was bigger. Deeper. Perfect for soaking.

"No. You are staying here until you go." He stopped in front of me. "Please. I am begging of you."

I tilted my head. He looked upset. His accent was thicker, his words not as precise as usual. His eyes held a wariness I wasn't used to seeing. I recalled his phone call in the early morning hours and the anxiety I had heard in his voice. I stepped closer, cupping his cheek. "What is it, Egan? What is wrong?"

He sighed, a long, heavy exhale of air, and leaned his cheek into my hand. He covered it with his much larger one, silent for a moment, his eyes closed. It was as if he was drawing strength from my touch. Then with another exhale, he straightened, opening his eyes and meeting mine.

"All is well. I am being a friend. You are tired. I am looking after you."

I opened my mouth to speak, but he laid a finger on my lips, silencing me.

"For my friend," he stated again. "Now, come."

I let him lead me to the bathroom, not surprised to

see the tub filled, a candle lit, and a large towel waiting for me.

"Are you tracking me?" I half joked. "Is that how you knew I was home and got all this ready?"

"I sense you near," was all he said. "You relax."

He backed out of the room, and I stared at the closed door.

I sense you near.

I tried to repress the delicious shiver I felt at his intimate words.

I failed.

I stepped from the tub, relaxed and warm, then realized I had no clean clothes to change into. Obviously, Egan had thought of that too, and on the vanity were a T-shirt and a pair of his boxers. I hesitated a moment, then slipped them on. The shirt came down past my thighs, and the boxers were loose like a pair of shorts. Egan had seen me in a bathing suit and this covered way more, so I decided simply to go with it.

I bundled up my clothes and headed back to the living room, suddenly starved. Egan glanced up, a strange look passing over his face, then he looked back to what he was doing with a small shake of his head. He muttered something under his breath, a slight smile tugging on his lips.

I stopped. "What?"

He looked up, his eyes no longer anxious. They were dark. Heated. A shiver ran through me at the barely held passion I could see in them. But his voice was mild as he spoke. "You are...*delightful* in my clothes." Then he indicated the high counter. "Sit and let me feed you."

It was the accent. That had to be it. There was no other explanation for why so many of the things he said to me sounded so intimate. Normally, he spoke carefully, choosing his words and enunciating them deliberately, his accent controlled. But when we were alone, or he was upset, angry, or in the moment, his control slipped and his accent came out stronger. I loved hearing it, but I never told him that.

He slid a bowl in front of me, and I inhaled deeply.

"Oh, I love your mushroom soup."

He grinned and placed a bowl for himself beside me. We ate in silence for a few moments. The dense rye bread was fresh and speckled with caraway seeds. The mushroom soup didn't taste like the kind that came from a can. It was thick, rich with spices, and laden with mushrooms. I loved it when he made it. He had told me in Romania that soup was very popular, and although I had tasted various kinds, this one was my favorite.

I eyed him surreptitiously. I loved watching him eat. His white teeth tore through the bread as if it had somehow insulted him. He chewed slowly, ate his soup carefully, his manners impeccable, and so in contrast with his appetite. It was voracious. I had to stop the thoughts that kept repeating in my head, wondering if all his appetites were the same.

He finished his bowl and stood, rounding the counter. He turned to the stove, opening the door and sliding out dishes. I finished my own soup, knowing not to interfere. Egan could cook like a dream. Romanian, Italian, Chinese, even simple, regular everyday things like burgers—any sort of cuisine. My favorites, though, were his Romanian dishes. I loved them. I was lucky if I boiled water correctly. I lived on salads, precooked chicken from the grocery store, or whatever hot foods the deli had ready. I could make toast and pancakes. Heat up something. That was all.

Egan held out his hand, and I gave him my empty bowl. He slid a plate in front of me. "Eat, *iubirea mea.*"

I stared at the full plate. Cabbage rolls, potato salad, and some sort of sausage-looking meat filled the plate. He'd made me the cabbage rolls before and the delicious Romanian potato salad, and I loved them both, but I had never seen the meat dish.

He sat beside me with a frown.

"You not like dinner?"

"No, I love it. But what is the meat?"

"*Mici,*" he said. "Beef, pork, spices. Delicious. Try it."

I took a bite and shut my eyes at the flavor. "*So* delicious," I praised him.

He nodded, looking pleased. He pushed a dip my way. "We usually eat it with mustard, but I like it with this."

I dipped the meat in a creamy dill sauce. "Wow. Is that Romanian too?" I asked, dipping another piece.

"No," he said with a laugh. "That's Egan."

I took another bite of the meal, and Egan watched me eat, leaning close to wipe a bit of dip off the corner of my mouth. I watched, fascinated, as he slipped his thumb into his mouth, licking off the sauce. He kept his gaze locked on mine, and I had to drop my eyes as a surge of heat went through me.

He grinned at my reaction and picked up his fork.

I had to be more tired than I thought. My reactions to him were all over the map tonight.

I lowered my head and concentrated on my meal.

EGAN

My God, she was beautiful. Sitting at my counter, eating my food, wearing my clothes. I wanted this every day. I wanted her to want that. But I couldn't seem to break through her walls. I saw how she watched me. The flickers of interest. Even the flashes of lust. But she refused to act on it. I had to figure out how to break through her resistance.

She moaned around a mouthful of cabbage rolls. I made all her favorites. I kept cabbage rolls in the freezer, always ready to heat up for her. The potato salad I made earlier, as well as the soup and *mici*. She loved the flavors of the olives, pickles, and tang of the dressing on the salad. Very different from the mayonnaise-based ones I had eaten here. She loved everything I cooked for her.

I wanted her to allow me to cook for her every day.

With a sigh, she laid down her fork. "Egan, that was incredible."

"More?" I asked.

She shook her head. "I'm as stuffed as your cabbage rolls."

I laughed at her statement.

"I'll send some to work with you for midnight snack."

She groaned. "If I get a break. We're swamped all the time."

I studied her, unable to stop myself from touching her. I ran a finger under her eye. "You are exhausted, *iubirea mea.*"

She narrowed her eyes. "What does that mean?"

"Buddy, friend, pal," I lied smoothly.

She eyed me in disbelief and reached for her water, sipping the liquid. I watched her delicate neck muscles flex as she swallowed. The way she licked her lips, catching the little drops with her tongue. I wanted those lips underneath mine. Her tongue in my mouth. Her skin gliding along my own.

She was incredibly lovely to me. The perfect height to kiss. Her long, dark hair hung straight down her back, often caught up in a bun at her neck. Her eyes were a deep, rich brown, her skin looking as if she had been freshly kissed by the sun. She had a beautiful smile and, even more important, a beautiful soul. She was kind, funny, and caring. A brilliant doctor. Sexy as hell without even knowing it.

And unattainable.

"I don't know if I believe you," she replied. "It doesn't sound like buddy, pal, or friend."

"What does it sound like?" I asked.

"Personal," she responded.

I stood, taking our plates. "Do not ask questions you do not want the answers to, my Sofia."

I could feel her gearing up to argue, but she stayed quiet. Surprised, I looked over my shoulder and saw she was yawning. She blinked, shaking her head. "I ate too much."

"No, you ate the right amount. You are working so hard. You need to rest."

"You're right. I'll go home. Thank you for——"

She never finished her sentence. I had swooped her into my arms, and I was headed down the hall before she realized what I was doing.

"Egan," she protested. "Put me down!"

I shook my head and carried her to my room. I liked how she felt in my arms. She did as well. I could tell by the way her body softened against me, nestling close. I laid her on the bed, pulling the blanket over her as she protested. I leaned over her, caging her in. "You are staying here." I pressed the button beside the bed. "This room will be dark and quiet," I explained as the blinds lowered, blocking out the late-afternoon light. "You can rest better. Your apartment gets too much light this time of day."

She tried to argue, and before I knew what I was doing, I kissed her. The second my mouth touched hers, something inside me settled. She gasped as our lips melded together, moving in perfect synchronization as if they had done it a thousand times. I didn't deepen the kiss but kept my mouth on hers in soft, light caresses. Then I lifted my head, our eyes locking.

"You will stay here and sleep. I will wake you later."

I drifted a finger down her cheek. "For me, Sofia. Please."

"You keep saying please."

"Because today, I need this."

"You kissed me."

"I needed that too."

"We're friends."

"Yes, we are. We are more too, Sofia. And soon, we will talk about it. But for now, you need to sleep." I pressed a kiss to her head and forced myself to leave her alone in my bed. I turned at the door, looking at her. Her hair was spread over my pillow, and I knew, later, I would smell her on my sheets. She watched me warily, and I smiled, flicking off the light, plunging the room into darkness.

"I'm here if you need me," I told her.

Shutting the door and walking away was the hardest thing I had ever done.

CHAPTER THREE

Egan

I checked on her frequently. I told myself it was because I wanted to make sure she was all right, but the truth was, I simply liked to look at her. She was curled up in a ball, holding one pillow, her head resting on the other as she slumbered. One long, sexy leg was on top of the blanket, and no matter how often I drew the blanket back over her leg, she kicked it off. I ghosted my fingers over her calf, wondering how it would feel to have her legs wrapped around me as I sank inside her. Felt the heat of her around my cock. Heard her gasps of pleasure as I took her.

I had to leave the room before I succumbed to the temptation.

I let her sleep as long as I could, sitting on the bed beside her and running my hand through her hair. It felt like silk under my fingers, and I grinned as she blinked awake. She was sleepy and soft, smiling at me without hiding her affection. "Hi," she murmured.

"Hello, *iubirea mea*. It is time to go to work. I made you coffee."

She sat up, accepting the mug and sipping it. "You make good coffee."

I chuckled. "I know."

"What time is it?"

"Just after ten. You can go and change. I made you some food to eat later and a snack for the car. I will pick you up in the morning."

"Egan, I can drive—"

I cut her off. "For tonight, indulge me."

She studied me, then linked her fingers with mine. She looked at our hands clasped together. Did she see what I saw? How right it was the way mine enfolded hers? Protected it? How well they fit together?

"That must have been some dream," she murmured.

I didn't reply, and she glanced up, meeting my gaze. "Fine, you can drive me tonight and pick me up in the morning. I get my waffles I missed earlier, right?"

I leaned forward and kissed the end of her nose affectionately. "You get anything you want."

She pushed me away. "Okay, I have to go get dressed."

I waited until she was ready and drove her to the hospital. "You work too much."

She laughed. "With HJ gone, I have lots of time on my hands. I love my job."

"I hate the nights. I worry with you out of the building. The things you must see in the ER."

She shrugged. "You see terrible things on day shift too. Holidays and full moons are the worst. And it's not forever. I really want to open my own practice with another doctor. But I'm saving up and waiting for the right partner. Our medical system is so broken right now, and we need more family doctors."

"I can give you money. Not a problem." I pulled up in front of the hospital, turning to her. "Anything you need. You ask me. It is yours."

"I can't do that, Egan."

"Why?" I demanded.

"I refuse to rely on anyone but myself. I will open a practice when I can do so on my own terms."

She unclipped her seat belt, and I covered her hand with mine. "You can rely on me, Sofia. I am not going anywhere."

She smiled sadly. "I'll see you in the morning."

"I will be here." I leaned over the seat, looking up at her standing next to the car. "Always."

She shook her head and walked into the hospital.

I returned home and called Damien. It was before dawn on his side of the world but I knew he'd be around.

He answered fast, sounding pleased to hear from me. "Egan, how are you, my friend?"

"Frustrated," I muttered.

Damien chuckled, knowing what I was referring to. "I warned you."

"You've been gone months," I replied. "I thought once you left and we spent more time together, Sofia would realize how good we are," I grumbled, running a hand through my hair. "Why does she push me away, Damien?" I asked. "She feels this. I know she does. I am at my end rope."

"You mean the end *of* your rope."

"Whatever. I am there."

"She has history. It makes her wary."

"I don't want to be part of her past. I want to be her future."

He sighed. "It isn't my story to tell. Raven told you to be honest with your feelings. Have you done that?"

"No. I worry if I do, she will refuse to see me. At least now, even if she suspects, she is part of my life."

"You can't keep going like that, Egan." He paused. "She went through some bad stuff. More than once. I'm not sure she can risk her heart again. Even if she wants to."

"No," I said emphatically. "This is different."

"I'm not sure she agrees."

I rubbed my aching temples, not wanting to discuss it any further. "How is Raven?"

His woman had been stalked by a madman. A highly clever one. It took us a while to find the perp, and he had kidnapped her before we were able to identify him. We got her back safely, but Raven had found it hard to move past what had happened, and she and Damien had moved to the island, where she felt protected again.

"She is doing really well. The longer we're here, the better she is. She's busy with the children and teaching. She smiles all the time," he said, his voice filled with affection.

"Have you asked her to marry you yet?"

"Yes. But we're not in a hurry. My mom is having hip surgery in a few months and can't travel until she heals, so we're going to wait. I would really like her here for it. Raven is wearing my ring, so I'm happy. We're committed to each other, and it's a formality, really. She is already mine."

"Lucky man," I mumbled.

"Bring Sofia and come for a visit soon," he insisted. "This place is magical."

I hung up and sat lost in thought. It felt as if I needed more than magic to make Sofia love me.

I needed a miracle.

I dozed some, made up the waffle batter, letting it sit as I drove to get Sofia. She was waiting outside, under the entrance. It was overcast and drizzling, the gray of the day matching my mood. She was quiet as she got in the car, and I handed her a cup of coffee. "Decaf," I explained. "So you can sleep after breakfast."

"I'll only take a nap," she replied. "I'm off for the next few days, so I want to be able to sleep tonight."

I glanced at her, something in her voice off.

"Are you okay?"

She nodded, her gaze focused out the window.

"Long night," was all she said.

Needing to touch her, I reached over and wrapped my hand around hers that was resting on her thigh. I squeezed her fingers and began to pull back. She shocked me when she grabbed my hand, holding tight. I was even more shocked when I saw a glimmer of tears in her eyes that she tried to hide from me. I had rarely seen Sofia cry. Once when she'd treated Missy, Marcus's woman, and listened to her ordeal, and once when Damien left. It hurt my chest to see her tears.

I held her hand in mine. "Did you lose a patient?" I asked quietly, knowing how deeply that affected her.

"No."

I left it alone, knowing if she wanted to talk, she would. Back at the apartment, she showered and once again donned a shirt of mine. I made the waffles she liked, watching helplessly as she pushed them around her plate, barely tasting them. I was on edge after my conversation with Damien, and I leaned over, pushing her hair away from her face.

"You didn't lose a patient, but something happened." I studied her eyes. There was an expression on her face and a look in her eyes I had never seen before. "Tell me."

"I helped work on a couple that came in after a car accident. Not my patient, but Dan needed another set of hands. The passenger died. The driver, Ann, survived."

"Spouses?" I asked.

"No," she whispered. "Best friends. Out celebrating her new job. They were going through a green light and were T-boned."

"I am sorry."

"After he died and she was told, I was walking past the lounge. She was in there, alone, staring out the window. She shouldn't have been out of the bed. She had some bad injuries as well. I went in to tell her and help her back to her room, and she started to talk to me about him. Felix was his name. Ann told me they'd been friends for five years. Best friends who did everything together."

I slipped my hand over hers, something telling me she needed my touch. She gripped my fingers again, holding tight. "She said that last week, Felix told her that he loved her. She told him she didn't feel the same way. She thought of him as a friend only. She cared about him deeply, but not the same way. Apparently he informed her that was fine. He'd give her time to get used to the idea, and once she figured out the truth, he'd be waiting."

Sofia was quiet, looking down at our clasped hands. "She said when she saw him lying on the gurney in the ambulance, she realized he was right. She was lying to herself. She loved him and couldn't imagine her life without him. That no matter how scared she was, she was going to tell him when he woke up."

"Except he didn't," I gently finished for her.

Sofia shook her head, her eyes bright with tears. "She said she would forever go through life regretting being afraid. That she hated the fact that he died thinking she didn't love him. She said she would never get over losing him." She was quiet for a moment. "I've never seen such heartbreak in someone's eyes, Egan. The regret and pain were overwhelming."

"You see yourself—you see *us* in her."

"Yes," she whispered.

I slipped my fingers under her chin. "Why do you resist how you feel, Sofia, *iubirea mea?*"

"Because I'm afraid."

Unable to stop myself, I cupped her face. "You feel something for me," I stated. It wasn't a question. We both knew the answer.

She shut her eyes. "Yes."

I leaned closer, my heartbeat getting faster. "Tell me why."

"Everyone I have ever loved has left me."

"I will not leave you."

"You don't understand."

"Understand what?"

A tear slipped down her cheek.

"They die, Egan. They always die."

CHAPTER FOUR

Egan

I poured us each a brandy. Sofia liked the flavor, and it would help relax her. I had a feeling I was going to need the liquor when she told her story.

I sat beside her, handing her the glass, urging her to drink it. She swirled the glass in her hands, staring down at the liquid. I took it from her, recalling how cold her hands were earlier, and I warmed the glass in mine, then gave it back to her. She smiled in gratitude and took a sip, letting out a long sigh.

"You can tell me anything," I encouraged her.

She didn't speak for a moment, running a hand through her hair and shutting her eyes. I remained silent, knowing she was gathering her thoughts. What she was going to tell me was pivotal to our relationship. I knew that as surely as I knew how strong my feelings for this woman were.

"When I was in medical school, I met Darren. We were friends who became more. Our goals were so similar. What we wanted from life was the same.

Become a doctor, do some good in the world. Get married, have kids. We were great partners. He asked me to marry him, and I said yes." She paused, meeting my eyes. "Are you sure you want to hear this?"

I had to stifle all my jealousy. Lock it down. I didn't want to think of Sofia with anyone else. I knew she had a past. I did as well. I had to remind myself that what she was telling me was exactly that. The past. I would listen, and then we could move forward. I kept my voice calm.

"Yes. I need to understand."

"We were doing a rotation in the same hospital in the ER. A patient came in, out of his mind on drugs. We had to get security and restrain the patient. He kept trying to attack us, and it was the only way to treat him. One of the staff helping didn't fasten the restraints tight enough on one side."

She fell silent, her eyes filled with tears. I already guessed what happened next, but I let her tell me the story in her own way. When she spoke again, her voice was thick.

"He got out of the restraints. He had a gun hidden in his clothing. He started shooting wildly, and Darren stepped in front of me and took the bullet meant for me. He died in my arms a few moments later."

"I'm sorry," I said. "That must have been traumatizing."

"It was."

"Did the patient go to jail?"

She shook her head. "He had a seizure shortly after that he never woke up from. He died later that night."

"Your fiancé was a brave man. He must have loved you a great deal."

"He died because of me."

"He died protecting you," I said gently. "His choice and, for that, I consider him a brave, honorable man."

I saw the tremor in her hand, and I took her glass, lifting it to her lips. "Take a sip, Sofia," I murmured. "Everything is all right, *iubirea mea*. Perhaps sharing the memories will help take away some of the pain, yes?"

She swallowed the brandy, the faraway look in her eyes still present.

"Did you have help getting over his loss?" I asked.

She shrugged. "When you're a resident, you don't have time for much except being a resident. Most of my friends were other residents. I had no family—my dad died when I was young, and my mom passed just after I got into medical school. But I had Damien. We'd been close all our lives since we were so near in age. And he was great—always willing to listen or take me out if I needed it, but he was busy too. I was given a little time off for bereavement, but I had to go back and finish my rotation. The first time I walked back into that room, I almost lost it." She swallowed. "It took me a long time to get over losing him."

I set down the glass in my hand and shifted to the table in front of her. I took her hands in mine. "Of course it did."

She sighed, the sound shaky and sad. "But I kept going. I wanted to keep our dream alive. Become a doctor and open a practice. Slowly, I was able to move forward. I concentrated on my career. Made that my priority. A few years later, a cop came in with an ambulance. Will was concerned about the woman who had been brought in. He suspected domestic violence and wanted to help her. I worked the case, and he got her away from her abuser." She rubbed the back of her neck. "He came back a few times to say hello and finally asked me out."

"And you had a relationship with him."

"Yes. For two years. He was a great guy."

"I wouldn't expect you to fall for someone unless they were," I said dryly.

That made her smile, even though I felt the way she was tensing. "What happened?" I asked.

"He was on the job. Called to another domestic disturbance. It was the same abuser he'd dealt with before, but a different woman. There was an altercation, and Will was shot. He was brought in and died in surgery."

"Jesus."

"I was working, and I knew he was brought in. I saw him before surgery. His last words to me were that he loved me. I didn't say it back." She met my eyes, her tears overflowing. "I wanted to, but he passed out and they rushed him away. I never got to say it."

"Like the woman earlier."

"Yes."

I squeezed her hands.

"I can't be involved with you, Egan. What you do, how dangerous it is. If something happened to you, I don't think I would survive it."

My heart rate picked up at her confession. I shook my head, dropping her hands and cupping her face.

"I am out of Hidden Justice. I have been for a while. I run a gym. Work at Elite with Leo. Paint pictures."

"And blow things up when you can."

"I demolish the odd building, yes. Safely. Legally."

"You still help out with HJ when needed."

"I am strictly behind the scenes. Computers, and yes, the occasional demolition. Again, I'm invisible. I have never been an active agent. Always behind the scenes."

"I worried about Damien for years. He's safe now, but you're not—you're still on the fringes. I can't take another loss, Egan." Her voice dropped. "Especially you."

I tightened my hands, forcing her to meet my eyes. "Why? Tell me why."

She covered my hands with hers. "I can't. I can't be with you. I can't risk it."

"You can. You can choose to be with me instead of alone. The men who loved you in the past would want that for you. They would want you happy. I want to make you happy."

"You—"

"I will give it all up. Right now. No more freelance jobs. Nothing but the gym and working with Elite."

"I can't ask you to do that."

"You're not. I am telling you I would do that for you. For us. That is my job, Sofia. You are my world."

Her eyes widened at that statement. I kept talking.

"But I could be a plumber and still die suddenly.

There are no guarantees in life, Sofia. As a doctor, you know this. I could have a weak heart. A blocked artery. Get hit by a bus crossing the street. You wouldn't refuse to love me because of those odds. Why refuse to love me because of my past? What matters now is the future. Our future."

For a moment, there was silence, the only sound between us her harsh breathing.

"I have the same fears," I said quietly. "Losing you. Your job is not without its dangers as well."

She frowned, obviously never having given that idea much thought.

"I cannot fathom not having you in my life, Sofia. Having to suffer your loss. But it is a risk I am willing to take."

"I'm scared."

"I know. But, Sofia, you have feelings for me already. If I were gone tomorrow, wouldn't you mourn my loss?"

"Yes," she admitted.

"Then face it with me. Admit to your feelings. You already know mine."

"I'm so torn. My head says one thing, my heart another. Some days I just don't know..." Her voice trailed off.

"Then know this. I love you. I love you less today than I will tomorrow. More than I did yesterday. Infinitely. I will love you for the rest of my life. And I want to share the rest of my life with you."

She stared at me. "Love like that doesn't exist."

"It does. It is how I feel about you, and it will not

change. It exists. *I* exist. Trust me, and I promise I won't let you down."

More tears flowed down her face. "Egan..." she breathed.

"Choose me, Sofia. Choose us. Let me love you."

Her whole body shook.

"Say it, my Sofia. Say the words, and let's move forward." I leaned my forehead to hers. "Don't keep living with regrets."

A long shudder ran down her spine. "I have feelings for you," she whispered.

I smiled at her words, knowing her feelings were greater than she could express. But for now, I would take them.

"Deep ones?" I whispered, pressing a kiss to her skin.

"Yes."

"Deep enough you want me to kiss you?"

"Yes," she repeated, the one word a soft breath over my skin.

I pulled her onto my lap. "Thank God."

I kissed her face, tasting her tears. Her fear. Her body trembled in my embrace, and I tucked her closer, surrounding her. She wrapped her arms around my neck, and I held her, letting her feel me, giving her my strength, letting her lean on me. I would give her anything she needed, whatever it was. Whenever it was. As long as I could hold her, as long as I knew she felt something for me, we could work on this together.

Then I covered her mouth with mine.

Finally.

SOFIA

I had imagined kissing Egan for a long time. Tamped down every instinct to do so when it came to him. Ignored the flashes of lust, the desire that coursed through me when I would see him. I had to. I knew with Egan, it couldn't be casual. Nothing between us was. It was intense and compelling. Overwhelming.

But the moment his lips touched mine, I knew it was something else.

Life-changing.

Explosive.

His full lips were soft, warm, and caressing. Tender and sweet.

Until his tongue flicked on my bottom lip, and I opened my mouth for him.

Then he became everything I secretly hoped him to be.

His mouth commanded. Controlled. Possessed.

What started as gentle and exploring changed.

It was carnal. Deep. Wet. Passionate.

He hauled me higher up his chest, then stood, turning and sitting on the sofa so I straddled him. He caged me in his arms, banding them around my waist like bars of iron. Our chests melded together, making me wish our clothing was gone. Even through the fabric, I felt his heat, the temperature warming me, making me pliable and soft. Making me his to mold and shape.

His tongue slid along mine in sensuous passes. He

explored my mouth, his taste lingering. Brandy, mint, and Egan.

He was delicious. Addictive.

He made low noises in the back of his throat. His chest rumbled. He never stopped touching me, his hands delving under my shirt, dancing over the skin of my back, gripping my hips, pulling me closer, flicking over the sides of my breasts, his fingers caressing my nipples.

And all the while, his mouth making love to mine.

I had never been kissed like this. Never known a man to convey so much with his lips while not speaking a word. I felt his desire, his need, his want.

His love.

It settled into my bones, saturating my body. Spread into every crevice, drip by drip. Life-affirming. Life-altering.

He pulled back, dropping his head to my shoulder, turning his face into my neck, his breath hot on my skin.

"We have to stop."

"Why?" I whimpered, seeking his mouth again.

With a groan, he took my lips, nipping, tasting, pressing soft kisses to them.

"You are tired, *iubirea mea*. You need to rest. If we don't stop, I won't be able to control myself. There will not be sleep for hours. If even then."

I cupped the impressive erection trapped between us. "Maybe I don't want you to."

He groaned, the sound torn from his throat. "When I make you mine, it will be forever, Sofia. I want you to be sure."

I stilled, and he met my eyes, his voice raspy. "I will

wait."

He stood, taking me with him. He carried me down the hall, setting me on his bed and pulling the blanket over me. "You will sleep. I will watch over you," he said simply, sliding in beside me, leaning up on his elbow.

"You'll be bored."

"No. I will rest too. I didn't sleep well last night. My body sensed your turmoil."

"Pardon me?"

He traced a finger over my cheek. "My parents had a connection. They always said they could feel the other person's emotions. I used to laugh at them, thinking they were crazy—old folklore. But I get it. I feel you, Sofia. In my chest. In my mind. I know when you hurt. I feel your sadness. When you need more care. More distance." He frowned. "I hate that one, but I give it to you."

"Why have you been so patient?" I asked. "It's been over two years."

He lifted one shoulder. "I knew you would be worth it. I had your friendship. Your trust. I had faith, in time, the rest would follow. My connection to you was too strong for it not to." He tucked the blanket higher. "Sleep. Know I am here and will watch over you. Then when you wake, we will step forward." He leaned down and pressed a kiss to my head. "Together."

With a small sigh, I shut my eyes. I could feel Egan's warmth beside me. A solid weight of strength. I lifted my arm, settling it on his hip, and he pulled me tight to his chest, draping his arm over my waist. I buried my head into his chest and breathed him in. He always smelled so good, and I knew the cologne he wore was one of his own creations. Sensuous and deep, the notes of sandalwood, musk, and citrus were perfect on him. I sighed in contentment. "I love how you smell."

He kissed my head, not speaking. I began to drift when I heard his voice again.

"Soon you will be soaked in me, Sofia. Where I end, you will begin."

I liked the sound of that.

I woke up slowly, warm, more rested than I could remember feeling in a long time, and wrapped around Egan. He was leaning against the headboard, reading. I had my head on his stomach, my arms enfolded around his waist. I was curled into a ball beside him, the blankets pulled high over my shoulders. A plush pillow was under my head, and Egan stroked his fingers through my hair in gentle passes, pausing on occasion to turn the page. I peered up at him, studying him for a moment. He wore glasses, simple black frames that made him even sexier than usual. His chest was bare, a smattering of hair glinting in the light from the bedside table. He lifted his hand to turn the page and glanced down, meeting my eyes. He smiled as he shut his book, drifting his fingers down my cheek.

"Hello, *iubirea mea*. You are awake." He looked pleased. "You slept well."

I cleared my throat. "Yes, I did. What does that mean—those words you say in Romanian? I know it's not friend."

His eyes crinkled, and he shook his head. "No. It means 'my love.'"

"I see. You've been calling me that for months."

"You have been that for even longer," he said quietly, pulling off his glasses, meeting my gaze. His eyes were dark and intense. "I began to worry I would never be able to tell you how I felt. But I hope we are past that now." A smile broke out on his face. "I mean, you are in my bed."

"I was sleeping."

He tilted his head, studying me. "And now, you are awake," he murmured, his voice low and raspy.

We stared at each other, something hot and powerful building between us. I didn't know who moved first, but suddenly I was under Egan, his weight pressing me into the mattress. Our eyes locked. "You're naked," I whispered.

"I always sleep in the nude." He lowered his head, rubbing his chin across my breasts. "You're in my shirt."

My nipples tightened at the sensation of his caress. Still holding my eyes, he opened his lips and sucked one through the thin cotton. I gasped at the feel of his mouth and teeth, the suction. I felt it everywhere. He moved to the other nipple, and I groaned, sliding my hand into his hair.

"You like that, my Sofia? You like my mouth on you?"

I whimpered as he pushed up the shirt, dropping wet, open-mouthed kisses to my stomach, tracing his tongue along my rib cage and returning to my breasts. The feel of his mouth on me was intense. Wicked.

I wanted more. I wanted to feel him everywhere.

He sat up, taking me with him. The shirt was pulled over my head. My underwear disappeared, and he laid me back down, hovering over me, his gaze raking up and down my body.

"Tell me you want this, Sofia. Or tell me to leave. But tell me now."

"Stay," I pleaded. "But I haven't brushed—"

He cut me off, grabbing a pack of breath mints and slipping one on my tongue and then his. "All right?"

Before I could answer, his mouth was on mine. The strong mint flavor gave way to his taste. Egan. I knew I wanted to taste him the rest of my life. I flung my arms around his neck, and we kissed endlessly. Long, deep, passionate kisses. Soft, gentle brushes of our mouths. Soul-wrenching, carnal kisses, so hot I was certain I would melt. I traced over the muscles of his back, marveling at the strength under my fingers. I gripped his biceps, clutched at his neck, ran my toes up and down his legs.

He licked my skin, sucked at my nipples until they were red and swollen from his teeth and mouth. He traced his tongue up my legs, kissing behind my knees, running his mouth between my hip bones, touching me everywhere except where I wanted him the most.

"Stop teasing," I begged.

He slipped his hand between my legs, his caress gentle. He groaned at the wetness he found. He explored me, teasing my clit, making my back arch as he went deeper, sliding one, then two fingers inside me. His erection nudged at me, and I wrapped my hand around him, stroking, wanting to give him the same pleasure from my touch as he was giving me. He was hot and heavy in my hand, the perfect size length and girth with a slight curve to the end of his cock. He was going to be amazing inside me.

I cried out as he circled my clit—small, tight loops that made me whimper.

"Please, Egan," I begged. "Please."

He hovered over me. "There has been no one since I met you. No one."

"I'm clean," I replied, pulling him closer. "I want to feel you."

He slid in slowly. Inch by glorious inch, I felt him stretch and fill me until we were flush. His curve rubbed against my G-spot, making me groan in anticipation. He stilled, meeting my eyes, the moment overwhelming for us both.

"No going back, Sofia. You are mine."

"Yes," I gasped. "Yours. Please. Now, Egan. Move now."

With a low growl, he did. Lifting my leg over his shoulder, he settled even deeper. He began to thrust, his movements powerful and claiming. My orgasm came fast, detonating with no warning, forcing a long cry to escape my mouth. Egan covered my lips with his, riding out my pleasure. He tossed my other leg over his shoulder, rising up on his knees.

"More, Sofia. You are going to give me more. I have waited for you, for this. I want it all."

He drove into me relentlessly. He slid his hand between us, playing with my clit. He groaned and hissed. Muttered in Romanian. Cursed in English. Sweat beaded on his forehead. Our skin slid together. The bed creaked. I gripped his sheets, trying to hold myself in place. He let one leg fall, and he leaned forward, gripping the headboard and changing the angle. His face was a study in contrasts. Intense. Focused. Ripples of pleasure making his lips curl. His gaze never left mine as my eyes widened and I gripped him. "Egan!"

"Yes, my love. Give it to me."

I exploded again, locking down. I pulsed around his cock, my muscles clenching him as he gasped and shut his eyes, his orgasm washing over him. He called out my name, fisting my hair and bending low to kiss me. I felt his pleasure in the warmth of his mouth. Tasted his ecstasy. Reveled in my own. Until our bodies had to stop and he lifted his head. Our eyes met again, mine sated, his seeking. He slowly disengaged from me and pulled me into his arms as we lay on the mattress, our breathing ragged and loud. He pressed innumerable kisses to my face and head, murmuring quiet words in between them.

He lifted my face to his and kissed me. "Are you all right, my love?"

"I'm good. Sleepy." I frowned. "Hungry."

"Go back to sleep. I cook for you after."

"Hmm," I replied, already slipping away. "So good, Egan. We were so good."

I felt the press of his mouth to my head.

"I know."

CHAPTER FIVE

Egan

She fell asleep, and I watched her as she slumbered. She was finally mine. She hadn't said the words yet, but I knew she felt them. She wouldn't have given me her body if she didn't. I knew that about her. I could feel it in her kiss, hear it in the way she said my name. How her body molded to mine when I held her. The smile she gave me when I least expected it. Unguarded, sweet, filled with emotion. And now that we'd had sex, she would confess her feelings soon.

I stayed for a while, mesmerized by her. How her dark hair spread over the pillow. The way her lips pursed and smoothed, a tiny sigh escaping her lips on occasion. As I eased from her, she frowned, reaching out her hand. I slid my pillow toward her, and she gripped it, whispering my name. I bent and kissed her, stroking the hair away from her face. She was so beautiful.

And now, she was mine.

The smile stayed on my face as I showered and went

to the kitchen to make coffee. It was late afternoon, but I needed the jolt of caffeine.

I answered some emails, talked to Leo, then I called the gym, speaking to Mack, one of my managers.

"Everything okay?"

"Smooth as silk," he responded. "Have some membership applicants for you to look over."

"Great. I'll be in tomorrow."

"Someone was here looking for you. Didn't leave their name."

"Oh?"

"A guy—big, muscles, dressed like a bouncer. Rather sour-faced and had a crazy hairdo. Asked for you by name. I said you weren't in, and he seemed to think I was lying."

"Odd."

"He said he would be back. Refused to leave a name or a card so you could get in touch. I assured him if he had a complaint about the gym, I could help. He just laughed and walked away."

"Was the camera on?"

"Yeah. I already forwarded it to you."

"Okay. Maybe someone looking for a job."

Mack laughed. "Well, word is this is the best gym to work at."

I laughed with him. "See you tomorrow."

I opened my laptop, studying the video Mack had sent. He was right. The guy was young and toned, and his hair stood out. He frowned the entire time he was talking to Mack, dressed in a shirt that showed off his muscles. I zoomed in on the tattoos on his arms, unsure of the symbols. I got a screen capture and decided to run it through a program.

Arms slipped around me, and soft lips nuzzled at my throat. Instantly, I forgot about anything else but that. I shut the laptop, spinning on the stool, and tugged Sofia into my arms. I fisted her hair, exposing her neck, and I kissed up the delicate column until I reached her mouth. I didn't hold back, kissing her until she was trembling in my arms. I loved this more vulnerable side to her. The way she responded to me, letting me take control.

I dropped my head to her neck. "You taste so good."

"Must be an improvement on earlier."

I chuckled and lifted my head. "You tasted perfect then too. If you think a little morning breath is ever going to keep me away from your mouth, you have a lot to learn."

She rolled her eyes but gripped my shoulders. "You taste like coffee."

I kissed the end of her nose. "I'll get you some."

I slid off the stool, lifting and depositing her where I had been sitting. I got her a mug of coffee and leaned on the counter across from her. "I thought you would sleep longer."

She shook her head. "I want to sleep tonight."

I arched one eyebrow. "And you're so sure I'm going to let you?"

For a moment, she blinked, then she began to laugh. "I know you will. You always put my welfare first. Even ahead of your rather impressive cock."

"*Rather impressive?*" I repeated. "You seemed thoroughly impressed earlier."

She took another sip of her coffee, her eyes dancing. "Meh. I was sleep-deprived. I can't rely on my memory."

"Is that a fact? Are you telling me, Sofia, that you require another session with me to improve your memory?"

"A *session*?" She laughed. "It might help."

"Well then, far be it for me not to come to your aid." I lifted her off the stool and strode back down the hall. "A man has to do what a man has to do."

She bit down on my neck, soothing the slight burn with a swipe of her tongue. "Good idea, Egan. Show me how manly you are. Really hard."

I followed her down to the mattress.

Really hard.

I could do that.

The next morning, I cooked her breakfast, watching as she ate heartily. "I love watching you eat the food I make for you."

"I could get used to it," she confessed. "Your cooking spoils me."

"Good. We can move in together upstairs. Bigger place. I will cook for you every day."

She gaped at me. "I don't think so, *mio uomo*."

"What does that mean?" I asked. She had never called me anything but Egan.

"Friend." She smirked. "With a big ego. I am not moving in with you."

I eyed her suspiciously, but I didn't push it.

"Why not?"

She shook her head, looking frustrated. "You're like a runaway train. We have barely begun and you want to move in."

I shrugged. "It makes sense."

"It makes no sense!" She threw up her hands. "Egan, it's too fast."

"Well, soon, then. Your place is small. My place is small. Upstairs is bigger. We can have it, and I can rent out these places. Make more money for Damien."

She snorted. Actually snorted. The sound made me grin.

"Damien doesn't need the money. Otherwise, he would have rented upstairs already."

"He has," I told her. "To me."

Again, she gaped. "Come again?"

"I pay rent for upstairs, so when you are ready, we can move."

"If you're paying rent upstairs, why are you still in the apartment down here?" she asked, obviously confused.

I leaned over the table and brushed my fingers down her cheek. "To be closer to you."

Her eyes softened, a smile tugging on her mouth.

"Damn you, Egan. You say the sweetest things."

"So, yes?"

She stood, shaking her head. "No, you impatient man. Not yet."

She walked down the hall, muttering under her breath, but I grinned.

Not yet.

It was as good as a yes.

I wondered if I could convince Sofia to marry me before Damien and Raven. We could travel to the island as husband and wife.

It seemed doable.

The next morning, I got ready for the day.

As much as I hated to leave her, I had businesses that needed me, and I knew Sofia needed some downtime and space from me. She was a thinker. She would take the events of the past days and mull them over. Dissect them and overthink. It was the way she processed things. I had to let her do her thing so she could settle into our relationship. I could only pray she didn't decide to stop it. I kissed her long and deep enough before leaving, to tip the scales. That, plus the fact that I dressed to head into Elite, wearing a suit. Her eyes lit up when she saw me. I knew the businessman aspect helped soothe her nerves. It cemented the fact in her head that my HJ days were behind me and what I did now posed no threats.

At Elite, I sat with Leo, and we met with two prospective clients. Both were celebrities who would be in town for filming and would require round-the-clock protection. We agreed to the right person, the contracts, and the length of term. After they left, Leo sat back with a grin.

"The docket is damn full. We may need to hire a couple more people."

"Awesome. Damien set off the trajectory well."

"You help."

"Sorry?"

"You look like a hit man. Talk like a gentleman. Act like a gun for hire. You're the whole package. Clients love you." He grinned. "You're the most requested bodyguard we have. I've added a premium rate for your services." He winked drolly. "And the word 'unavailable' drives up the price fast. I have one client willing to pay a small fortune for you for a private function."

He handed me a folder, and I glanced at it, my eyebrows shooting up at the quote.

"They aren't serious."

"They are. It's Malcolm Weston's daughter's birthday. She wants a movie night with her friends, he wants her protected. He's high-profile enough to warrant it."

"And rich enough to afford it," I finished. "But I can't look after an entire group of girls." I rubbed my forehead, thinking of the drama a group of teenagers could cause.

"No, you and three others. But you, specifically, watching the daughter."

"When is it?"

"Soon. It's a Friday night."

"Fine. Get all the particulars."

"Awesome."

I shook his hand and left, heading for the gallery that displayed my paintings. I was pleased when I got there to find two had been sold. Carmen, the owner, smiled widely. "They loved them, Egan. Now, I will have two blank spots. Perhaps you have something I can fill them with?"

I laughed. "Soon. I have one done, and the second is almost finished. They're a duo."

"Oh, those sell so well. What is the subject?"

"A place I like to go and unwind. It's a spring and fall view."

"Perfect. How soon?"

"Next week," I promised.

"I'll have your payment ready as well."

She air-kissed my cheeks and headed to her office. I wandered the gallery, absorbing the light textures and colors. The canvases layered in oils. Delicate watercolors. Bold charcoal. Rough pottery. Sculptures of heavy, dark metal. I loved art in all its mediums. A painting caught my eye—a small one, not by an artist known to me. Whimsical. Images of lovers so faint you had to squint to see them woven into the canvas. But once you saw the image, it became sharp. Their expressions were tender, passionate, sad. Joyous. All the emotions associated with love. The man was massive, his large frame dwarfing the woman. I could feel his possessiveness in his embrace. The way he held her, the fierceness of his expression. He would kill for her. Die protecting her.

Carmen came from her office. "Interesting piece, isn't it? Everyone sees something different. Jealousy. Possessiveness. Sex."

I saw more.

"I want to buy it. I would like to take it with me."

She smiled. "You've never bought a piece before."

I studied it again. "I like it. It will be a perfect gift for my woman."

She blinked, then laughed. "Your *woman*. Another surprise. I'll have it prepared for you."

I nodded, still studying the image. Sofia would love it as much as I did. I was certain of it.

At the gym, I walked around, making sure everything was up to my high expectations. I sat at my desk, returning a few calls, when Mack knocked on the door. "He's back," he informed me. "The pushy guy from the other day."

I sat back, running my hand over my chin. "Bring him up here."

A moment later, Mack escorted my visitor in. He was tall, well-muscled, and fit. His eyes were nervous, his gaze flying all over the place. His hands were balled into fists, and he looked ready to fight at any given moment, his entire body giving off a nervous energy. He looked like a thug for hire. His nose had been broken several times. He had some faint scars on his arms and the backs of his hands. The oddest thing about him was his hair. Bright gold and cut into a mohawk. It added inches to his height, yet seemed out of place.

He approached the desk, his voice deep when he spoke. "Egan Vulpe."

I stood. "And you are?"

"Alex."

"What can I do for you, Alex?"

"I wanted to meet you."

His statement put me on guard, and I chose my next

words carefully. "If you want a personal trainer, you can inquire downstairs."

He scoffed. "Not a trainer. I wanted to meet the great Egan Vulpe."

"Do we know each other?" I asked, my nerves beginning to hum with anxiety.

"No. But we will. I look forward to it."

I leaned forward, resting my fists on the desk. "I do not like cryptic conversations. I do not know you, nor do I plan to. Now, unless you want information on the gym, I suggest you leave."

"You will be hired."

Hired? He wanted a bodyguard?

"If you are looking for security, contact Elite. If you are looking for a gym, talk to Mack downstairs. Otherwise, there is no other business in which to hire me. Now, I'm a busy man, and you have taken up enough of my time."

I sat down, pointedly opening my laptop and ignoring him. My rudeness didn't faze him in any way. He sauntered to the door and headed down the steps. I turned on the camera, watching him leave. He paused just before he walked out the door, staring directly into the camera. He opened his fists fast, mimicking an explosion. Then he grinned widely and walked off.

What the fuck?

I called Damien immediately. He listened to what had occurred and looked at the image I had captured. "He sounded North American," I said. "But at times, his words had an accent in them. Like he had picked it up over the years."

"What kind?"

"Old country. Russia, I am guessing."

"Hmm," Damien said. "Interesting."

"I ran him through some databases. No hits," I said. "But he knows my past, or at least part of it. I don't know what he wants."

Damien was quiet. "You could have an unwanted admirer."

I groaned. "Just what I need."

"I'll run the picture through the HJ system. See what I can find."

I sighed. "That would be great. I never expected to need that sort of access again."

Once Damien had left Hidden Justice and turned over the role of Watcher to someone else, all the equipment had been removed and stored elsewhere. Any access was removed—except, of course, for the man himself. The software we had at Elite was nowhere near as powerful or encompassing.

"I still have some pull," he stated mildly.

I laughed at his understatement. Then, hearing voices in the background, I decided to let him get on with his day. "I will let you go. Let me know if you come up with anything."

"I will. He could have come across some old snippet about you. Or heard rumors. He could be a wannabe."

"Or wants to rob a bank and thinks I could break him in through the basement. He didn't seem overly bright. More muscle than brains. I think he's been watching too many movies."

Damien laughed. "Not to change the subject, but Sofia called me earlier."

"Oh?"

"It appears you have made some progress with my cousin."

I thought about the *progress* I had made. How enjoyable it had been. But I wouldn't share that with Damien. "Yes. We have talked. I know her past, and she is willing to give us a chance."

"You should tell her yours. Be honest."

"I know. I will. Tonight. Once I have cooked her dinner."

And made love to her so thoroughly that she wouldn't care much about my sordid past. But I didn't say that to Damien.

"What does *mio uomo* mean?" I asked.

"Friend with a big ego," he replied.

I had to laugh. "She told you to say that."

He laughed too. "Loosely translated, it means 'my man.'"

I liked that.

"Good luck." He paused. "Treat her well, Egan. She's my family."

"She'll be mine as well," I assured him. "And my world."

I hung up.

CHAPTER SIX

Sofia

I spent the day relaxing and doing a few errands. I video-called Damien and talked to him, confessing that Egan and I were closer. I didn't go into details, but he knew what I meant. He was pleased, telling me I couldn't do better than Egan.

"He's been crazy about you for a long time, Sofia," he said. "His patience has been astonishing."

"His past, his future, still worries me," I confessed. "But he's right. People can die for lots of reasons. Refusing to love him on a what-if is wrong. And he is pretty awesome."

Damien chuckled. "He thinks you're perfect."

"I'm hardly that."

"Don't worry. I'll tell him lots of stories, so he knows."

I rolled my eyes. Damien grinned. "Come for a visit here. It's so beautiful."

"I'll talk to Egan about it. How's Raven?"

"She's great. And Missy has recovered so well. I know she'd love to see you."

I nodded thoughtfully. After what Missy had been through, she deserved to be in a place that made her happy and with a man like Marcus. I knew he adored her and would ensure her safety and happiness. And Raven and Damien made an awesome couple. So did Julian and Tally. I didn't know Matteo and Evie as well, but the rare times I had met them, they'd seemed lovely. Egan had mentioned the island more than once. I had to admit, the idea of sun, sand, and a quiet place to relax and spend time with Egan was tempting.

"I'll talk to him, and we'll see if we can plan something."

"Great. I'd love to see you, my favorite cousin."

I laughed. "Your only cousin."

He shrugged. "Still favorite."

We chatted a few moments more, then said goodbye.

I heard the elevator, and I went to the door, knowing it would be Egan. I would have to ask him his thoughts on a trip. I had a feeling I already knew the answer.

I opened my door before Egan could knock. My breath caught at the sight of him. Egan everyday was handsome and sexy.

Egan in a suit was devastating. Suave, sleek. His jacket fit his broad shoulders and tapered waistline to perfection. He had loosened his tie, the top two buttons of his shirt open. I wanted to tuck my finger into the gap and pull. Tear open the shirt and expose the taut muscles it hid. Listen as the buttons hit the floor, then peel off his jacket and shirt and rub my chest against his.

I blinked at the idea. I had a feeling Egan wouldn't object in the least.

As if he knew what I was thinking, he set down the

flowers and package he was carrying and yanked me into his arms. He covered my mouth with his, pushing his tongue in and stroking it along mine. He slipped his hands under the shirt I wore, spreading them wide across my back, pressing his fingers into my skin. He groaned low in his chest as he deepened the kiss. I clung to his shoulders, caught up in a vortex of emotion. Passion flared, and I gripped him harder, whimpering. I registered the sound of my door closing as he kicked it shut. He moved his hands lower, hoisting me up. I wrapped my legs around his waist, and he slid me onto the kitchen counter, his mouth never leaving mine. His erection pressed into me, and I flexed my hips, grinding against him. He groaned again, easing back from my mouth and dropping his head to my neck. His ragged breath was hot on my skin.

I traced my fingers over the back of his neck. "How was your day, dear?"

He looked up, his green eyes even darker than usual and intense. "Not as good as the next few moments are going to be."

I lifted my eyebrows. "Few moments? Egan," I teased, "I expected far more stamina from you."

"You will have no complaints."

Then he covered my mouth with his again and carried me down the hall. In my room, he set me on my feet, tugging my shirt over my head. I pushed his jacket off his shoulders, pulling at his buttons. A couple popped off in my haste, and Egan gripped the sides of the shirt, tearing it open and peeling it off his body.

"Jesus," I whispered. "It's like the Hulk."

He laughed, and in seconds, my wish of feeling his bare skin on mine came true. His chest hair rubbed on my nipples, the abrasion on my skin making me shiver. We fell onto the bed, kissing and touching. One moment I was under him, the next on top. His hands were everywhere, exploring and leaving a trail of fire wherever they landed. I pushed up on his chest, looking down at him. He gazed back at me, his adoration blazing. "I have been thinking about you all day, my Sofia."

"Thinking about this?" I asked as I shifted, lifting myself and grasping his rigid cock. I kept my eyes locked on his as I guided him in, sinking down on his massive erection, feeling him fill me perfectly. He grunted in satisfaction, holding my hips.

"How beautiful you are," he murmured. "Taking my cock. Ride me, my love. Take what you need."

I began to move, the sensation of him overwhelming. The curve to his cock hit me right where I needed it. He was thick and hard and fit inside me so well. He rolled his hips in time with mine, and soon, we were moving rapidly. He pulled and pinched at my nipples, gripped my hips, slid his hand between us, toying with my clit. I arched my back, crying out. I reached behind me, playing with his balls, stroking his sac. He cursed and muttered, sweat breaking out on his skin. We moved together faster.

"Egan," I pleaded. "I need more."

He sat up, covering my mouth with his as he drove

deeper inside me, the angle changing. Our chests rubbed together. He surrounded me. His tongue tangled with mine. He gripped my ass, stroking and cupping the cheeks, sliding his finger sensuously around the puckered hole. He used my wetness to slide in one long finger, and my body locked down around him. My orgasm was hard and fast, skyrocketing me into oblivion. I cried out, letting my head fall back as Egan used his teeth and tongue on my neck and shoulders. He kept moving, drawing out my orgasm, gasping as his own hit him. He buried his face into my neck, breathing my name, thrusting and claiming me until he was spent. Until our bodies stopped moving from exhaustion.

Then he slowly lowered us to the mattress, his arms still holding me like a vise. He pressed endless kisses to my head, stroking up and down my back in long, gentle passes.

I looked up, meeting his warm gaze. "So, hello."

He grinned. "I would like you to greet me that way every day, please."

I had to laugh. "So polite."

He rolled us, slipping from my body and hovering over me. "I have waited so long to have you, Sofia. This is like a dream."

I cupped his face. "Was it worth the wait?" I asked quietly.

He trailed a finger down my cheek. "Every moment. I would wait a lifetime for you."

I smiled. "No more waiting, Egan."

He gathered me in his arms. "I was worried you

would have regrets today. Want to talk," he admitted. "Want to take a step back."

"You know me well. I was overthinking this morning. I called Damien, and he told me he thought we belonged together."

"We do," he agreed. "I believe we are soul mates."

With a sigh, I snuggled into his warmth. He pressed a kiss to my head. "I like you like this, *iubirea mea.*"

"Like what?"

"Relaxed. Soft." He paused as if searching for a word. "Vulnerable. I like you like this with me."

I lifted my head. "I can't be that way in the outside world. As a doctor, I have to be strong. For myself. My patients. With only Damien for family and support, I had to learn to rely on myself. Be strong." I traced a finger over his chest, tickling the smattering of wiry hair. Then I pressed a kiss to it. "With you, when it's us, I can let my guard down. Just be Sofia."

He lifted my chin. "My Sofia," he said softly. "I like this is ours. Just Egan and Sofia."

I smiled. "Yes. Just Egan and Sofia."

He bent and kissed me. "Perfect."

EGAN

We ordered a pizza and sat on her sofa, eating the simple dinner and sipping wine. She put her flowers in a vase, touching the petals softly. "I haven't been given flowers in a very long time," she admitted. "I love how they smell."

I decided to buy her fresh ones every week so she would have the scent of them around her all the time.

After we ate, I gave her the painting. She opened it, setting it on the chair and stepping back, studying it.

"It's erotic and yet so unintentionally soft," she whispered. "Look how he is holding her. Like he is ready to defend her." She tilted her head, quiet for a few moments. "Her warrior." Her gaze met mine. "Like you."

"Me?" I asked, surprised at her words.

"You look at me as if you would slay the world for me."

"I would. Nothing will harm you. I will not allow it."

"*Mio guerriero*," she whispered. "My warrior."

"I will always be your warrior," I vowed. "I would protect you to my dying breath."

A shadow passed over her face, and I was quick to reassure her. "Nothing is going to happen to me, Sofia. We are going to have a long, wonderful life together. Watch our children grow. Bounce grandchildren on our knee and spoil them."

She lifted her eyebrows at my words, and I had to laugh. "I know. I am going fast. But it is how I see our life unfolding."

She shook her head, but she didn't say anything.

And she smiled.

To me, that was a good sign.

With a long exhale, I settled the barbell back in its place and sat up. I stretched, feeling the satisfaction of my muscles pull and ease. I grabbed my bottle and drank deeply, the cold water refreshing and needed. Grabbing a towel, I rubbed at my sweat-soaked skin, sitting for a moment and looking around the gym. For a midweek morning, the place was busy. The classes going on at the moment were full and most of the machines taken. I grunted in gratification. My business was doing well. So was my personal life. For the first time in what felt like forever, I was happy.

After wiping the weight bench and tossing the towel, I headed to the shower. I wanted to get clean, finish some paperwork, and head over to Elite Security and do some work there with Leo before he left for the day. Then I planned to head home and cook dinner.

Sofia and I had spent a lot of time together on her days off. I put aside every thought other than her and enjoyed the feeling of being with her. Ever since my dream had occurred, I'd wanted, needed to be close to her. I luxuriated in the feel of her wrapped around me as she slept. How it felt to be inside her, listening to her moans and whimpers as we made love. Hearing her gasps and pleas as we fucked. Holding her after the passion had passed, no matter how it was expressed. We talked and laughed, neither of us wanting to go out or break the bubble. I still needed to talk to her about my past, and I would. Soon. But I was enjoying the moment and being selfish, afraid it would end.

When she returned to work, I changed my schedule slightly. I started earlier at the gym, meeting with Leo and working at Elite early in the afternoon. I was home by the time she woke up, and we could have dinner together and spend time with each other before she napped and then headed to the hospital. Every night when she left, I couldn't settle until she let me know she arrived at the hospital. A few nights, I was able to convince her to let me drive her and pick her up in the morning. Those days, I also spent the night painting, then crawled into bed with her for a few hours, making love to her before she fell asleep with a satisfied smile on her face.

Those were my favorite days.

I used one of the showers in the locker room, wrapping a towel around my waist when I finished. As I dried off, I checked the room, pleased to see everything the way I liked it. Clean, orderly, and up to my high standards. I went overboard on every detail. Even the lockers were lined in cedar, so your clothes smelled fresh when you were ready to put them back on.

If you had a membership at my gym, you got the best. Top-of-the-line equipment and instructors. Private workout areas and showers for those who preferred them. Staff who knew what they were talking about. The best hot tub, swimming pool, and sauna money could buy. Fluffy towels. High-end shampoos and soaps. It was all provided with the steep membership fee I charged.

We had a men's locker room. A women's locker room. An all-gender one. Anyone was welcome in this gym. You could use whatever area you were comfortable in, and if none of them was for you, then small, private rooms were available where you could change, shower, and be at ease. I wanted all my clients to be happy.

I was towel-drying my hair when Mack walked in. "Egan," he said, looking worried.

I frowned. "What's up, Mack?"

"There's someone here to see you."

"Again?"

"Different someone. He insists what he has to say is private and refused to discuss it with either Sharon or me." He paused. "I don't recognize him as a member. Or the guy with him. In fact, they don't look like they want to be in a gym, never mind join one. They're suits."

I lifted my eyebrows in puzzlement. I didn't like these unexpected visitors. I hadn't seen or heard from Alex again, and Damien had found nothing on him. I had put him out of my mind, convinced he'd seen me at an event and was simply trying to get an in at Elite or the gym and going about it in a strange way. "Did he say what it was about?"

"No. He insisted on speaking only with you."

"Where is he?"

"At the front desk."

"Take him to the office. The general one. Not mine. Offer him a juice."

Mack grinned. "Doesn't look like the juice type, boss."

"What type does he look like?"

"Coffee with a side of handgun with a silencer, to be honest."

That made me pause, but I smiled. "Get him coffee.

Make sure the cameras in the office are on. I'll be there soon."

"Okay."

He left, and I pulled on a pair of jeans and a black T-shirt. I ran a hand through my short hair and over my scruff. I spritzed on my favorite cologne from my collection and headed up to my office. I tapped on the cameras and studied the men waiting for me. Neither was familiar, but I had to agree with Mack. They didn't look like they wanted to join the gym or belonged here. I doubted they wanted to complain about a piece of machinery or the temperature of the pool. They were both reclining in visitor chairs, their legs crossed. One sat perfectly still, but I had a feeling his eyes were taking in every detail. The other man was on his phone, scrolling. I returned my gaze to the one sitting still. There was an air about him I recognized, even on camera.

Despite his calm expression, perfectly tailored suit, slicked-back hair, and shiny shoes, malice clung to him. He was someone you didn't want to cross. I studied him carefully. His hair was dark, as were his eyes. His face was unusual. Slim nose, heavy brows, smooth skin. I found it hard to judge his age. I had the feeling the skilled hands of a surgeon had a lot to do with his appearance.

What the hell did he want from me?

I made sure the extra cameras behind the desk in the office were running and grabbed a juice bottle, deciding to play up the gym aspect until I knew what they wanted.

Then I headed down the steps and walked into the general office. The men stood as I entered the room, and I nodded at them.

"Gentlemen," I greeted them. "I was told you wanted to see me. Forgive my keeping you waiting. I was just cleaning up from a workout."

The one I identified as the boss stepped forward, extending his hand. "Mr. Vulpe, thank you for seeing me."

I shook his hand, noticing the lack of grip and the coldness of his skin. Definitely the boss. He specialized in issuing orders and not getting his hands dirty. He was weak. His sidekick simply nodded at me, standing to one side of his boss.

I frowned. "I fear you have me at a disadvantage. You know my name. I don't know yours. Or why you are asking to see me. My managers could give you a tour if you want a membership."

"I am not here about a membership."

I sat down, taking a sip of my juice, every instinct on overdrive. "Then why are you here? And, more importantly, who are you?"

He sat down, unbuttoning his jacket. His tie was navy, matching his suit, a ribbon of darkness against the white of his shirt.

"Ivan Jones. My card."

I took the card, studying it. "You're in construction?" I asked mildly, even more wary. If he was in construction, or his last name was Jones, I was the Queen of England. As cultured as his voice was, I could detect a trace of a rougher accent at times—even stronger than my own. It put me on edge.

He inclined his head.

"I'm not looking to sell the building or do renovations."

"I'm not looking to buy it. I want to hire you for a job."

My eyebrows rose in surprise. "A job?"

"Your name was given to me by Barry Sinclair. He says you are the best demolition man he knows."

I was surprised Barry would give out my personal information.

"I work for Barry on occasion. If you need a building demolished, you can hire his company and request my services. I don't do freelance."

"This is a special job." Ivan's eyes were frosty, his tone equally so. "Private."

"Not interested."

"What would make it interesting?" he asked. "Name your price."

"There isn't a price. I'm not interested."

"There is always a price."

"Not for me."

"I would give you the best crew. Everything needed to complete the job. My nephew would make sure you had everything."

I paused, then asked a question. "Alex, I presume?"

Ivan pursed his lips and nodded. "I know he is here. My apologies. He gets ahead of himself."

I stood, indicating the meeting was over.

"As I said, if you want a building demolished, hire

Barry's company. Request me. If I am available, I will work on it. If not, his company is top-notch. He can bring down a building without my input."

Ivan remained seated. "This job requires the highest discretion and talent. I would make you a very rich man for one job."

I had zero desire to have anything to do with this man. The second I'd walked in the room, every instinct screamed at me to get out. He was dangerous. His card lied. He lied. This wasn't about construction. This was something else. He may have gotten my name from Barry, but he was here for another reason.

One I wanted no part of.

"I do not need a job from you to be wealthy. And as I said, you'll get the best from Barry's company. I'm not interested. Thank you for the offer, and I wish you a pleasant afternoon."

He unfurled himself from the chair, anger drawing his mouth down and making his eyes narrowed and furious. "I had hoped you would be reasonable."

"I am very reasonable. I'm simply not accepting jobs from strangers. I'm a busy man."

He glared at me. "Yes. Your gym. Your cologne. Your *paintings*," he said softly. "Quite the Renaissance man, are you not, Mr. Vulpe?"

I stiffened, my first instincts correct. If he was only looking at hiring me, he wouldn't have dug so deep into my life. But I refused to let him see my fears.

"I stay busy. Now, if you will excuse me, gentlemen, I have other things to attend to."

Ivan crossed his hands in front of him.

"Is that your last word? You are saying no to me?"

I nodded. "I am not interested in a job working with you."

He laughed. "It would not be *with*, it would be *for*."

"Which is why I am saying no. Good day."

He studied me. "We will meet again."

"I hope not."

He spun on his heel and left, his sidekick following him out the door, leaving it open. I walked to the door, watching as they left. I raced up the steps to my office, studying the cameras that tracked their departure. Ivan stepped into a black car, the windows tinted so dark they were impossible to see through. His sidekick followed him, and the driver sped away. I got the plate and sat back, rubbing my lip.

My dream from days before floated through my mind. I hadn't been involved in a building being demolished for months. Then I had that dream and he showed up not long after? I shook my head to clear it and to stop my thoughts. It was a coincidence—that was all.

Still, I decided to head to Elite. Use the computers in the basement to do some digging. Then, I would head home to have dinner with Sofia.

I did what I could at Elite, my mind too anxious to concentrate. I got nowhere with my inquiries, so I gave up and headed home. The need to see Sofia was overwhelming. I wanted to call her and hear her voice, but I knew she was sleeping. Tonight was her last night, and she was always tired by the time the last shift rolled around. By going home, I could look in on her then make some more calls.

She was the priority.

Perhaps then, I would discover why a Russian mobster was pretending to be someone else and wanted to hire me.

CHAPTER SEVEN

Egan

I opened Sofia's door quietly, grateful I had a key. I peeked into her room, glad to see her asleep. She was under the blankets, except for one sexy leg that rested on top. By now, I knew better than to try to tuck it in. She would kick it off almost immediately.

I went closer, matching my breathing to hers. Long, slow, deep breaths that helped me to relax. I could smell her perfume, the light, citrusy scent filling my lungs. She was fine. Safe.

I wanted to wake her, hear her voice. Make love to her. But I left her alone. I would come back in a couple of hours and make her dinner. Drive her to work and pick her up in the morning. I decided I would take the day off tomorrow and spend it with her.

I returned to my place and called Damien. It was late on his side of the world, but I knew he would be awake.

He answered fast and worried. "Egan? What's up?"

"My blood pressure," I muttered. "But not for the reason you think."

"What's going on?" he asked.

I sat back and told him what had occurred today. About the way the vibe and instincts had increased every moment I spent in the company of "Ivan Jones." I also told him my hunch that Ivan had confirmed and the fact that the oddly behaved Alex was his nephew.

"You checked this Ivan out?" he inquired.

"Yeah—briefly. The business is registered and looks legal. It's owned by a numbered company, which is owned by yet another one. Lots of layers to peel back. I need to concentrate on him. Something isn't sitting right with me. And when I called Barry, he told me he'd had an inquiry but never gave my name specifically. He said he'd told the caller he had a top-notch crew and could handle any job." I sighed. "Leo and I did some digging, but the software isn't the same as what HJ had. I hacked into what I could with my resources, but aside from his card and name, I don't have much to go on. There isn't a website or place I can start from. I need access."

"You can't get to the HJ software without the system code and log-in. You know how deeply I encrypted it. And there is nowhere I can send you to get access."

I missed the hidden office in the building where Elite Security was located. The system and incredible machines were all gone to another secret location. There were new leaders, new teams. The rare occasion I was called in, I had a contact, a meeting place, and directions. Need-to-know basis only. I never thought I would need access to the powerful system Damien had run again.

"But _you_ can get access," I said quietly. "I need your help."

"And you will get it. Do you have a sketch?"

"Even better. I have a picture I can send."

"You're sure he's Russian?"

"He covered the accent well, but I heard it. And his demeanor was telling. His approach was way off. He was too forceful, too direct. He is used to issuing orders."

Damien was quiet. "I don't like the sound of this, Egan. What does he want blown up?"

"No idea. But he's decided that I must be a demolition expert for hire."

Damien chuckled. "Wonder where he got that idea?"

"That was a long time ago, and I got out of it. Way before HJ. And all the jobs I did after HJ were legal."

"Sometimes the past catches up with us when we least expect it. Julian can tell you all about that."

"I know."

"You need to watch your back."

"I'm aware."

"Okay, send me the picture. I'll do some digging. I'll chat with the others. Maybe now you've said no, he'll look elsewhere."

"I have a feeling he won't. His veiled threat said it all. But if he tries, I know how to fight back. I'm not being dragged into that world again."

"I know." He paused. "Have you told Sofia?"

"No. She's asleep, and I'm not sure if I should tell her."

"You have to. She needs to be aware. On alert. You can't hide this from her."

I groaned. "She might use it as a reason not to let this relationship go forward."

"I think that ship has sailed, Egan. She has admitted to me she has feelings for you."

"Will she still think so if she gets worried about my safety? It's such a trigger for her." I ran a hand through my hair in frustration. "Or her own safety. If she gets worried she might be in danger because of me, she will pull back."

"Have you been out on the town much?"

"No. Not at all. We're pretty much homebodies."

"Then there's nothing connecting you except living in the same building. But other people live there as well, so it's not obvious. But you should be careful—stick to the homebody thing."

"I will. I've been careful since Alex's unusual visit. I haven't noticed anything. No tails, nobody watching. Nothing. We swept Elite for bugs, and I did the same with my car, this place, and the gym. Nothing. I'm being cautious."

"Still, you should tell her. She hates being lied to, and she would see an omission as the same as a lie."

"I will."

I rubbed my aching temples, not wanting to discuss it any further, but knowing that he was right. "Look into Ivan Jones for me."

"I will."

We talked a few moments more. Everyone on the island was well. I was pleased to hear it, but after I hung up, I sat forward, resting my head in my hands.

I knew I had to tell Sofia. She needed to know the truth. But how she would react troubled me. I cursed Ivan Jones and whatever had brought him into my life. I had finally broken down Sofia's walls, and now, because of him, I might find them re-erected.

And this time, I doubted anything would bring them down again.

SOFIA

I woke up to the scent of something delicious. I smiled into my pillow, knowing Egan was in my kitchen and making us a meal to eat. I glanced at the clock, surprised to see I had slept longer than usual. I got up and had a quick shower, then headed to the kitchen.

I watched Egan for a moment, caught up in the image. He had a tea towel slung over his shoulder and another tucked into his waistband for a makeshift apron. He was busy chopping, his brow furrowed in concentration. I could smell garlic, spices, and tomato sauce. My mouth watered at the aroma and the vision of the sexy man preparing the food.

He didn't look up, but he spoke.

"I know you are there, Sofia. I feel your eyes on me."

I sauntered forward, standing beside him. I slipped my arm around his waist and leaned against his shoulder. "You look so sexy in my kitchen. Any kitchen, really."

He chuckled and pressed a kiss to my head. "I am making you cutlets and pasta."

"My favorite."

He smiled. "I know."

He finished his task and moved to the sink, washing his hands. "You slept well, *iubirea mea?*"

"I did. For too long, though."

He shook his head. "You are tired. You are always tired by the last night. I am driving you tonight and picking you up."

"Egan," I began, but he shook his head, stopping my words.

"It is what is happening," he said. "Now, sit down, and I will bring you dinner."

I sat down with a frown. Something was off with him. He was tense, his accent thicker. That was always a clue to his frame of mind.

He brought over dinner and sat down with his own plate. "I assumed no wine."

"No, not when I have a shift."

"Tomorrow, then," he said, picking up his cutlery and beginning to eat.

He was quiet most of dinner, which wasn't unusual. Egan wasn't much for small talk, although he usually had some questions about our time apart. How my shift was the night before? Had there been any interesting cases? Any amusing incidents? Did I eat the snack he packed me? But today, he was withdrawn, and I noticed that although he ate, it wasn't with his usual gusto. He pushed the food around on the plate, barely finishing his meal.

I studied him, seeing the worry in his expression. The tension in his shoulders. More than once, I felt his gaze on me, and when I would meet his eyes, I caught a glimpse of such sadness, my heart ached. Something was up. Something big.

And I was determined to know what it was.

I finished my meal and complimented him. I insisted on helping him clean the kitchen, although there wasn't much. Egan always cleaned as he cooked. But we put the food away, stacked the dishwasher, and took a cup of coffee and sat on the sofa. I was shocked when Egan sat across from me, not beside me. I had also noticed the lack of physical contact from him. Aside from a quick kiss and squeezing my hand once, he hadn't touched me. That was highly unusual. He normally couldn't keep his hands to himself.

My stomach felt like it was tied in knots.

Outside, the sky was a dull gray, a slight drizzle hitting the glass.

"I hate this sort of weather," I murmured.

He met my gaze. "Oh?"

"It's just enough rain for the roads and sidewalks to be slick. People don't pay attention. The ER will be full of accidents."

He nodded silently, sipping his coffee. I put down my mug, the sound of the ceramic hitting the wooden table loud in the room.

"Whatever you have to tell me, Egan, just say it."

He began to shake his head, but I stopped him. "No.

Something is wrong. The way you're acting, I can see it. Feel it. Talk to me." I took in a deep breath. "Are you regretting this? Regretting us? Was the idea better than the reality?"

He looked shocked. "No, Sofia. Nothing like that. I love you. That has not—*will not*—change, no matter what. I am sorry, my love, if I gave you that impression."

"But something is wrong."

He paused then nodded. "Yes. I have something to tell you, and your reaction worries me."

"Why?"

"I am afraid *you* will decide to stop this. Stop us. And I cannot face that moment."

I frowned. "Egan, I won't—"

He held up his hand, cutting me off. "Do not say words you may take back."

Something in his tone scared me, and I pulled my legs up to my chest, wrapping my arms around my knees. "Tell me," I pleaded.

He told me about the strange visits he'd had. First, Alex, then the men today. Realizing that the two drop-ins were related. The feeling of being threatened.

He sat down, running a hand through his hair. "Damien is using his resources to see if he can find information."

"You think this man wants to hire you for some demolition?"

"Illegal demolition, yes."

"Why would he think you would be willing to do something like that?"

He glanced past my shoulder to the window. His

gaze was unfocused for a few moments, then he met my eyes.

"I was not always on the right side of the law, Sofia."

"You mean Hidden Justice?"

He shook his head slowly. "Unlike Marcus or Damien, I wasn't brought on board HJ through the normal channels. I didn't go to the police academy or have military training."

"What are you saying?"

He scrubbed his face. "My father was a specialist. He defused bombs. Built them. He worked for the government. He was brilliant. I was always fascinated by his work, and he let me sit with him a lot. I learned very early in life how a bomb was made. How to take one apart. We would make small devices and go into the country and blow things up—like a tree stump or whatever. I loved it. My mother hated my fascination with it, but she allowed it because she knew if I was with my father, I was safe. She said more than once if I was left on my own, she was afraid of what I would do."

I smiled and nodded, wanting him to keep talking.

"We were just a middle-class family. Struggling. My mother's parents were gone. My grandmother—my father's mother—was alive and lived with us. She died when I was eight. Neither of my parents had siblings. No other family holding them there, and the country was volatile at times. Times were hard. My father lost his job due to cutbacks. An opportunity came up, and we left everything behind and came to Canada and started over."

"Did you like it?"

He shrugged. "I was resentful of being taken from what I knew, but I liked it here. It was more modern, the city was bigger. My father had a job that gave him a steady income, and my mom worked in a coffee shop. We lived in a small house, but it was nice. He worked for a construction company, razing buildings. That fascinated me too, and he often let me go to work with him." He smiled grimly. "When I was eighteen, he told me I knew more about bombs than he did. That the student had surpassed the master."

"So you went into the same field? Demolishing buildings?"

"My parents wanted me to have an education. My father held three degrees, and he wanted me to explore my options. I had always been ahead at school. I skipped grades nine and eleven, I tested so high. But I tried to please them, so I went. But university bored me, so I quit and I went to work."

He stood and began to pace, his voice and accent thick when he spoke. "I was twenty-two when my parents went on a trip. They had been saving for a long time to go back to Romania and see old friends. They had been gone two weeks when I got a notice that they had been killed in a train accident. It derailed, and the car they were in had no survivors."

"Egan," I whispered. "I'm sorry."

"I found out it was an attack. Planned and executed. The small group that did it were militants, wanting attention. They got mine. They killed innocent civilians to get their name out there. Using a bomb."

He met my eyes. "I was furious. Consumed by grief.

I went after them. Put myself deep undercover, with no one knowing. The few friends I had here thought I was on an extended trip. I knew no one back in Romania any longer. I wanted revenge—to make the men who did this pay for my loss. To give some justice to others who had lost so much that day as well. It took a long time. I plotted and planned. Got into the group. I killed them all." He laughed without humor. "Locked them in a room and blew them up the way they did to my parents and all the other lives they took."

I shuddered at the cold look in his eyes. The flatness of his voice. The doctor in me wept at the thought of the lives he'd taken. The daughter in me understood his need for vengeance.

"And?"

He kept pacing. Walking around the room, picking up a piece of sculpture or a small picture, holding it in his hands, then setting it down and continuing to move. He strode past me, and I reached out, taking his hand and pulling him down beside me.

"Tell me."

"I took out the group, but there were others. I became a self-taught mercenary, tracking them down. Taking them out. I was known as the silent bomber. The deadly ghost. I could walk in and plant a bomb and never be seen. I had no identity. You never knew who I was until it was too late. If you were on my radar, that was it. I got you. I razed buildings. Defused bombs planted to hurt innocents. Even though I wanted to help people, and I did, I had a reputation. A scary one." He shut his eyes. "I loaned my talents to some groups I probably should not have in the name of revenge. I did that for three years. Then one day, I couldn't anymore. I didn't want the violence. The blood. I couldn't bring my parents back, and I was fast slipping down a slope. A dangerous one. Right and wrong were becoming blurred. I walked away and came back to Canada."

"How did you get into Hidden Justice?"

"Along with bombs, computers fascinated me. They were the only classes I took that I enjoyed. I kept teaching myself, and I learned how to write programs, hack, do all sorts of things. I could build a computer and dismantle one the way I could a bomb. I had heard of Hidden Justice. Whispers and rumors—the way they extracted vengeance. I dug deep but found little." He smiled, a real one this time. "But Damien spotted *me*. He dug into my trail, and one day Marcus appeared on my doorstep. He knew enough about me to be dangerous, yet he didn't threaten me. We met other times. I told him the complete truth, filling in a lot of blanks for him, but he was unfazed. Told me about the manifesto at Hidden Justice. Gave me a chance to come on board and make a difference—this time, legally. Or at least as legal as HJ is. I could be a good guy again. Help people."

"And you have."

"I have killed a lot of people, Sofia. Done things I'm not proud of, but those days are behind me. I know right from wrong. I won't cross that line again."

"But you're worried that now I know your past, I'll leave you?"

He sighed. "My past, plus there might be someone

else who knows it. Who might threaten me, and I know how you worry. That the idea of something happening to me might push you away."

I was quiet as I mulled over what he had told me. His past hadn't shocked me. Damien had hinted once that it was dark. Egan was a different man now; of that, I was certain. He showed it in the way he lived, the way he acted. The loyalty to his friends. The tenderness he showed me. The thought of someone threatening him did frighten me, but it angered me more than anything.

"Egan, I—"

I was interrupted by my phone, and I glanced at it with a frown. "I'm sorry, I have to take this."

I answered the call from the ER. Hearing about the mass casualty coming in, I agreed to head in right away. Egan was already on his feet by the time I hung up, grabbing the car keys. "Come, Sofia. I will take you."

In the car, I called the ER back, getting more details. Egan drove fast, skillfully going around other cars and getting me to the hospital in record time. "We'll talk more," I assured him as I climbed out of the car.

He indicated the doors of the ER. "Go. They need you."

I hurried away, stopping as a thought occurred to me. I turned, but Egan had already driven away. I wanted to tell him everything was okay. That when I said we would talk, it would be only to set aside his fears. But he was gone.

I planned to settle it in the morning.

CHAPTER EIGHT

Egan

I watched the news on the multivehicle accident that Sofia had rushed away to help with at the hospital. She was right when she said this weather was dangerous. Some people were overcautious. Some didn't take the slick streets into account. Some drove too slowly. Some too fast.

It all culminated in a horrific crash on the busy streets of Toronto. Nine cars, one truck, many humans, and even a dog were injured. I knew she would be busy for hours. I hoped she would be able to save some lives. The commentary on the news stated several people had sustained life-threatening injuries.

I paced the apartment, thinking of what I had told her. I had barely brushed the surface of my time spent on the wrong side of the law. There was simply too much to tell. Marcus, Damien, the powers behind Hidden Justice, knew of my past. Buried a lot of it. Scrubbed some.

None of it would ever be scrubbed from my

memories. Some unintended people were hurt in my quest to rid the world of those who killed to get their name known. I regretted it deeply. Hidden Justice had appealed to me because of their mandate and the way they eliminated those whose crimes were clear and left no room for doubt. They also protected the innocent. I had prayed more than once that those I helped save made up for the lives that I had taken away before.

I had found a small bit of peace once I became a member of HJ. My mind was clearer, my grief dissipated. I had always loved art, and I began to paint, losing myself in the beauty of the simple canvases I liked to create. I started to channel my extra energy into workouts, adding layers of muscle to my body. I stumbled upon the art of perfume making by accident. I attended an exhibit with perfume makers and struck up a conversation with a couple who was working on a new line of fragrances. The process had always fascinated me. Angelica and Warren Dubois were warm, personable, and talented.

"I like this one," I mused to Angelica, inhaling the fragrance on the slip of blotter paper. "Is that a trace of pine in the blend?"

"Yes," she said, sounding delighted.

"And cypress. Cedar as well. A touch of bergamot. Very woodsy. Masculine."

"Exactly."

She handed me another one. "Tell me."

I waited a moment then inhaled. "Fresh, like water. Citrus, but unusual. Grapefruit, maybe?"

She clapped her hands. "Yes."

She held up her wrist. "Here?"

I sniffed. "Ah, jasmine. Lily. Freesia? Delicate. Very pretty."
"You have a good nose, Egan. You should come visit our lab."
"I would love to."

Visiting their lab was an incredible learning experience. Talking to their staff. Listening to their objectives. I invested in their company, and they allowed me to work behind the scenes with them, using my unknown talent of my nose. I was proud of the line of fragrances we created. They sold well, and I enjoyed having my own scent no one else could purchase. I had helped create a complementary one for Sofia. It had slighter different notes than the citrusy one she wore now, but I knew she would love it. I had mixed a few light florals with citrus and some water elements. The result was creamy, soft, and subtle. I had received the first bottle last week and planned to give it to her as a gift.

If, that is, she still wanted to be with me.

I always knew she would have to be told about my past. And I had hoped she would accept that it was my past and I was beyond it. Now, thanks to the mysterious stranger entering my life, I'd had no choice but to tell her the truth now and hope she could handle it. But I was worried.

Worried that I might be too much for her.

I paced and agonized. Checked the news for any updates. Looked at my phone for messages I didn't expect to come. She would be too busy. I wondered if she would stay later than the end of her shift. If that happened, she would text to tell me. I would pick her up whenever she needed me to.

I tried to sleep and failed. I worked out in the small gym down the hall, lifting weights and running on the treadmill until my legs shook with exhaustion.

Still, there was no sleep. Finally at five, I gave up and made a pot of coffee. I took my mug and stared out the window at the breaking dawn. I was startled when my door opened and Sofia walked in.

"Sofia?" I asked, confused. "What are you doing here? Your shift—"

"A few of my colleagues came in early. They knew what happened last night and arrived early to cover so we could go home and rest."

"Was it terrible?"

"Yes. We lost three people, but the rest have all been treated or sent to surgery. I hope there are no more deaths." She shook her head. "A useless tragedy all because someone was impatient and refused to slow down in the rain."

"I'm sorry."

She lifted one shoulder, still not coming closer. I had to swallow before I could speak again.

I set down my coffee. "You never called."

"I took a cab, Egan." She approached me, tugging off her coat and leaving it on the sofa. "You've been up all night, haven't you?"

"Yes."

She stopped in front of me, cupping my cheek. I shut my eyes, leaning into her caress. "You think I'm going to leave you."

I heard the tenor of her voice. The gentleness only she would allow me to witness.

Was she trying to let me down easily?

"Yes."

"I'm not going anywhere, Egan." She cradled my face between her palms. "Look at me."

I opened my eyes, meeting her gaze. It was tired and beautiful. Filled with patience and something else. Something she had never allowed me to see before now.

Love.

My heartbeat picked up. "Sofia?"

"I can't walk away, even though I'm scared. We'll face whatever comes our way together."

"Why?" I asked, needing to hear the words. Desperate for her to say them.

"I love you, Egan Vulpe. So much."

"My past?"

"Is just that. Your past. It shaped the man you are now. The man I love. You are a warrior. My warrior. *Mio guerriero*."

My heart quickened at her endearment.

"And your worries?"

"I have to let them go."

"Tell me why," I asked again.

"Because living without you now would hurt more than losing you in the future. I want whatever happy times we have in between."

I stared at her. "Nothing is going to happen to me."

"Then we get to live a long, wonderful life together," she whispered. "If that's what you want."

"It is." I covered her hands with mine. "What do you want, *iubirea mea?*"

"You, Egan," she responded simply. "Just you."

86

I yanked her into my embrace and kissed her. Every emotion I was feeling—relief, wonderment, joy, and love —was in that kiss. She threw her arms around my neck, kissing me back with equal fervor. I lifted her, carrying her down the hall. I was going to show her with my body what I was feeling in my heart.

Until she was saturated in me.

Until she was writhing and screaming my name in ecstasy.

And then I would start again.

The room was quiet, aside from our rapid breathing and the rain that tapped against the window. Sofia rested in my arms, her hair splayed beneath her. I stroked my fingers through her tresses, liking how silky they felt on my hand.

"Sofia."

"Egan."

I smiled and pressed a kiss to her head. "You must be tired."

"No, actually, I'm still running on adrenaline."

"May I ask you something?"

She tilted up her head. "You can ask me anything."

"How did you get involved with HJ? I assume because of Damien?"

She sat up, leaning against the headboard. The blanket fell away, exposing her lovely breasts. I stared at them, then laughed as she tugged up the blanket. "Eyes up here, Mr. Vulpe."

I smirked and met her gaze. "Not my fault you're so beautiful."

She shook her head. "Back to the subject at hand."

"I know where I'd like my hand," I retorted, wiggling my fingers and winking.

She blinked then began to laugh. I loved the sound of her amusement. Full, rich, and loud. It was at odds with her more serious persona that most people saw.

She stroked my cheek. "You make me happy."

I captured her hand in mine and kissed the palm. "I like to hear that." I sat up and faced her. "And I would like to hear your story. I've always wondered."

She tilted her head. "I remember the first time I met you."

"Oh?"

She nodded. "You were new to the crew. Marcus had brought you on board, and you were moving in to the building. I was coming home from my shift, and you were in the hallway talking to Damien."

"He introduced us."

"Yes." She smiled, a soft, almost-shy smile that did something to my chest. "I thought you were the sexiest man I had ever seen. So tall and strong. Confident. You kissed my hand and said my name. I knew right then I was in trouble and I had to avoid you."

"You did a good job, my love."

"I failed, though."

"Does that upset you?" I asked.

"No. Not really. At least, not at the moment," she confessed.

I laughed and tapped the end of her nose. Always

honest, my Sofia was. "That wasn't the first time I'd seen you."

"It wasn't?"

"No. I recall the exact moment I saw you as well."

She pulled her knees to her chest. "Tell me."

It was off topic, but I wanted to tell her. "I had met with Marcus several times. Listened to his offer, thought it over. I was still concerned, and he asked to meet again, and this time, he brought Damien with him. He wanted us to meet and talk. Not business—he never talked about HJ in public—but on a personal level. Let me meet someone I would work closely with. We met at a small restaurant close to the hospital. You came in to get a takeout order on your way home. Damien got up to say hello to you. I saw you and was smitten. You were in your scrubs, your hair up, no makeup, and I thought you were the most beautiful woman in the world. I asked Marcus who you were, and he said you were Damien's cousin. I was relieved because I was worried I was going to have to kill a man I had just met and quite liked." I grinned at her. "But he was talking to the woman I had already decided would be mine. I would have to eliminate him."

For a moment, there was no reaction. Then she laughed again.

"You are incredibly caveman-ish, Egan."

"For you, yes. I had never experienced such intense feelings for a stranger before. You left, and Damien returned to the table. I asked him why he hadn't introduced us, and he said he wouldn't do that unless I was part of the team. He was very protective of you. I told Marcus I was in."

She gaped at me. "Because of me? You agreed to be part of HJ because you wanted to meet me?"

"It was the, ah, tip of the ice cream?" I responded, then frowned. "No. The tip of the sundae."

She chuckled. "The cherry on the sundae. The tip of the iceberg is the other saying."

"Well, it was both. You were the deciding factor, and I knew we would have a deep connection." I grinned at her. "I was right."

"That was a long time ago."

"I know. But I had to prove myself to Marcus. To Damien. I had to earn their trust before I could earn yours. And I knew from the moment I met you it was going to take a long time. You had a sadness about you, a thick wall that I had to break down. It took time, but it was worth it, *iubirea mea*."

She clasped my hands, and I lifted them, kissing her knuckles.

"Now I wish to hear your story."

She studied our hands, then sighed. "When Damien began working with Hidden Justice, he didn't tell me. I thought he had a programming job that kept him busy and he went on a lot of business trips. He moved in to this building, and I was only ever here once. He would come visit me, or we'd meet in a restaurant."

"Too many secrets here."

"Yes. I never really thought about it. He was a bachelor and busy. We spoke a lot, and he was always there if I needed him. We got together regularly, and I had never really been the sort to just drop by to say hello, so nothing tweaked. But one night, we were supposed to go out to dinner, and he asked if we could postpone. He said he wasn't feeling well. I checked on him the next day and he sounded okay, and he agreed to come over to my place for dinner that night. He seemed off. He didn't hug me, which was unusual. I ordered in food, and he picked at it. That told me something since he has always had a big appetite. He was pale and he kept wincing. He looked tired, and I noticed he was sweating. When I asked, he said he was still getting over the flu. I told him I thought it was something else. He denied it."

"And?"

"I put my hand on his shoulder, and he flinched. I got mad and demanded to know what was wrong. I refused to let him leave, and finally, he showed me his arm. He said he'd had an accident and gotten some stitches. I knew he was lying. I knew a gunshot wound when I saw one, but I was mostly concerned about the fact that his stitches were infected and a couple had popped. I cleaned him up and restitched him. I had some antibiotics in my bag and made him take them. He stayed the night so I could watch him. I called in a favor and got my shift covered, and by the next day, he was getting better. Then I told him I wasn't stupid and knew what a gunshot wound looked like. I told him he had thirty seconds to start talking or I was going to the police."

"I bet he didn't like that."

She tossed her hair. "I didn't give a damn. I wanted the truth."

I leaned forward, grasping her neck and pulling her to me. I kissed her until she was breathless, then released her.

"What was that for?"

"You looked so fucking sexy, talking all tough and haughty. *I didn't give a damn,*" I mimicked her. "So fierce, my Sofia."

"Should I continue? Are you done?"

"For now."

She blinked. Touched her lips. Then kept talking. "Damien told me everything. What he did. How he got involved. He'd been at a raid and took a bullet at the top of his shoulder. He hates doctors, and although Marcus had him looked at and the wound stitched up, Damien didn't tell anyone it was getting infected. He was sure it would heal. I was furious at him. For lying to me. For risking his life. For not taking better care of himself." She huffed. "He told me it was rare for them to get hurt, but it did happen on occasion. I made him drive me to his place and show me HJ. I was still angry when Marcus walked in on us. I told him off, including how Damien wasn't looking after himself. How his men needed an in-house doctor for their injuries. Someone who could care for them and follow up."

"What did Marcus do?"

"He listened to me. Let me rant. Agreed he needed that. Then told me Damien had informed him I disliked the hospital I was at, but he knew that I had to work. He offered me a position as their primary caregiver."

"And you agreed."

"Not at first. He showed me the room he could set up, promised me all the top medical equipment. Assured me anything that was more serious, he had connections for proper medical care in the hospital. Showed me this apartment where I could live as part of the deal. Explained more about what HJ did. How they helped save innocent lives. I was still angry about Damien, but it was tempting. I told Marcus I was worried about that world. I didn't want to be part of an illegal operation. He assured me I would remain safe and anonymous. Damien explained the layers of secrecy they had, and although they were deep under cover, they weren't illegal. They were ghosts. Disavowed by the people who funded them for their own safety. I thought about it, met some of the team, and decided to do it. HJ paid off my student loans and paid me a salary. They got me on part time at the hospital I wanted to work at so I had income and a place to practice my skills. The same place where I still work, except now I'm full time. I became the in-house medical care for HJ."

"How did Damien feel about it?"

"He wasn't happy with it at first, but he agreed it was the best solution. Aside from the new address, my life didn't change that much except I knew what was going on. I worried, but I trusted Marcus and Damien."

"Do you regret it?"

"No. Damien was right. It was often scrapes or accidents. They were always well prepared and wore protective armor. I could remove a non-life-threatening stray bullet without question. Stitch someone up if things got physical. Care for someone if they became ill. No questions, no records, all invisible—the way HJ worked. Major cases, like when you were all injured, went straight to the hospital. Missy was the exception. Marcus was determined to keep her here."

I laughed. "We all know why. He was obsessed with her from the first moment he held her. He trusted no one outside his people. He knew you would care for her, although if you had insisted, he would have taken her to the hospital."

"He was lucky she wasn't in worse shape. I had my doubts at first, but she was strong. Still is."

She was quiet for a moment. "When Damien decided to leave HJ, I decided it was my time too. I got on a steady rotation at the hospital and settled down."

"You never moved from here, though."

She smiled ruefully. "I know."

"Why?"

"You were here. Despite my fighting this, fighting us, I couldn't bear to move away from you."

"That is why I stayed. To be close to you." I shifted over, cupping her face. "I want to be even closer."

"To move in together."

"Yes. For now. Then I want to marry you, have babies, and live a long, full life with you."

"Marry?"

"We can wait on that. Start on the babies first. Whatever you want."

"There you go again, Egan."

I stroked her cheek. "I have been waiting, Sofia.

Patiently. Now that I have you, I want everything. And I want it all with you."

"Can we just date for a bit? Get to know each other? Maybe once you see how boring I am, you'll change your mind."

I laughed at the absurdity of her statement. "That will never happen, but yes, we can date for a while. But I will keep asking."

"I'd expect nothing less, Egan."

I leaned close and kissed her. "*Excelent.*"

CHAPTER NINE
Egan

Sofia finished off her breakfast and picked up her coffee cup. I watched her with an indulgent smile on my face. We had spent the day yesterday staying in the apartment, making love, often napping. I answered some emails. We chatted via video with Damien, who grinned at seeing us together, asking when the move upstairs would be happening. Sofia had rolled her eyes, refusing to answer. We did, however, watch the sunset on the rooftop, sipping wine and relishing the nice evening. She murmured something about enjoying gardening, and I swept my arm out.

"All of this, Sofia. We can use all of this. Plant what you want. I can use lots of vegetables for cooking. You can put pretty flowers on the table."

"We don't have to live on the top floor to use it," she pointed out.

"More convenient," I assured her.

That got me my own eye roll. But I noticed she disappeared for a while, and I was sure she'd gone to look at the apartment. It took up a lot of the top floor, the rest empty. Marcus had thought of adding another smaller place on the same floor but liked his privacy too much. Damien couldn't be bothered. I thought it would make a great studio space. The light was perfect.

I kept that to myself. I had shown patience waiting for Sofia, and I could do it again. When she decided she was ready, we would move forward. In the meantime, I got her in my bed and my life. I wasn't complaining.

"Are you headed to the gym?" she asked.

"Elite," I responded. "Leo has a new client he wants to discuss."

"When is your teenager nightmare?" she teased.

"Friday. I am dreading it."

"Who is the new client?"

"No idea. Apparently another bigwig needing our services. Leo is hiring a few more bodies since the bookings are climbing."

"Are they dangerous? Damien always said no, but I wondered if he was trying to protect me again."

"Dangerous? No. Celebrities hire us because they are concerned about their safety, usually because of overzealous fans getting too close. Political people need us to get them from point A to point B and keep the harassers out of their face. Businessmen get hit on for money and, yes, threatened at times, but usually by people fairly harmless, more annoying than anything. Sometimes it's more intense than others. This party is for a girl who's father is a rich tycoon. He worries about her safety—about her being kidnapped. She has a bodyguard for everyday, but she wants her birthday to be at a public theater. To go bowling with her friends and have pizza. Again in a public place. So I'll stick close, make sure nothing happens to her. Her regular bodyguard will be there as well. Our guys will sweep the perimeter and check on the guests. Make sure no one gets in who shouldn't be there."

"Wouldn't it be easier if her father just rented the whole theater and restaurant? Sounds as if he could afford it."

"That is exactly what he wanted to do. But she wants to do a normal birthday like her other friends. Go to the theater and sit with everyone. Eat pizza with other parties going on around her. 'Be normal,' she told her father. Luckily, it's only a dozen kids. We prebought the seats in the theater, including those around her, made sure the lanes beside hers are being used by our people, and booked the party room at the bowling alley for the pizza and dancing. That was as far as her dad was willing to go, and she accepted it. She gets out, and he has a little peace of mind. At least as much as he can have with a teenager."

Sofia smiled. "Sounds like a good party. Nothing extravagant."

"No, nothing over the top. She is amazingly grounded for someone who could be spoiled. But it is what she wanted. Her friends won't know that some of the other people around them are bodyguards. Or that they're being watched as carefully as they are. The parents do, but we agreed to keep it on the down-low so Iona—the daughter—and her friends can have a fun time."

"Will you watch the movie? Bowl? Eat pizza?"

I shook my head. "I'll watch her and the crowd in the theater. The same at the bowling alley. I'll always be on my guard, keeping an eye on her. Not eating popcorn or pizza and not bowling."

"What if she wanted you to?"

I frowned. "I highly doubt that. She is used to bodyguards, so she wouldn't expect me to join in the *fun*." I shuddered. "I hope."

Sofia laughed at my discomfort. "What if I wanted to go to a movie and out for pizza? Or go bowling?" she asked, looking mischievous.

I leaned close. "I would take you in a heartbeat. But I warn you, I am an excellent bowler, and just because I love you, I won't give you special treatment. I play to win. And I wouldn't share my popcorn."

"Even if I asked nicely?" she whispered.

I groaned, leaning my forehead to hers. "Dammit, woman, you know I would. I would give you anything you asked me for."

"I thought so. So a movie and bowling night?"

"I would prefer to dress up and go to dinner. Somewhere I can show you off and then take you dancing. Hold you in my arms."

"We can do both. Some fun nights, some dress-up nights."

"Perfect." I paused. "But…"

"I know, you want to be cautious until you're sure that gangster guy is gone."

"Damien will probably have something for me in a couple of days."

"Then we can just hang out here." She nudged my

leg with her foot. "I'm sure you can come up with something to keep us busy, Egan."

I grabbed her leg, pulling her close. She squealed and giggled as I tugged her onto my lap. I covered her mouth with mine.

"I'm sure I can."

Leo grinned at me. "You look happy."

I grinned back. "I am."

"Finally convinced Sofia to give you a chance?"

She'd given me much more than a chance, but I kept that to myself. "Yes."

"Congrats. You make a great couple."

"So, who is this new client?"

"I've only spoken to his assistant, which isn't unusual. He's in town for meetings and needs security. Your name was brought up."

I looked at the file. The name Roman Brock meant nothing to me. "What kind of business?"

"Import/export, according to the assistant. I looked it up. Not much to see. Started overseas. Has a warehouse here for distribution. According to what I could find, he makes trips here often. In fact, he does a lot of traveling."

"Has he used security before?"

"He has his own, but according to his assistant, he usually adds a local."

I shook my head. "So basically a hired gun for a day?"

He pushed a contract my way. "An expensive one."

I whistled at the dollar figure. "That's what you quoted them?"

"That was their offer. I'm not going to argue with the client."

I crossed my legs, frowning. "Seems awfully high for a day of me standing close. Why not just add another member to his team? He must trust his security leader. Why a stranger?" I pushed at the contract. "And why so much? Is he worried about an attack? Has he been threatened?"

"I asked the same questions. He said this is Mr. Brock's usual protocol. He prefers an unknown bodyguard. Someone not involved with him or his business added to his team during a trip. He explained that we had been recommended and to ask for you specifically. He assures me although this man is wealthy, there are no threats. Mr. Brock is cautious and always brings extra security to meetings with new clients as a precaution. It's only one day. You'd be on the clock from six a.m. to eleven p.m. His last meeting is at nine and in his hotel. Once he is safely back in his room, you're done. You'll go with him to five different meetings. The fee is higher because it is short notice and they assumed I would be pulling you from another job." He pushed a file my way. "I ran him through our system. He is legit."

"Well, it would certainly add to the bottom line."

"So, you'll do it?"

I pursed my lips. It all appeared straightforward, although over the top. Three security guards for one man who didn't expect any trouble, traveled often, and ran an import/export business? It seemed odd, but Leo had checked him out and he was legitimate. I scanned the file Leo handed me. Brock's business was very successful, and he always had security around him. It all checked out. I had to admit, I found most wealthy people hard to understand at times. I thought many of them had unusual quirks, and perhaps added security was his. Still, it was only a day, a shit-ton of money, and it would be different. I could dress in a suit, wear dark glasses, and enjoy being a tough guy for a day. Listen to a rich man talk business. Maybe I could learn a thing or two.

"Sure."

I dropped by the hospital on Friday on my way to the birthday party. I double-parked my car and went into the ER, waving at some staff I recognized. It wasn't the first time I had dropped off food for Sofia.

I spotted her at the nurses' station, busy jotting down something. I snuck up behind her and wrapped my arms around her waist, dropping a kiss to her neck.

"Dr. Mitchell," she scolded. "How many times must I tell you, not at the nurses' station?"

I growled deep in my chest. "Who the hell is Dr. Mitchell, and why would he be kissing you?"

Sofia began to laugh, turning her head with a droll wink. "Gotcha." Then she indicated the wall in front of her. A glass cabinet showed our reflection. She had been teasing me.

"You will pay for that, woman," I whispered into her ear.

She turned with a shake of her head. "What are you doing here, Egan? Don't you have a job…" Her voice trailed off. "What are you wearing?"

I looked down. "Iona asked that the bodyguards dressed casually to blend in more. Her father agreed. So, I am casual."

She grabbed my hand and led me to the staff room, which was empty. "You look anything but casual," she said, then flung her arms around my neck, kissing me. "You look so hot."

I highly doubted jeans and a black T-shirt with a jacket was hot, but if she thought so and wanted to kiss me to prove it, I was good with that. I yanked her tight to my chest and kissed her back, wrapping her long ponytail around my fist and tugging on her hair so I could kiss down the column of her neck. She whimpered then pulled away, running her hands down her white coat and shaking her head.

"I get carried away with you."

I grinned. "Come back, and I'll carry you elsewhere and make you feel good. There must be an empty room, yes?"

She shook her finger, admonishing me. "I am at work."

I grabbed her finger, kissing it in contrition. "I only came to bring you food before I go to the job. I made you soup."

Her eyes softened. "Thank you. You are so good to me."

"I like being good to you. But you're still going to pay for that stunt, Sofia." I dragged her back into my arms and kissed her. Hard. Wet. Deep and possessive. I kissed her until she was shaking, her whimpers music to my ears. I stepped back, liking the flush on her cheeks. The way her lips were red and swollen from mine. The glazed look in her eyes.

"You're mine. Don't forget it." Then I winked. "Have a good night. If I survive the teenagers, I'll see you in the morning. I'll be waiting for you in my bed. Naked." I paused. "Hungry. And ready to be appeased. Think about that the next time *Dr. Mitchell* pays a visit."

She grinned, not at all worried. "See you later, then."

I left, stopping one of the nurses. "Is there a Dr. Mitchell here?"

"No."

Satisfied, I nodded. "Good."

I ignored Sofia's laughter I heard behind me. Although I loved making her laugh, I kept going.

I walked out the door, not even the sight of a parking ticket dampening my mood. I was already looking forward to the morning. I'd be happy to play doctor for Sofia. Or her patient. Whichever got her hands and mouth on me fast.

If I survived tonight, that was. Somehow I had a feeling dealing with criminals might be easier than teenage girls.

I only hoped I was wrong.

Being Friday, the movie theater was crowded. But we got the girls into their seats, popcorn, snacks, and drinks in hand. They were all surprisingly well-behaved and down-to-earth. Not a diva in the bunch. They said please and thank you. They talked among themselves, laughing, and sharing jokes. Not a single cell phone was out unless someone wanted a picture, and it was used, then slid into a pocket. Iona looked happy, excited to be out. I had two female Elite guards with their kids in the row in front of the girls. They blended perfectly. At the end of each row was another guard with their family. I was going to be behind them, in the seat directly in line with Iona. A couple of other sets of parents, including Iona's, would be beside me. The girls were well protected.

I was speaking with Malcolm, listening to the girls and watching the theater, when someone gasped. I tensed, then relaxed when I realized one girl had dropped her popcorn. She was upset, bending to pick up the almost-empty container. The movie would start in five minutes, and I held up my hand to stop one of my men from moving. "I'll get another one," I said. "Malcolm, you and your wife take your seats."

I hurried to the concession stand, getting another popcorn, keeping my eyes on the door. As I turned, I saw a man enter the theater, and the hairs on the back of my neck stood up. It looked like Alex, the height and bright color and cut of his hair familiar. I dodged the lineup behind me, entering the theater and scanning the crowd. Iona and her friends were fine, and there was no one out of place. I didn't see the bright-gold hair anywhere. I gave the popcorn to Mike and asked him to watch for the next few moments.

I covered the theater fast. I couldn't see Alex anywhere. If, in fact, it had been him. I returned to the seats as the previews finished, sitting down. "Eyes open," I muttered into my earpiece. "I thought I saw something. Tall guy, bright-gold mohawk. Keep on the lookout."

As the audience became engrossed in the film, we watched the room. I scanned it over and over. And while I never saw anything amiss, I couldn't relax. My mind went a hundred miles an hour. How would Alex know we'd be here? Had the system been hacked? Was I being followed and I hadn't noticed? As soon as this party was over, I planned to head to the office and do some deep digging. I would contact Leo as well on the way to the bowling alley.

The movie finished, and as agreed, we waited until the crowd was mostly dispersed to take the girls to the cars. They were all chatting about the movie, in love with the lead teen heartthrob.

"Did you like it, Egan?" Iona asked me.

"Yeah, it was, ah, great."

She nodded enthusiastically. "I know, right? It appeals to every age group. He is so dreamy!"

I only smiled, not wanting her to know I hadn't watched a second of the movie and if Mr. Dreamy appeared in front of me, I would have no idea.

At the bowling alley, we went right to the private room. Presents and pizza were waiting. I left men on the doors and checked out the entire building. I saw nothing out of the ordinary, but my anxiety didn't lessen. I called Leo to tell him what I thought I had seen.

"How would he know?" he asked. "Our firewalls are solid. Damien and you built the system."

"I don't know," I replied. "Maybe he's following me?"

Leo snorted. "I doubt there is anyone who could follow you and you not know, Egan."

"Maybe a new hire got befriended? Said something out of turn?" I said, grasping at straws.

"Highly doubtful."

He was right. We only hired the best. And the best never talked.

"Still, I'm going to check the system."

"Okay. Let me know."

"I will."

The group ate pizza and drank far too much soda. They moved to the lanes and began to divide up. Iona came over, looking nervous.

"What's up?" I asked, concerned. Everything seemed fine, although I still felt wary.

"I wanted to ask if you'd be on my team. We're one short."

I began to say no when I caught her father's eye. He nodded, and I realized I had no choice. "One game," I said.

She grinned, wide and toothy, clapping her hands. She made that noise only teenage girls could make—a high-pitched squeal that seemed to come from her toes, it was so loud. She hurried back to the girls, who all looked pleased.

Inwardly, I groaned. Beside me, Mike chuckled. "You've got a fan."

"God help me," I muttered and went to pick up a pair of bowling shoes. I returned, slipping off my own shoes and sliding them on. I stood and joined the girls. I stayed in the mode, watching the area, not speaking much, although I clapped with the rest of them and smiled as they teased and taunted one another. None of them took it seriously, and they all seemed impressed with my ability. I hadn't lied to Sofia. I bowled well, and I made sure Iona's team won. None of them cared. They all got tiaras to wear to celebrate, and I jokingly let her put one on me, although I removed it as soon as they returned to the room for cake and presents.

I took off my borrowed shoes and headed over to the counter to return them. That was when I saw him. Sitting in the corner, drinking a beer. There was no doubt it was Alex. I approached him, keeping my face neutral. He smirked as I got close.

"What are you doing here?" I asked, my voice low with anger.

He shrugged. "It's a free country. I'm having a beer."

"Go have it elsewhere. Stop following me."

He shook his head. "I'm not following you. I was here first."

I felt the anger grip me at his lie. He knew my schedule.

"I saw you at the theater."

He didn't deny it. He grinned, looking pleased. "I saw you looking."

I leaned close. "Get out, or I'll have you escorted out."

He tsked. "That's not very polite. I was just enjoying watching you with your little groupies." He shook his head. "Is that what you've sunk to now? The great Egan Vulpe? Babysitting children instead of using your talent?" Again, there was a slow shake of his head. "So much money and power you are letting slip through your fingers. So many detonations you should be creating."

"What I do or do not do is none of your business. Get out."

He finished his beer and stood. "I'll be seeing you around."

"I doubt it."

He laughed, the sound of it grating on my nerves. "Oh, you can count on it, Mr. Vulpe. We will find what you cannot live without."

Ice wrapped around my chest, but I kept my expression neutral. "You cannot take what I do not have," I lied.

He shook his head. "We will find it. I look forward to working with you."

"It will be a cold day in hell before that happens."

He smiled. It was twisted and evil. "Temperatures are dropping as we speak."

And he left.

CHAPTER TEN

Egan

The party was deemed a success by everyone. The guests, the staff, and, most importantly, by Iona and her parents. I breathed a sigh of relief when I shut the door of the limo and watched them be escorted into their house by their own security. My job was done.

Now I had to figure out why the hell Alex had shown up and how he knew about it. I drove to the Elite office, needing the powerful computers and server room there for the task.

At the office, I began digging. I followed trails, checked out firewalls and encryption. Called Damien and told him what had occurred. He wasn't pleased and signed in to his system even though it was the middle of the night where he was. We found nothing. No trace of being hacked. I scanned everything, including myself, and found no tracking devices. No listening equipment in the office. I was at a loss.

"How did he know?"

"Everyone has a talent," Damien surmised. "Maybe this Alex's is following someone undetected."

"I'll have to be more careful."

"I was going to call you in the morning."

"You found something?"

"Not much. I think your visitors are Russian ex-mobsters that have been off the radar for a while. I got a hit on Alex. I'm tracing it, but it's taking time."

"Ex?"

"He was involved in a lot of illegal activities. Crime for hire. Did a lot of dirty jobs. Suddenly disappeared. Files closed."

"You sound unconvinced."

"It feels...off. I found a few things, but not much. I get a feeling something is hidden. Something related to Ivan."

"Without a doubt. He's the leader."

"I will keep digging."

I had always trusted my instincts and those of the people around me. If Damien was suspicious, then so was I.

"So, what do they want with me? What could they want blown up?"

"I don't know. But be careful, Egan. I'll keep going." He paused. "They haven't discovered your connection to Sofia yet," he mused.

"No. And they won't. I will protect her."

"You can only do so much. You have to put her first."

"I will."

I hung up, now more anxious than ever. I paced the

office, then went home. I couldn't sleep, unable to relax. I scanned the apartment, Sofia's place. The garage. The car. Nothing. I checked my electronics, Sofia's. Everything was clean.

Finally, I gave up and made coffee, waiting for Sofia. I had to talk to her. I took my coffee and went for a shower, letting the hot water run over my shoulders and loosen the tight muscles. I soaped up using my own unique fragrance brand, then washed my hair. I toweled off, wiping the condensation from the mirror and studying my face. I looked drawn and worried. Tired and older than my years. I had promised Sofia honesty, and I would give it to her. If she felt worried and wanted to walk away, I had to allow it. Damien was correct. Her safety was paramount, and with this new information, I wouldn't blame her. I would hate it, but I would accept it. Until I found out what these people wanted, it might be better if she distanced herself from me. I rubbed my chest at the ache I felt simply thinking about it.

In my room, I sat on the edge of the mattress, letting the cool air dry my skin. I shut my eyes, feeling exhausted. Weary. Even my bones ached with it. With a sigh, I flopped back on the bed, keeping my eyes shut. I would get up in a minute and get dressed. Be waiting for Sofia.

I just needed a minute.

Or two.

SOFIA

I arrived home, fully expecting to be greeted by Egan. In my apartment, I had a quick shower and changed into a pair of loose pants and a sweatshirt. It was old and soft from being laundered so often, and it hung off one shoulder, the neckline loose and stretched. It was one of my favorites and spelled comfort to me.

Using my key, I let myself into Egan's place, immediately smelling the coffee. The apartment was quiet as I poured a cup and snuck a pastry he had on a covered plate on the counter. He always had something sweet around. Again, I was surprised he wasn't there, then remembered his words about waiting for me in his bed. I finished the sticky treat and the coffee and padded to the bedroom. I stood in the doorway, gazing at the sight that greeted me.

Egan was passed out on the bed. It looked as if he'd sat down and fell backward, falling asleep immediately. His hair was still damp from the shower, and he wore only a towel around his waist. His arms were stretched over his head, and his legs were splayed wide. His chest moved up and down in a rhythmic beat. I stepped closer, filled with wonder and longing.

How had I resisted this man for so long? His arms were thick and muscled. His pecs and abs defined. His long legs were toned and strong. He was gorgeous. Sexy, even in sleep. With his tousled hair, beautiful, sculpted body, and the symmetry of his handsome face, he was captivating. However, I noticed, although he slept, his gorgeous hands twitched, and the frown lines on his face and around his mouth were deep. His sleep wasn't bringing him any rest. Something had upset him, and judging from the dark circles under his eyes, he'd been up the entire night. No doubt, he'd sat down and finally gave in to exhaustion. He tried to match his hours to mine, staying up late and sleeping with me when I got home for short periods, before he went to work, leaving me to rest before my next shift. He was already tired before last night, and by this morning, he must have been exhausted.

I crept closer, watching him. The urge to touch, to kiss him, was strong. I wanted to do something to help him relax fully and to sleep deeply. I bit back my grin as I realized I knew exactly how to do that. I stepped between his legs, gently pulling on the towel, exposing him to my eyes. Even in sleep, he was at half-mast, and I touched his cock, barely tracing it with my fingers, smiling as he swelled, growing hard and long. A thick vein ran around him, the dark color and head tempting. I lowered myself, tracing the vein with my tongue, feeling him getting harder. He moaned in his sleep, clenching his hands.

"Sofia," he murmured, still asleep.

Resting my hands on either side of his hips, I engulfed him in my mouth, sucking lightly. He tasted of water, man, Egan. His scent surrounded me, his cock stretching my lips, hitting the back of my throat. He jerked, waking fully, and his hands flew to my head. "Sofia," he repeated. *"Iubirea mea."*

I licked the shaft, swirling my tongue on the swollen head. Teased the slit. He groaned, arching his back.

"More," he begged. "Use your tongue. Suck me."

I cupped his balls and took him deeper. I swallowed around him, and he cursed, fisting my hair. "Like that, Sofia. Just like that."

I played and stroked his balls. Moved my head. Pulled back so he was almost out, then sucked him back in. He groaned and cursed in Romanian. In English. Praised me. Begged me.

"Don't stop, please."

"Ah, take me deeper."

"Fuck yes, Sofia. Like that. Don't stop. Please don't stop."

"I want to wake up like this every day."

I met his eyes as I began to move faster. Feel the way he was swelling. Knowing he was going to come.

"You look so good like that," he panted. "With my cock in your mouth." His head fell back, his neck arching, the veins standing out. "Sofia, I'm going… You need to move… I can't…"

He called out a list of gods. Cursed and shook. Came in my mouth in long, hot spurts. His fists tightened in my hair, but he never hurt me. He spasmed and trembled. Then he went still, and with a final sweep of my tongue, I pulled off him, lifting my head.

He was breathing hard, his chest pumping up and down with the effort. I rubbed his thighs, feeling the muscles contract with my touch. He lifted his head, meeting my eyes.

"Good morning, *mio guerriero*."

With a roar, he sat up, dragging me to him. He tore my sweatshirt over my head, yanking down my pants.

He pulled me to his chest, rolling over on me, his mouth covering mine.

His kiss was blistering. Profound. Wet. Carnal. I now had both tastes of him on my tongue, and it made me crazy. He explored every inch of my mouth, his tongue deep inside me. Then he moved, licking and biting at my neck. Sucking at my skin. He wrapped his lips around my nipple, drawing it between his teeth. He went back and forth between the two, devouring them, making me gasp and plead with him.

Then he sat up, kneeling. He grabbed my legs and threw them over his shoulders, dragging me up his body until I was positioned by his mouth. "Did you like that, my Sofia? Waking me up with my cock in your mouth?"

His hot breath drifted over my core. I nodded, whimpering.

"You made me come. Now, it is my turn. But I will not be satisfied with one orgasm from you. I am going to make you come until I am satiated." He licked me once. A long, hot trail up my center. "As I told you last night, I am hungry, so hold tight."

I shivered at the dark promise in his voice. Our eyes locked as he buried his face into my core. He ran his tongue over me, tasting me. He turned his head to my thigh and drew the skin in between his lips, sucking hard and leaving a mark. He did the same to the other leg then met my eyes again.

"Everything between these two marks is mine. And what lies between them is the sweetest-tasting pussy I have ever known." He licked again, swirling his tongue around my clit and making me cry out.

"Who does it belong to?" he asked.

"You, Egan. Only you."

"Such a good girl," he purred. "You need to be rewarded for that."

"Yes, yes, yes," I babbled.

"My tongue and my fingers?" he asked. "Or my cock?"

"All of them," I begged. "All of them."

He smiled, one so filled with love and passion I caught my breath. "What a good answer. You deserve your reward. And you'll get it." He kissed my clit. "*Now.*"

The world ceased to exist. All there was, all that mattered, was Egan's mouth. His tongue. He licked and lapped. Stroked my clit with tender caresses, then sucked it between his teeth, nibbling softly. He worked it, sliding one, then two fingers into me. He strummed my clit in time with his movements, sending me over the edge. He added another finger, stretching me, making me whimper with need. He pressed his thumb to my sensitive nub, driving me to another orgasm, and before I could come down from it, slid two fingers into my ass as he kept fucking me with the other two, again using his thumb on my clit. I detonated again, unsure how he could draw such intense orgasms from me one after another. I cried out his name, riding his hand, begging him for something. What, I had no idea. But he did. He eased back, hovering over me, and thrust inside me, his cock hard and hot. I shouted out, my body locking down around him. He grunted and gasped, moving inside me. I gripped at his shoulders, and he kissed me. I could taste us both, feeling another wave of heat building within me. I wrapped my shaking legs around his hips as he began to move faster. Harder. Hitting me in a place I never knew existed. I flew higher, crying and scratching at his back, pulling at the sheets, sucking on his tongue, noises coming from my mouth I had never made before. He kept kissing me, his tongue fucking my mouth in time with his hips. We were pressed so closely together our skin meshed. Our breaths were shared. Our lips locked.

I was on fire, and I wasn't sure I would survive this. Survive him. I was convinced there would be nothing but a pile of ash left when he was done with me.

If he was ever done with me.

I soared upward, hurtling into the unknown. Until the room around me faded and the sky opened up, black and filled with stars. Blue and bright with the sun. Day and night colliding. I exploded, crying out his name, the sound echoing off the walls. Egan rode it out, pounding into me as he came. He filled me completely, shouting my name, pulling my hair, pushing on the mattress, driving us both deep into the plush bed.

Then he collapsed, shaking and heavy on top of me. Neither of us moved. Neither of us could. He mumbled something into my neck, his lips gliding along the sensitive skin. I was sure I was going to be covered in love bites. I was also certain he'd be pleased with his handiwork.

He lifted his head, his eyes drowsy. He pressed his mouth to mine, kissing me. The heat was gone, the desperation evaporated. Instead, I felt his adoration, his love, and his gratitude. He rolled off me, pulling me to his chest. "Sofia, my love."

I pressed a kiss to his skin. "Hush, just sleep, Egan."

"I have things to say."

"Later."

I felt for the extra blanket, glad I could reach it. I flung it over us and curled into his side. He fell asleep almost instantly. I lifted my head, studying him. The frown was absent, his forehead unlined. A low, snoring noise escaped his lips on occasion.

I smirked as I settled into his embrace. I wanted him relaxed and asleep.

I did my job well.

CHAPTER ELEVEN
Sofia

I woke up, the scent of coffee heavy in the air. I sat up, not surprised to see the other side of the bed empty. I ran my hands over the mattress. It was still slightly warm, and I could see the indentation from Egan's body. He hadn't been awake long. A look at my phone told me it was just after noon. He had slept with me for a long time.

I slipped from the bed and went to the bathroom. As I brushed my teeth, I looked over Egan's artwork on my body. Scruff marks were on my neck and stomach. A few on my thighs. My lips were still swollen from his possession earlier, and I had other love bites scattered everywhere on my body. Luckily, most in places I could cover up. The largest ones were on my thighs, and I shivered as I recalled the words he'd said as he marked me.

"Everything between these two marks is mine."

I had never been a woman who swooned over a possessive caveman. I always considered myself an independent woman, needing nothing from a man. Having lost the two men in my life who mattered romantically, I had done everything on my own, learning as I went. Refusing to rely on someone else for anything. And the few men I dated had been nice. Polite. Decent in bed, although I never felt satisfied.

I had nothing but satisfaction from Egan. Wild, unbridled satisfaction. He was an incredible lover. Giving, passionate, controlling, yet he gave me more freedom than I had ever experienced before. He encouraged my sexuality, loved it when I talked dirty, and always put me first. His body was spectacular, and he let me explore to my heart's content. I loved the way he explored me as well.

I shook my head, picking up his discarded T-shirt and pulling it on. He loved seeing me in his clothes, and I had to admit wearing them made me feel sexy.

I padded down the hall, stopping at the entrance to the living room. Egan stood, coffee cup in hand, staring out the window. He was frowning, seemingly deep in thought. He rubbed at his temples, then paused, turning his head. Our eyes met across the room, and his frown disappeared. His warm, sexy smile—the one only I ever saw—curled his lips. He held out his hand, beckoning me.

"Sofia," he murmured.

I went forward, letting him take my hand and pull me close. He pressed his coffee cup to my lips, and I took a sip of the fragrant brew.

"Mmm," I murmured. "Delicious."

He set down the cup, embracing me. For a moment,

I basked in his warmth. The solid feel of his body aligning with mine. He murmured my name, and I lifted my head, meeting his gaze. He looked despondent, worried. Before I could ask him, he covered my mouth with his and kissed me. Long, slow, and profound. I felt his love, his worry and fear. I felt the way he pulled me closer as if to mold me to him, for our skin to meld together so we were one.

Then I tasted his fear. The salt of his worry ran down his face, and I pulled back, cupping his cheeks. "Egan, what is it?"

He met my gaze, his tortured and sad. "I think we should stop seeing each other."

He led me to the sofa, sitting beside me, my hands clasped in his.

"What nonsense is this?" I asked. "You've chased me for years, and now you want to break up?" I didn't believe him for a moment.

He told me what had happened last night. Seeing Alex. Knowing that somehow he was being tracked.

"Damien and I cannot figure it out. I don't think they know about you, but I cannot take the chance. I cannot risk you, my Sofia. I would rather you be safe without me than in danger with me." He gripped my hands tighter. "You should go away. Go to Damien until this is done."

"No."

He lifted his eyebrows. "Sofia—"

I interrupted him. "I'm not leaving you, Egan. You want to live two separate lives outside this building? I understand that. No dates out, no more hospital drop-bys. No driving me to work. But when we're here, we're safe, right? Damien told me this place was locked down and any sort of scanning or listening device wouldn't work. Right?"

He nodded.

"Then, to the outside world, we just live in the same building. But I am not giving you up." I crossed my arms. "Don't even try to talk me into it."

A small smile curled his lips, then he shook his head. "They might already know, Sofia. I can't risk that."

I shook my head. "If they knew, they would have used that angle. They don't seem to be the type to pussyfoot around. They would have threatened you with me, but they haven't. You only drove me to the hospital a couple of times and dropped by once. From now on, we will be careful."

He sighed, running a hand through his hair. "I can't risk you being out on your own, my love. There are simply too many factors. Until I know all the players and what the hell they want with me, I have to put you first. I need you somewhere safe. Damien is the obvious choice."

"I am not running."

"It isn't running. It's being smart."

"I am not leaving you alone. Don't ask me to do that, Egan Vulpe."

He stared at me, then yanked me onto his lap. "Oh, my love, for you to be worried. I have not had someone worry about me like that for a very long time." He kissed me. "I love you for that. I love you so much. But I have to put you first."

"And I have to be here for you."

He studied me. "I do not want to give you up," he said quietly. "The thought of going back to being without you tears me up."

"Then don't."

"We have to take precautions."

"Fine."

"There will be a driver taking you to and from the hospital."

I pulled a face, and he held up his hand. "This is not negotiable."

"Fine."

"A bodyguard——"

I cut him off. "No. I will not have a bodyguard. The driver drops me off and picks me up. I don't leave the hospital during my shift."

"What if you are hungry?"

"I'll DoorDash. My fellow night nurse, Karen, has an account. I think she's their best customer. I won't leave the hospital."

"I want someone with you when you do errands."

"Egan," I said patiently. "If they are watching this building and suddenly see me with bodyguards, won't they assume I'm someone special? I think I should just go about my life. I'll be careful. I'll use Amazon Prime. I won't go out without your knowing. You can put a tracker on me—more than one, if you want. Add one to my phone like Damien did years ago."

"He did?"

I nodded. "I assume it is still on it. He always wants to mess around with my new phones, so I assumed that was why. It made him feel better, so I didn't care."

"I would feel better if you had someone watching over you for a while," he said slowly. "Much better."

"Nice try. I will agree to the driving. I will agree to a tracker or two. I will check in with you, and I will be careful." I held up my hand before he could argue. "If something happens and I get nervous or you think they know about us and will use it against you, I will go to Damien. I won't jeopardize you or us."

He huffed out an impatient noise, breathing heavily through his nose like a discontented bull. I tried not to smile. I wrapped my arms around his shoulders and snuggled close to him. "Don't make me leave you, Egan. I would miss you too much."

He held me tight. "For now," he agreed. "But if anything happens and I am worried…"

"I will go."

"No arguing."

"No."

He stood. "I will hold you to that, Sofia." He walked to the kitchen and set me on the counter. "Now, I will make breakfast."

"More like lunch."

"Whatever. I will cook and you will eat."

"So bossy."

"You like it."

I caught his arm and kissed him. "Maybe."

He met my gaze and grinned. In a second, he had

me tossed over his shoulder and was heading down to the bedroom. "You need to be reminded of who is boss," he muttered.

I held on to his ass, enjoying gripping the firm flesh.

He wanted to show me he was boss? I didn't object.

EGAN

Sofia smiled at me, contented and sleepy. I enjoyed seeing her in my bed. Watching her sleep. Knowing she was protected and happy. Sated. My favorite part of the day was when she woke, still drowsy and sweet, her defenses down. Then she was simply my Sofia.

I had to grin. I supposed I was every inch the caveman she told me I was.

"What?" she asked, covering a yawn with her hand.

Chuckling, I dropped a kiss to her head. "Nothing. I was thinking I love having you here."

"I'm only here for the sex and food." She paused, pulling the blanket over her shoulder. "And this bed. It's really comfy."

I began to laugh. "Okay, *iubirea mea*, whatever you say."

She smiled again, taking my hand and kissing it. She curled her fingers around mine and held it to her chest. For a moment, neither of us spoke, yet the quiet was filled with silent words that passed between our gazes.

Stay with me.

I feel safe.

I will protect you.
I want to be with you.
You make me whole.
I never want to leave.
I will never let you go.
I love you.
Always.

Sofia sighed, the sound soft in the room.

I tapped the end of her nose. "I have a gift for you."

"I don't need a gift," she protested, but she sat up, looking delighted.

Grinning, I handed her the gold box. She ran her finger over the sleek label and embossed lid. "So lovely," she murmured.

"Open it."

She lifted the lid and withdrew the elegant bottle. Mine looked as if it were carved from granite. Her more feminine container looked like etched crystal, the light playing off the facets. She studied it. "It is exquisite."

I took the bottle from her hand and uncapped it. I applied a drop to her wrists and inner elbows, then behind her ears, and added a touch at the nape of her neck. I recapped it and handed it back to her. She waited a moment and lifted her wrist to her nose, inhaling.

"Egan," she whispered. "This is beautiful."

"I helped design it for you. Only you, Sofia. No one else will have this fragrance."

"It reminds me of yours a little."

I smiled, tucking a long strand of her dark hair over her shoulder. "They complement each other. They each hold a few of the same notes, but yours are sweeter. Like you." I leaned forward, burying my nose in her neck and bringing her scent into my lungs. She smelled heavenly, the Asian florals and citrus the ideal combination for her. I turned my face and kissed her neck.

"Perfect."

I eased back before I followed my instinct to tip her over and make love to her wearing nothing but the fragrance I had created for her.

She cupped my face. "Thank you."

Beside her on the nightstand, her phone rang. She answered it with a frown. "Dr. DeSalvo."

I got up, pulling on some sweats, and went to get us coffee. I had just poured the steaming liquid into the cups as she wandered into the kitchen wearing one of my shirts. I loved seeing her in my clothes. It felt intimate.

She sat at the counter. "No, that's fine." She frowned. "No, just one. No plus." She listened for a moment. "Okay, Sally. We can be each other's dates." She laughed and said goodbye, hanging up. She took the mug from my hand.

"Dates?" I asked.

She took a long drink of coffee and ran a hand through her hair. "There is a dinner for the hospital to raise money in a week. I had forgotten about it, and Sally was calling to remind me I had to pay for my ticket. She knew I was seeing someone and asked if I was bringing them." She regarded me sadly. "I assumed you couldn't go with me since we're doing the whole 'not together' thing. So I only got one ticket. Her husband is working, so we'll sit together."

I covered her hand, hating the note of disappointment in her voice, even as it pleased me. She would like me to go with her. Sit beside her. I wanted to as well, but the need to make sure she was safe was stronger.

"When is it?"

"Thursday next week."

I opened my laptop, scanning my calendar. "Leo had mentioned a charity event. We're doing security for it," I said, meeting her eyes.

She nodded. "They always get some extra security. The doctors, the auction items."

"I'll get Leo to add me. I can't be with you, but I can be there. Maybe we can sneak in a little rendezvous in the dark somewhere," I offered, teasing her.

She gazed at me, a glint of humor showing through. "A tryst, Egan? Groping me in the dark?"

"Whatever you want, my love." I traced her cheek. "Whatever the next benefit is, I will escort you. Show the world you are mine."

"Caveman," she muttered, lifting her coffee cup to her lips to hide her smile.

"Your caveman," I assured her.

"How about you get your caveman ass in gear and make me something to eat?"

I turned to the fridge. "Your wish, my command."

"Omelets?" she asked hopefully.

I picked up the eggs. "Omelets it is."

CHAPTER TWELVE

Egan

L eo laughed when I asked to be added to the roster for the hospital event. "It's run-of-the-mill stuff, Egan. Standing by the auction table, looking fierce so no one thinks to slip a pair of earrings they're admiring into their pocket," he teased. "We donate our time every year because of Sofia. We do all their events."

"I want to be close to her," I explained. "I cannot escort her, but I can watch her. Pay the regular guys, but add me, no charge."

"Okay," he agreed easily.

"And I need a driver for her." I handed him her schedule. "Nondescript car. Two drivers, varying their schedule. But they make sure she gets into the hospital and the apartment building safely. They open her door, and they watch her walk in. I want them armed. If there is any trouble, they act. No questions."

He nodded. "Why don't we add a fake car service sign to the car? If anyone sees it, it looks like they're hired. As if her car isn't working or something."

"Good idea."

"Darnell and Samuel would be good," he mused. "Big guys, fast, well trained. Both ex-cops and good men. They'd watch over her."

I nodded in agreement. I knew them both well. They were strong, fast, and often requested by our celebrities. They were excellent marksmen and would keep Sofia safe. Damien had hired them and they had great respect for him, so they would take this assignment personally. "Okay. Bring them in so I can talk to them, please."

"Sure."

He typed for a few moments, speaking as he did. "Any ideas on how Alex knew your schedule?"

"No. The system is clean. No one has tried to hack into the software. Sofia and I come up clean for tracking devices. Nothing on our cars, our persons, anything. Damien could be right, and this guy could be an amazing tail. Hiding in plain sight. I'm being extra vigilant."

He glanced up. "Hiding in plain sight. Like Raven's stalker?"

I suppressed a shudder. "I hope not." Andy had been a nutjob of epic proportions and kept us guessing and chasing him for weeks.

"Maybe we need to add some equipment around you. Some cameras to see if we spot some coincidences that aren't coincidences. The same hat behind you as you walk somewhere. The same van six vehicles down, that sort of thing."

"Not a bad idea."

He frowned. "There are bugs now that I can't even trace without specific equipment." He glanced around. "This building is safe, especially this office. Your apartment should be okay as well, but out there..." He trailed off.

"I'll be careful what I say."

He nodded. "You can't be too cautious until we figure out what they want. Why they want you specifically. No offense, but there are lots of people who could blow up a building for them."

"I know," I agreed, not offended at all. Leo was right. There were others who could bring down a building, and I needed to know why they were focused on me.

And how they'd found me.

———

Life seemed normal for the next week. Sofia was picked up and dropped off every day. She waited in the car until her driver assessed the area and gave her the okay, and they stayed until she had walked in, not leaving until she was safely in the building—either the hospital or the apartment block. She had no idea that if they were uneasy, she would remain in the car, and they would leave with her and take her somewhere safe. I wasn't taking chances with her. She did agree to another tracker in her purse and on her phone, which surprised me. Then I realized Damien had spoken to her. He had told her to take it easy on me and cooperate.

I appreciated his backup.

I had two of our ex-HJ agents follow me from a distance. They changed all the time, and I was never able to spot them right away. But they, in turn, never spotted anyone following me. I didn't see Alex again, and there was no contact. Still, I was worried. I knew they were simply biding their time.

The day of the charity event, I pulled out my tux to get ready. I was going early as was our protocol, to check everything out. Sofia's driver would pick her up along with her friend Sally and bring them to the event. I was contemplative as I got ready, tucking in my shirt, making sure my bow tie was straight, and adding my favorite cuff links to the sleeves.

I didn't want to be attending as personnel. I wanted to sit next to Sofia. Be able to wrap my arm around her. Laugh and talk with her. Dance with her after. Peruse the auction tables and buy her something that caught her eye. She had only shaken her head when I told her what I was thinking, and she assured me these events were as boring as any other charity dinner.

"Lots of people wanting to be important. So much chatter and money being thrown around," she said. *"The meals are the same, the speeches too long, and the liquor flows far too freely. I rarely dance unless someone I know is there and we take a turn on the dance floor. I dislike the dinners, but we are asked to support. I'm usually one of the first to leave."* Then she smiled. *"At least I'll have an excuse. Tonight, I'm working, so I can't drink, and I can leave with an emergency if I have to."*

Boring or not, I still wanted to be the one beside her. I shook my head to clear my thoughts and added some cologne, reaching for my suit jacket. I would carry it with me and put it on when I arrived to avoid some wrinkles. I heard my door open and the sound of Sofia's quiet footfalls. She was getting ready at her place, but it was too early for her to be done.

She walked into the bedroom, wearing a short robe. Her hair was down, a dark wave of silk that tumbled over her shoulders.

She clasped her hands as I turned to face her.

"Put your jacket on," she murmured.

I did as she requested, pulling down my sleeves.

"My, my, Mr. Vulpe. You are one fine specimen of a man all the time, but in a tux?" She waved her hand in front of her face. "You slay."

I smiled at her words and moved in front of her. "You are beautiful."

"I haven't gotten ready yet."

"You are still the most beautiful woman in the world."

She ran her hand up my chest, resting it over my heart. "Thank you."

"I dislike the fact that I will not be here to watch you leave, so I have asked Samuel to call as he gets close, and he will meet you at the door and walk you to the car."

"Egan, you are going to worry yourself into an early grave about me. Please relax."

I lifted her hand and kissed it. "When this is over, I will."

"Will it be over?"

"Yes. Between Damien and I, we will figure it out." I pulled her into my arms and kissed her. "I have to go."

"You need to relax," she repeated, running her hand down my chest. "I feel your tension."

"I will later."

"You'd enjoy your evening better if you were." She tugged on my cummerbund. "I can help you."

"Sofia," I warned, my body beginning to respond to her closeness. It always did. "I'll be late."

"Oh." She pouted and spoke in a hushed whisper. "But I was hoping to persuade you to fuck me in your tux."

My jaw dropped. "What?"

She leaned up, nibbling on my neck. "Drop your pants and take me hard and fast, Egan. I'm so turned on just looking at you, I'll come quickly." She sucked my earlobe into her mouth. "I'll make sure you do too."

My cock responded. I shucked off my jacket, tossing it over the chair. Wrinkles seemed unimportant now. So did being late. They could scope out the room first without me.

I carried her to the bed, dropping her onto the mattress. "You better be naked under that robe."

"Totally."

I yanked on the sash and tore open the soft material. She was naked. Her nipples were stiff—rose-colored pebbles waiting for my mouth. The way she rubbed her thighs together, I knew she was wet and aching.

She needed my cock to ease that ache.

"This will be fast, Sofia."

"And hard, Egan," she replied, lying back, opening her arms and legs wide. "Don't forget hard."

I reached for my pants.

"Not a problem."

I stood at the edge of the room, scanning the large area. It was rapidly filling up, guests, staff, and employees circulating. Trays of champagne were being carried, glasses lifted off by well-dressed invitees. Large centerpieces of flowers perfumed the air, the scent heavy in the room. I recognized a few people, greeting Sofia's coworkers with a dip of my chin and the occasional handshake. I wasn't there to mingle, but do a job—as easy as this one was.

Then she walked in, and the room faded away. When she paused in the doorway, our eyes met across the room, and my focus narrowed in. I saw only her. Only her sensual beauty.

She wore a deep green dress that looked stunning against her skin. The skirt ended mid-calf, the luminous material glowing in the lights, the high heels on her feet making her legs seem endless. The bodice dipped low, the swells of her breasts visible. Her long hair was swept up in a knot at the base of her neck, showing off the delicate column of her throat. Wisps hung around her face. She wore more makeup than usual, making her eyes seem larger in her face, her lips glistening and inviting. The shawl she wore slipped, and I spied the slope of her bare shoulder. I knew how that skin tasted under my lips. How soft it was. She was artlessly sexy, while still being elegant and classy.

Despite having had her only a couple of hours ago, I

felt my cock stiffen, and I had to turn away, breaking our eye contact. I made another sweep of the room, walking slowly, making my way toward her. I stopped when I reached her side, standing and observing the crowd.

"You take my breath away, *iubirea mea*. You are beyond exquisite."

"I'm glad you think so," she responded.

"So does every other man watching you."

She laughed softly, shaking her head as a waiter offered her champagne. "I think you are a little biased."

Her coworker Sally came over, handing Sofia a glass. "Iced tea," she said. "Looks like we're drinking, but we're not."

I smiled at her and tilted my head in acknowledgment.

"You clean up well, Egan."

I threw her a fast wink, and she laughed.

"We need to mingle, Sofia."

Sofia looked at me and I nodded. "Go enjoy your evening. I'll be watching."

I felt the brush of her hand over my back as she moved away. "I know."

The dinner and the speeches were over. People were dancing, some still perusing the auction items. It would close in about an hour, then there would be more dancing for some, and for others, it would be the time to depart. As Sofia claimed, it was fairly dull, but the keynote speaker had been interesting and passionate, and I planned on donating some money to the cause of the evening. Funds were being raised to upgrade the pediatric oncology area of the hospital. As the speaker claimed, the area gave the kids a chance to escape from their treatments. They unveiled the plans, and I wanted to help make sure they achieved their goal. But at the moment, something else was on my mind.

I watched, annoyed, as Sofia was asked yet again to dance. Even if she tried to say no, she ended up on the floor with yet another admirer. Another man holding her in his arms. She was graceful and classy. It had been difficult enough to stand by and watch her during dinner. Laughing, talking—relaxed and beautiful. Unknowingly sexy in her guileless mannerisms. She seemed oblivious to the admiring stares, the frank appraisals of many of the men. I, however, noticed every single damn one.

The room had gotten warmer with the large group of people, and she had slipped off her shawl after dinner. The first time she stood, I saw the way the dress dipped low in the back, exposing her beautiful skin. I had to endure other men touching the bare skin of her back as they danced. Holding what was mine. Feeling the softness of her flesh. How it stretched over her spine. More than once, I had to hold myself back from walking over and ripping someone's arm off when their hand drifted too low for my liking.

It was when the newest doctor in the ER asked her to dance that I lost it. He was younger than me. Handsome. Cocky and sure of himself. The way he held her was too tight. Too aggressive. More than once, I saw her head shake and she stepped back, putting some distance between their bodies. Seconds later, he was pressed up into her again.

Leo had decided to work the event as well. He enjoyed the occasional easy-to-handle event, and this hospital meant a great deal to him. They had saved his life when he was brought in after a vicious beating at the hands of a perp we were after at the time.

He sidled over to me. "Um, if you are going to mentally murder the man, you might as well go over there and break them up," he said. "Everyone in the room is accounted for. We've seen nothing suspicious, and I don't think Sofia would object. Consider yourself off the clock."

That was all I needed. I moved toward her, skirting around the dancers on the floor and appearing at Sofia's side. I heard enough to step in right away.

"I said no, Dr. Slater. I don't date colleagues, and besides, I have a boyfriend."

"Where is he, then?" he challenged.

"Right here," I growled. "And unless you want to lose your hands, I suggest you move them."

He stopped moving, glancing at me. Young and good-looking, yes, but he was soft. His muscles lacked any great definition, and he was weak. As soon as he saw me, he stepped back, holding up his hands. "Just dancing, man."

"And now it's my turn."

Ignoring him completely, I swept Sofia into my arms and twirled her away. As soon as I held her, inhaled her lovely fragrance, I relaxed. She leaned her head on my shoulder with a small laugh.

"Hello, caveman."

"You said you never dance," I growled.

"Tonight seems to have been the exception," she agreed. "Must be all the new staff."

"I tried," I said. "I couldn't take it anymore. All those men touching you." I ran my fingers over the silky skin on her back. "Touching what is mine. He's lucky I didn't break his hands."

She tilted up her head. "Don't do that. He is a gifted surgeon."

"He's weak to be a surgeon." I sniffed.

"Not everyone is built like a brick shithouse, Egan."

I had no idea what that meant, but I was certain it had to do with my size. I scoffed. "How he stands on his weak legs and performs surgery is a mystery to me. And how old is he? He probably still needs naps in the afternoon."

She laughed low in her throat. "He's old enough. And he is strong—he's just built differently from you. If you weren't so jealous, you would see that. Plus, he's an amazing surgeon, and the patients love him. When he's in doctor mode, he's brilliant."

I didn't like her praising him.

"He was pressuring you."

"He was asking me out. He asks me every shift. Every shift, I say the same thing. No. He's a hopeless flirt, but he is harmless. He will have already forgotten about me and moved on." She looked around. "See?"

I followed her line of vision. He was already dancing with someone else, not looking at all upset.

I grunted. "I don't care. All of them need to back off. The rest of tonight's dances are mine."

"I thought—"

I cut her off. "We're in a room surrounded by my people. I don't see anyone out of place. You can go to work shortly, and I will go to the apartment." I pulled her closer. "But when you get home in the morning, Sofia, I'll be waiting. It'll be payback for this dress and the stunt you pulled earlier."

"You don't like the dress?"

I looked down as I spun her. "I love the dress. It looks exquisite on you. It'll look even better on the floor by our bed."

She pressed her lips to my ear, her voice low and raspy. "And you didn't enjoy fucking me?"

I had to shut my eyes as I thought of the blistering orgasm I'd had. I had done exactly what she wanted. I had taken her fast and hard, barely five minutes passing once I was buried inside her. My release had left me shaken, loose, and determined to have her again as soon as possible. I could never get enough of her. I had left her on my bed, curled up and smiling in pleasure. I planned on her smiling that way again.

"Maybe not payback. Reward."

"Oh, I like that idea," she said, then laid her head on my shoulder. "But I love dancing with you, Egan. You are an amazing dancer."

"Having you as a partner helps."

"Whatever it is, I want to do it a lot."

I didn't look around before I pressed my lips to her head.

"Consider it done, my love. Consider it done."

CHAPTER THIRTEEN

Egan

The sun was shining brightly overhead. I wiped my brow at the heat, shutting my eyes and inhaling the breeze as it drifted it over my skin. There was none of the smog or humid air I had grown used to, living in the city. Instead, the air was crisp, clean, the scent of the forest and water strong. I opened my eyes, staring up at the sky. It was clear, blue, without a cloud in it. I sat up, looking around me. I recognized this place. To my right was a stream, the sound of the water bubbling and dancing audible as it traveled along the rocks. Ahead in the clearing was a small house, the pitch of the roof and the old wooden door familiar.

I stood, running a hand over my hair. I had grown up in that house.

How had I gotten here?

By the house was a tall tree, the branches hanging low, providing shade. Sitting in a chair, alone, was a woman. She was bent low over a task, but I recognized her. The brilliant white of her hair was bright in the sun. The bent shoulders were from years of hard work.

My grandmother. *Bunica.*

I walked toward her, taking everything in. The lazy smoke drifting from the chimney. The swing hanging from the tree not far from where my grandmother sat.

I stopped in front of her, still confused. She looked up, her hands never ceasing their busy work. A bowl of peas sat in her lap, and she separated the tiny green orbs from their shells efficiently, somehow creating two piles within the dish.

"Ah, *micul meu leu,* I have been waiting." She always called me her little cub.

I kneeled beside her. "*Bunică?*" I asked. "How are you here? How am I here?"

"I have to warn you. But I do not have much time." She shook her head sadly. "You do not believe, but I must try."

I glanced down. I wasn't a boy, but a grown man, yet she knew me.

"This is a dream."

"It is the only place I can reach you. Egan, you have danger around you. Grave danger. You must protect what is yours. Do what you must to ensure it is safe."

"I am trying."

She cupped my face, her skin buttery soft, the ends of her fingers callused. "There will be a crossroads. You must choose. Choose wisely."

"*Bunică?*"

She looked around. "I must leave, but you have to listen to me. What your heart needs must be protected at all costs. Remember your strength. Do what you must. If you lose your heart, the world will no longer be your home, Egan."

Her dark eyes, always filled with love, met mine. "You do not believe, but listen and remember. Heed the warnings in your dreams. Know what has passed will come full circle. Do what you must." She pressed a kiss to my forehead. "*Micul meu leu*, it will be hard, but you can do this. *You must.*"

The bowl fell to the grass, and I picked it up. I lifted my head, but the chair was empty. I stood, looking around, frantic. "No! *Bunică*, come back. I don't understand. Help me.*"

I spun on my heel, but the house was fading. Blackness was settling in all around me. I ran toward the structure, but it was gone in the blink of an eye.

I looked over my shoulder. The tree was gone, the landscape empty.

"No!" I shouted.

"Egan?" A quiet voice said my name. "Wake up."

My eyes flew open, and I sat up, my breathing harsh. Sofia sat up beside me, rubbing my arm. "Egan," she murmured in comfort. "It was a dream. Just a dream."

I turned to her, pulling her into my arms. Feeling her warmth, I relaxed and lay back, taking her with me. I wiped at my eyes, shocked at the dampness I felt on my fingers.

"Do you want to talk about it?" Sofia asked. "Was it a nightmare?"

"Not a nightmare. I was back in Romania. By the house I grew up in. My grandmother was there. Shelling peas," I added with a small smile. She'd always stayed busy. If she didn't have a task to do, she made one. Knitting and sewing were her two favorite things to do.

"That sounds nice. But you cried out."

I couldn't tell her what had happened. I didn't understand it. "She left too soon. I wanted her to stay," I said by way of explanation.

"I'm sorry."

I pressed a kiss to her head. "Go back to sleep, my love. I am fine."

It didn't take her long to drift off. She had slipped away from the event and went to work, and as soon as the dinner was over, I dropped by the ER, using the back stairway and getting her attention quietly. She joined me in the stairwell, her makeup gone, her hair up, still the most beautiful woman I had ever seen.

"What are you doing?"

"I had to see you." I pulled her into my arms and kissed her. I held her close, breathing in her scent.

"Will you go away with me, Sofia?"

She pulled back with a frown. "Go away?"

"A weekend—a few days. Just us," I added. "Do you have time?"

She smiled. "I have so much vacation, yes, I have time. Where will we go?"

"I don't know, but I want to be alone with you. Perhaps a cottage up north. Or somewhere else. Somewhere we don't have to hide."

"Yes." She smiled and kissed me. "Yes, I will."

"I will plan it."

"Perfect."

I kissed her again. "Go back to work. I will be waiting in the morning."

"With my reward?"

I chuckled. "With whatever you want, iubirea mea.*"*

When she got home, what she wanted—or, more importantly, needed—was some sleep. I had fed her and brought her to bed, thinking I would lie with her for a while. I had fallen asleep and dreamed of my grandmother.

I mulled over her words. The meaning.

Was she talking about Sofia?

Something else?

My grandmother was right—I didn't believe in the power of dreams or voices from the past. Yet that was twice in a short time period that I had heard her voice.

And it had been so real. Her voice had been clear. She had been clear. And her words struck a chord deep within me.

"Do what you must. If you lose your heart, the world will no longer be your home, Egan."

Sofia was my heart. And my home. A world without her was a place I didn't want to inhabit.

I looked down at the woman slumbering in my arms.

I would do whatever I had to do to protect her.

No matter what.

My dream stayed with me all day. I made the rounds, dropping off the finished paintings at the gallery and talking to Carmen for a while. At the gym, I sat with Mack, going through membership applications, discussing some repairs that needed to be done.

"Anything out of the ordinary happen lately?" I asked, flipping through the documents. I paused to study one, handing him back the application. "This one is not complete."

He took it with a frown. "I didn't notice that. Sorry. One of the other staff must have accepted it. We had quite a few people come ask for a tour."

That was good. Business was excellent, and my gym had a stellar reputation. Hand-selecting the members made it attractive to many. I nodded and kept perusing the paperwork.

"You mean any more strange visitors?" he asked as he slid the papers into another file.

I sighed. "That or anything else? Anything out of the ordinary?"

He frowned as he gave my question some thought. "Not that I can think of. The shower backed up in the women's locker room again. I had to fine two members for fighting in the men's locker room and breaking a door."

"What were they fighting about?"

"Which one of them got to take out Cindy. They were quite upset when I informed them staff was not allowed to date members. More upset than the fine and the week suspension."

I chuckled. "You didn't mention she was your fiancée?"

He grinned at me. "I might have withheld that information."

I shook my head, my hand stilling at one of the applications. "Who accepted this one?" I asked, holding it up.

He took it from my hand and scanned it. "I don't know. I don't recall seeing it before." He frowned. "That's odd. I went through these the other day. It wasn't there then." He scratched his head. "I don't think it was."

I took it back, the name staring back at me. Ivan Jones. He had been here. In my building. Walking around.

What was his game?

I flipped the pages, noticing most of the spaces were blank. His name, phone number, and what I assumed was a fictitious address were filled out on the front. He wanted me to see this application. For me to know he'd been here.

"I'll handle it," I said.

Mack left, and I turned to my computer, going into the security feed. I scanned the footage, stopping when a familiar face was in the frame. Alex. Not noticeable with his hair tucked into a beanie and scruff on his face. He wore casual clothes and leaned on the counter, talking to one of the female staff. I rubbed my chin. Yesterday was Mack's day off, which explained why he hadn't said anything about seeing Alex again.

Alex said something to the staff member, and she disappeared into the office. In seconds, he had rounded the counter and went directly to the membership file on

Mack's desk and added the form I was currently looking at, putting it on the bottom of the pile. Then he returned to his position at the counter, looking up and winking at the camera.

He knew I would be watching this. He wanted me to see it.

I glanced down at the number on the form. It was different from the one on the card Ivan had given me. I finished what I had to do and headed to Elite.

I pulled a burner cell from my desk and dialed the number.

"Mr. Vulpe. You got my message."

"You think you're clever, Ivan. Sending Alex in. Dropping me a message. A little boring, actually."

The silence on the line made me smile.

"You haven't been in touch."

"I told you I wasn't interested."

"Does five million interest you?"

I didn't hesitate. "No."

"Ten."

I huffed out a long, impatient breath. "I will make this as plain as I can. There is no amount of money that would be enough to get me to work for you, Ivan. I am not interested."

"You're wasted, is what you are. You should listen to my offer. What the future could hold for you. Wealth. Power. Fear when your name is spoken. Respect. I can give it all to you."

"Except I am not interested in any of it. Find yourself another lackey. Or better yet, get out of the country and go bother someone else. I am not available to you for any price."

He was quiet, the only sign he was still on the line was his sharp breathing.

"Are you certain of that?" he asked, something in his voice making the hair on the back of my neck stand up. I kept my voice neutral.

"I am not interested."

"Perhaps the next message will change your mind."

He hung up.

I tapped on the computer in front of me. His signal pinged off so many towers it was impossible to trace. He could be on the other side of the world for all I knew.

But he was here. I could feel it.

I rubbed my lip as I contemplated the situation.

His threat was vague but still troublesome. And annoying. He and Alex were getting on my nerves.

I called Damien. He answered, listening to what I had to say, then sighed.

"I'm still digging, Egan. It bothers me that I can't get a lead on him."

"Maybe it's nothing."

"Or something so big that it's been so deeply encrypted, even HJ can't get to it."

"Is that possible?" I asked.

"Anything is possible."

"But HJ—"

He interrupted me. "Runs in the Western world. Our ties aren't strong in other parts of the world. It takes longer. I don't have the resources. The language. I'm pulling in a few favors, but it's going to take time."

"I understand."

"I spoke with Sofia earlier. She said something about you going away?"

"For a few days. I found a cottage up north by the water. Private and secluded. I think we can both use the break." I blew out a breath. "I've got a plan to shake any tail that might be on me."

"Good. Enjoy it, and I'll be in touch."

"Okay."

I drove to the coffee shop, parking the car, and sliding my sunglasses on before I exited the vehicle. The place was busy when I walked in, and I placed my order, then headed to the back, stepping into the men's room. Inside, Samuel waited. He was almost as tall as me, and with sunglasses on and wearing identical clothing, it would be easy to think we were the same man from a distance. I handed him the car keys, sunglasses, and we exchanged jackets. "She's waiting," he murmured.

"So is your breakfast."

He grinned and headed out. I pulled a baseball hat low over my forehead and added the sunglasses I had in my pocket. Then I used the hall, exiting through the back door. I hurried to the waiting car and slid into the driver's seat.

I started the vehicle and pulled out of the lot, quickly driving away.

"Please tell me you at least brought coffee," Sofia

asked from the back seat where she lay hidden. "This is the worst taxi service I have ever experienced."

I laughed. "Soon, my Sofia. We'll clear the traffic and be on the 407 soon. I will get you coffee and anything else you want."

She was quiet for a few moments. "Can I sit up now?"

I glanced in the rearview. The street was empty behind me. The windows were tinted, the car private. "Yes."

She scrambled into the front seat, clipping on her seat belt.

I took her hand. "Hello, my love."

"You sure know how to excite a girl, Egan. Your 007 moves are impressive."

I laughed. "If I am being followed, they're waiting for me to come out of the coffee shop. If they are trailing you, they will think you are working a double shift when no car shows up for you. Neither of their efforts will be successful. They will follow fake Egan back to the apartment. We will be long gone."

She sighed. "And we'll be alone."

I lifted her hand and kissed it. "Yes."

"Tell me about the cottage. You haven't said anything."

"It's on a small lake. You can only get there by boat. It's private. Secluded, with its own beach. We'll stop in town to get supplies and go to the marina."

"Someone will drive us there?"

I smirked. "I will."

"You can drive a boat?"

"Yes."

"Is there anything you can't do?" she asked.

"Stay away from you," I responded.

She sighed and rested her cheek on the headrest, her face turned my way.

"I don't want you to try."

"Good. Now, we have a three-hour drive ahead of us. Sleep. I'll wake you when we get there. I want you rested." I paused. "You won't get much sleep once we're there."

She laughed softly and reached for my hand, shutting her eyes. I knew when she fell asleep. Her breathing evened out, and her hold on my hand loosened but didn't break.

The miles passed by in a blur, the roads mostly empty since it was midweek. It made the trip easier and gave me comfort knowing we weren't followed. Someone tailing me would have been easy to spot on the wide-open roads behind me. When we arrived in the small town, I woke Sofia up by leaning over the console and nuzzling her tempting mouth.

"*Iubirea mea*, wake up."

Her eyes fluttered open, and she smiled against my mouth. "Hi."

"We need to get some groceries. I brought some things from home, but we need more."

"Okay," she agreed easily.

An hour later, I shut the trunk, trying not to laugh. We'd been to the grocery store, the bakery, liquor store, and the farmers market set up on the main street. We had enough food to feed a small army, never mind the two of us for a few days. But everything she picked up, exclaimed over, or sampled and hummed in delight, I bought. The boat was going to be full.

I parked at the marina, and we found the boat. It took several trips to load everything up, and I parked the car in the lot as I had arranged. Then we were off, plowing through the water, the wind in our hair, the lake stretched before us. Sofia stood in front of me as I guided the boat toward the small cove where the cottage was located. She was beautiful in the sun, the light playing on her hair, her smile wide. I was looking forward to the next few days of having her all to myself. From the excitement in her eyes, I sensed she felt the same way.

"Egan, this is beautiful!" she exclaimed.

I set down the last of the bags on the counter, looking around. I had purposely not shown her pictures of the cabin, wanting it to be a surprise, and I was pleased as I explored it with her. The A-frame log cabin was open concept, a large fireplace the focal point of the main floor. The kitchen was a gourmet cook's dream with the high-end appliances and gas range with a built-in griddle and grill. The soaring ceilings and view were impressive, the walls of hand-hewn logs smooth and beautiful under my fingers. The staircase led to a loft that overlooked the main floor and was the only bedroom in the place. The space held a king-size bed, and its rich linens and warm-colored walls made the room romantic. Spectacular was the only word for the lofty view. Overhead, the skylights would be great for gazing at the stars. The bathroom had a huge walk-in shower with multiple heads I looked forward to using. Everything was luxurious and spacious, exactly as the owner had promised. And there was no one around for miles.

We unpacked everything and went outside to explore. There was a screened-in gazebo if the bugs were bad, plus a fire pit and the large dock and boathouse. The water was deep and clear, ideal for swimming. A hot tub was positioned at the side of the house, surrounded by a cedar deck. I planned on sitting in the swirling water tonight with Sofia beside me.

Naked.

Sofia slipped her arm around my waist as we stood on the dock. I squeezed her close, enjoying the moment. She gazed at the vista in front of us, then turned and looked at the cottage. "It's perfect," she murmured. "It takes my breath away."

I looked down at her, not bothering with the view. She was far more beautiful.

"Yes, it does."

SOFIA

I felt his arm tighten around me, and I knew he wasn't gazing at the water.

He was staring. At me.

The way he looked at me—the intensity and focus—made me feel beautiful. Sexy. Wanted. I also knew if I met his gaze what would happen next. He would kiss me. Swoop me into his arms, and in five minutes, we'd be back in the cabin, on that huge bed, naked. Our skin would rub together, and we would be lost to each other.

It took two seconds for me to decide that was fine with me.

I looked up at him, our gazes clashing. The intensity I was expecting was there. So was the focus, but there was also so much love and passion, it made my breath catch in my throat.

"Egan," I whispered.

He smiled, lowering his head and capturing my mouth. "Sofia," he breathed against my lips. He cradled my head, kissing me. It was slow, gentle, and filled with emotion. He explored my mouth as if he had never kissed me before, learning me all over again. I clung to his arms, whimpering, kissing him back. His scent surrounded me, caught in the warm breeze that swirled around us. He lifted his head, and I frowned, going up on my toes to follow his mouth.

He ran his thumb over my lips. "I was never big on kissing until you," he confessed.

"Why?"

"It never felt as if it was part of the moment. It was simply a means to an end," he said honestly.

"And now?

"The instant I saw you, I wanted to kiss you. Every time I do, it's not enough. I want more. You have the sexiest mouth. I love the way your lips form words. The way they shape around my name. How you taste." He caressed my lips again with his thumb, the callused tip stroking just inside my lower lip. "It means so much. I can't explain it."

"I like kissing you too." I looped my arms around his neck. "I like doing other things with you, too."

He lifted one eyebrow slowly. "Such as?"

"Take me upstairs and I'll show you."

"You don't want to go for a swim?"

I blinked. "A swim?"

"The water is beautiful."

"And cold."

"It's summer."

"*Late* summer. Almost fall."

He grinned, a mischievous look in his eyes. "I would warm you up after."

I began to back up. "Egan, no!"

He grabbed me, sweeping me into his arms. I squealed, then relaxed as he turned to head up to the cabin. He'd only been teasing. Then he turned and headed straight for the end of the dock. I let out a yell as we hit the water, the cold lake surrounding us. I came up gasping. Egan grinned at me, treading water, looking amused.

"See? Beautiful."

"It's freezing!"

He laughed and tugged me close. He wrapped his arm around me, holding me. I felt the heat of his body soak into mine, even in the cool water. "I'm all wet," I complained as I wrapped my legs around him. The cold actually felt nice. The jolt had woken me up fully and felt good on my skin.

"I'll warm you up and get you wetter," he promised, kissing me again, all the gentleness and lazy strokes of his tongue from earlier gone. He devoured me, pressing me tight to his chest. He pulled back, breathing harshly. "Now I'll take you upstairs and fuck you."

I grinned. "Maybe you're the one who's fucked."

He frowned, but before he could figure it out, I used his body as leverage and lifted myself up, grabbing his head and dunking him. Laughing, I swam away, hearing him come up sputtering and cursing.

"Now you're in trouble," he said, heading my way.

I loved to swim, and I was good at it. Very good.

"Bring it on, Vulpe," I called over my shoulder, swimming faster.

"I'm bringing it, Sofia," he warned. "Hard."

"Promises, promises."

Then he caught my foot and pulled me toward him. I got away, squealing like a teenager. He laughed and came after me. I went under and came around behind him, climbing on his back. He bucked me off and caught me before I broke the surface. We splashed, chased, and dunked each other, laughing and carefree. The sun was warm, the water cool, and the heat between us was blistering and constant. We kissed between battles, and Egan licked at the water on my neck, latching on to the juncture and biting down, making me groan. I cupped his balls and stroked him, feeling his need. He pulled off my shirt, sucking my erect nipple between his lips, the heat of his mouth burning. Piece by piece, our clothing ended up thrown to the dock or sinking in the lake. Egan maneuvered us to the steps, and I grasped at the railings as he lifted my legs to his waist. He thrust forward, the snap of his hips fast and hard. He was cold. I was hot. We both gasped for different reasons. He wrapped an arm around me, anchoring me to him, and gripped the wooden rail with his other hand. He began to move. Hard, short, wild thrusts. He devoured my mouth. He groaned low in his chest. Grunted. Breathed his oxygen into me and took mine. I began to shake, my orgasm coming quickly. He hissed his approval as I milked him, and he grabbed my ass, holding me close as he spasmed, the heat of his release filling me. He stilled, freeing my mouth and easing back. He pressed three kisses to my lips, his touch light and affectionate, then he dropped his head to my shoulder, a final long shudder of pleasure rippling down his spine.

"I think I lost my underwear," I whispered into his ear.

"I think I lost the feeling in my ass."

I grabbed at it, squeezing it firmly. "It's still there."

He lifted his hand from the water. "So's your underwear."

I began to laugh. He lifted his head, joining me, our amusement loud in the stillness surrounding us.

"I think we may have scared the fish."

He grinned. "Then my job here is done."

I shivered and he frowned. "Okay, playtime is over. Up to the cottage and we'll dry off and have a nap."

"Not sure I can move."

He smiled and kissed me again, then turned me around. As I began to climb, I looked back at him. "Our clothes are wet. We didn't bring towels."

"Then you'd better run."

On the dock, I clutched my shirt, no idea where my leggings ended up. I began to hurry to the cottage, but Egan caught me, throwing me over his shoulder. He moved fast, muttering the whole time about his junk swinging in the breeze, making me laugh.

I smacked his ass, admiring the way it flexed as he moved.

If this was how our break began, I was looking forward to the next few days.

Egan's heartbeat was a steady rhythm under my ear. His chest rose and fell with even breaths. Our bodies were pressed together, and he slowly drifted his fingers through my hair. The late-afternoon sun glinted on the skylights overhead, filling the room with its warmth.

I let out a sigh of pure happiness. I had never felt such contentment. Been so peaceful. With Egan, I was safe, loved, and secure. It was a feeling I wanted to get used to.

He cupped the back of my head, his voice low and affectionate when he spoke.

"Good sigh, Sofia? Or are you bored?"

I snuggled closer. "I am never bored with you, Egan. I was thinking I have never felt so content and happy. I love being with you."

"Ah, *iubirea mea*. You have no idea how long I waited to hear you say that. You make me whole. Complete. I love being with you as well."

He paused. "I want to be with you the rest of my life."

There was a time his words would have frightened me. When I would have pushed away and said no. But now, his declaration filled me with a sense of rightness.

"How do you see our life, Egan?" I asked quietly.

He was silent for a moment, but I felt his heartbeat increase. Felt the way his hold tightened. He went back to stroking my head.

"I see us with a family," he responded. "Happy."

"I love being a doctor."

"I would never ask you to give that up. I know how long you went to school, how many sacrifices you made to become one." He took in a long inhale of air. "Do you want children, Sofia?"

"Yes, I think so."

"Then you can do both. I will be with our children. I can work from home. Paint. Oversee the gym. Arrange care for when I need to go to a meeting."

I lifted my head, meeting his eyes. "You would do that?"

"I think being a father is a very important job. It makes me no less a man to raise my children while their mother works. One less gym in the world means nothing. But one talented, caring physician can make a huge impact."

"What about…" I trailed off.

"No. I will not do anything dangerous. Once we are

committed to our life together, it is gone. No more explosions. No more HJ. Nothing. Like Damien or Marcus, I will give it up. You, us, mean more."

"What about Elite?"

"I can help Leo behind the scenes. Put on a tux and look tough on occasion. But nothing high risk or profile." He smiled as he traced a finger down my cheek. "I am wealthy enough I never have to work, Sofia. Nor do you. But I understand your calling, and I would never deny it."

I stared at him in wonder. "You are incredible."

He smiled. "No, I am smart. I love you. I want you happy. Telling you to sit at home while I work and you waste your talent and schooling is a recipe for disaster."

I was amazed by his words.

"Now, Matteo had offered us a house on his island if you want a totally different lifestyle."

"What?"

He chuckled. "There is a hospital on the mainland. Easily accessible and always in need of doctors. Damien said you would love it there. We could live happily in a very safe place. You could be a doctor, be close to Damien, have me, and I will still look after the babies."

"And everything here?"

He shrugged. "Is a placeholder. Part of my life I can leave behind. As long as I have you, my paintbrushes, and lots of babies, I am happy."

I sat up, looking at him. "Egan, have you ever changed a diaper? Held a baby?"

He sat up as well, looking insulted. "Sofia, I can dismantle a bomb in minutes. Implode a building without disturbing anything around it. Take apart and put back together a number of weapons in seconds. I think I can figure out a diaper. Or how to hold a baby."

I gaped at him, and he began to laugh and tapped the end of my nose.

"I have visited the island many times. Held the babies, rocked them. Changed and fed them. I love that part of visiting. I can hardly wait to hold my own. To watch our children thrive." His gaze darkened. "To watch you grow round with them and know they are safe and warm within your body. You will make the sexiest mother-to-be."

"You will be an amazing father," I whispered, fighting the thick feeling in my throat and blinking at the moisture in my eyes.

"What is this?" he murmured, wiping his thumb over my cheek where a tear fell.

"I can't believe this, Egan. I can't believe you. I don't know how I got so lucky to have you love me."

He pulled me into his arms. "I am the lucky one, my Sofia. You are my dream. And together, we will figure out our life. Here. The island. A house elsewhere. Wherever you are is my home." He pressed a kiss to my head. "You are my home."

I shut my eyes, letting his words sink in.

"You are mine," I replied.

"Then we have everything we need."

CHAPTER FOURTEEN

Egan

Candlelight flickered over Sofia's face, highlighting her beauty. I sipped my wine, watching her as she stared over the water. She had her chin propped up in her hand, and she wore a small smile, looking content. I loved watching her expressions. She had become much more open with me now that she had let her guard down.

She turned her head, meeting my eyes.

"You're staring."

"You're beautiful. I like to look at you."

She indicated the window. "The view is far more spectacular."

"I disagree. Your beauty puts it to shame."

She picked up her wine, a soft color flushing her cheeks. "Stop."

"Why should I?"

"You're embarrassing me."

I lifted one shoulder, smiling at her indulgently. "Why does it embarrass you that the man you love thinks you are the most beautiful woman on this earth? You should be pleased."

"I'm not used to it," she admitted.

"You will grow accustomed."

She shook her head, but I saw her smile as she lifted the wineglass to her lips. I slipped my hand into my pocket and pulled out a box, sliding it across the table. "For you."

Her eyes grew wide and slightly panicked. I chuckled. "Not a ring, Sofia. A small token of our trip for you to remember."

She took the box and opened it, delight written across her face. "Those earrings I admired earlier when we were walking around! But I didn't say anything. How did you..." She trailed off. "Egan, they are lovely."

"I saw how you looked at them. And they suited you. When I told you I had left my phone, I ran back and got them. Please wear them for me."

She took them from the box, fastening them on her ears. The colors of the topaz against the gold were pretty. They glittered in the light and suited her. She could wear them every day, even at the hospital. A small golden topaz sat on her earlobe, and a larger smoky-colored one hung under the lobe, held together behind the ear so all you saw were the stones.

She stood and came around to my side of the table, bending low and kissing me. "Thank you," she murmured against my mouth. "I love them." I received another kiss. "I love you."

She sat down before I could respond the way I

wanted, which was to pull her onto my lap and kiss her senseless.

"You are spoiling me, Egan. The painting, the perfume, this trip." She touched her ear. "And these."

"I like to spoil you. I plan on doing it for the rest of our lives."

"Do you know what my favorite gift is?"

"The earrings?" I guessed. She had been surprised, enthusiastic, and gracious with all the gifts, so I was curious which her favorite had been.

"No." She reached across the table and took my hand. "Your heart."

For a moment, I said nothing. Then I cleared my throat. "Thank you."

Our meals arrived, and we looked at each other. I glanced up at the waiter. "Could you box these up for us, please?"

"Is everything all right, sir?"

I met Sofia's eyes. "Everything is perfect."

I looked around, making certain we hadn't forgotten anything. I walked down to the dock, where Sofia waited. I wrapped my arm around her waist, tugging her back to my chest.

"Saying goodbye?" I asked.

"Can we come back?" she whispered.

"Yes. You tell me when you can have more time off, and I will book it. I know the owner."

She turned in my arms. "It's been magical, Egan. I love it here. Just us."

I bent and nuzzled her lips. She was right. It had been magical. No stress, no phone calls, no worries. Her and me alone. We'd eaten well, made love often, fucked a few times, and talked. Shared. Teased and laughed. Sofia's walls were down completely, and I never wanted them resurrected.

"We'll come back," I promised. "If you love it here, I'll buy a place, and we can come all the time. I'll ask Bentley if he is interested in selling this one."

She gripped my arms, tilting her head back to smile at me. "You would, wouldn't you? Buy a place just to make me happy."

"I would do anything to make you happy, but it would be for me as well. I love how relaxed you are here. You're with me every moment."

"I wish I didn't have to go back to the hospital, but a few days were all I could get at short notice."

"I know. I have that job the day after tomorrow as well as a few coming up in the next while. We'll head back to reality, but you book a week or two as soon as possible and I'll give the dates to Bentley and rent this place again."

Her eyes lit up. "Maybe Thanksgiving? It would be beautiful in the fall."

"Bit cold for swimming, but the hot tub would be well used."

She nodded enthusiastically. "I'll put in the request."

"All right." I tightened my arms. "We have to go, my love."

"I'm ready."

Hand in hand, we walked to the boat. She stopped twice to glance over her shoulder, and I knew how sad she was to leave. I decided to contact Bentley as soon as we were back in the city.

My phone rang, and I answered on the Bluetooth. "Mack," I greeted him. "What's up?"

"Some pipes burst in the gym overnight, Egan. The ceiling collapsed, and the gym was flooded."

"Shit," I swore. "So, a lot of damage, I assume."

He didn't sugarcoat it. "Yeah, there was. It was extensive."

"Anyone hurt?"

"No, but there were some electrical issues caused by the water. We're lucky there wasn't a fire."

"I'm on my way back into town. I'll be there shortly. You have the insurance information, right?"

"Already called."

"Okay. I'll see you soon."

I hung up, and Sofia placed her hand on my arm. "Egan, I'm sorry."

I patted her hand. "Not the news I wanted to hear today."

"Why would the pipes burst?"

I shrugged. "Any number of reasons. The building is older. Perhaps a weak spot. Until I get there, I won't have any idea."

"Can I help?"

"No, my love. I will take you home first, make sure you are safe, and head there."

"Okay. I'll be waiting when you get back."

I squeezed her fingers. "I'd like that."

I surveyed the damage with a low whistle. Because the gym was in the lower level of the building, the destruction was bad. Machines ruined, the floors and walls soaked. All the electrical wiring unusable. The insurance adjuster shook my hand and told me they would launch a full investigation as to the cause, but it appeared as if a pipe had simply given way and the water had poured into the space. "Old pipes sometimes crack. There could have been a sudden spike in pressure or a blockage. Shame it happened in the middle of the night when no one was around to monitor it."

"I'm covered though, right?"

He nodded. "You upped your policy to include water damage, which is why your rates were so high. I suppose now it was worth it." He glanced around. "This is pretty severe, though."

"How long until we can reopen?"

He shook his head. "It will depend. Walls, floors, insulation, all of that will have to be replaced." He met my eyes. "It might be cheaper to close and move. Take a payout and use that toward the costs."

I wasn't happy with that thought. I spoke with Mack, and between us, we got the important things from the office and desk, called the staff, and Mack promised he would send emails to our clients explaining the closure. I would have to come up with a game plan for the members. Until then, a handwritten Closed sign was hung on the door.

I walked around, looking at the damage. In the main gym where the pipe had burst in the ceiling, water still dripped. It was too dark to see much, but I studied the pipes, noting the jagged metal edges. I took some pictures, and after talking to a few other people, left the building so the insurance company could do their work.

Back home, I spent hours making calls and finding a couple of places that would allow my members to use their facilities temporarily. I got the information to Mack, knowing it wasn't going to be a good solution in the long run. My members were used to top-notch services. But until I knew what was happening, it was the best I could do.

I rubbed my temples, all the relaxation and peace from my time away with Sofia gone. I felt a slight headache coming on. This was a huge disaster, and it was going to take time to figure it all out.

Not what I needed right now.

I touched base with Leo, pleased there was nothing new or odd happening. No Alex sightings, no notes, nothing. I checked the camera footage from the apartment and the gym, finding zero. Sadly, the cameras had been off in the main part of the gym when the break happened. Once the gym closed, they shut down overnight. I would have to change that once I made a decision about the building.

In the meantime, I wasn't stupid enough to think Ivan had given up, but I was hopeful. Maybe he'd found someone else to blow up his building.

Without Sofia beside me, I was restless and didn't sleep well. The next morning, I headed to Elite. Leo and I talked business for a while, then I got all my instructions for the next day. I had looked into Roman Brock, finding little. He was wealthy, rarely photographed. There were a few pictures of him with his family, but they were blurry. He obviously guarded his privacy well. I still didn't understand his request. Something felt strange, but I had nothing to go on, and the job was booked.

My phone rang, and I saw Carmen from the gallery's name show up on the screen.

"Hello, Carmen," I greeted her.

Her voice was raspy. "Egan," she began, then cleared her throat.

"What's wrong?"

"We had a fire this morning."

I stood. "I'm on my way."

The gallery was only a few blocks from Elite, so I ran, stopping in shock in front of the small building that used to contain the gallery. All that was left was a smoldering pile of ash and debris and some walls that looked as if they would crumble at any given moment. The buildings on either side of it were also destroyed. Firefighters and police were working, dousing the flames and keeping the crowd under control. Hoses were running, the sound of the water reminding me of the gym and the broken pipe.

I found Carmen, hugging her hard. "Are you all right?" I asked.

"Yes," she said, none of her usual confidence evident. Her face was soot-streaked, and she reeked of smoke.

"Was anyone hurt?"

"Next door. The manager was badly injured. I was at the front of the gallery when it happened. He was apparently in his stockroom and was close to the area. The force of the blasts blew through all the buildings."

"What happened exactly?"

"They think a gas leak. They've been doing work on the streets around us." She pressed a hand to her mouth. "All that beautiful art."

I thought of the canvases I had in the building. The new ones I had dropped off. All the sculptures and glass the building contained. The other paintings and works of art. A fortune, gone in a second.

"It can be recreated. As long as you're okay," I murmured comfortingly.

I looked back at the burning rubble. I met the eyes of a police officer, who came over. "Mr. Vulpe?"

I shook his hand, recognizing him from yesterday at the gym. "Officer Whyte."

"Is this your building too?"

"No." I shook my head. "I had some artwork in the gallery."

"Hell of a coincidence. Not your week," he said.

"But it's a good thing it wasn't a weekend or the street wasn't busier. It could have been a lot worse."

He went back to his task, and Carmen looked at me curiously. I explained about the burst pipe in the gym and the damage. She laid her hand on my arm. "Egan, I'm sorry."

I shrugged. "I am too, but I'm more grateful no one was injured. Equipment and art can be replaced." Officer Whyte was right. If it had been the weekend, the street would have been swarming with people. The casualties could have been great. The same if the water had set off an electrical fire. The devastation would have been total.

I couldn't stop the shudder that ran down my spine at the thoughts. Or the unease that settled into my mind. Were the two incidents really a coincidence?

My gut told me no.

"Egan," Sofia murmured, hugging me tightly. "How awful."

She sat back, picking up her coffee. She sipped it, watching me. "Are you okay? That is so much to think about. The gym, the gallery…"

I finished my coffee and set the empty mug on the table. "I'm fine. Upset about the losses, but that's why I have insurance." I crossed my legs. "There was a similar incident when I first opened the gym. The ceiling upstairs in my office collapsed. One of the tenants hadn't reported a leaking toilet and it weakened the floorboards, and the contents of the washroom ended up in my office." I laughed as I recalled the mess. "Right then, I upped my insurance. Never thought I'd need it, but here we are." I sighed. "The danger of old buildings. The gas leak, though? Horrible anytime, but the timing is just ironic. One right after another."

She swallowed, her eyes widening at my words. "Do you think they're related?"

"I don't know," I replied honestly. "It occurred to me, and I will be checking into it."

"They say bad luck comes in threes."

I chuckled. "I don't believe in old wives' tales."

"Maybe we should go to a hotel for a while," she mused.

"I thought about it," I admitted. "But this building is safe. I know it inside and out. I can protect you best here."

"I wasn't worried about me."

I stood and kissed her. "I know." I pulled her to her feet. "Let me feed you, then I need some extra kissing time. I won't see you tomorrow."

She followed me to the kitchen. I had made her mushroom soup since that was her favorite and some sandwiches. She could eat the leftovers tomorrow since I wouldn't be here.

"You leave early?" she asked.

"Around five. I won't be home until late." I smiled at her. "You get a whole Egan-free day."

She frowned, and I couldn't resist teasing her. "There was a time that would have pleased you."

"No, I would have made you think so, but I wouldn't

have liked it then either. Now, I hate it."

Her confession warmed my heart. "I like hearing that."

"I like saying it."

"I'll be here when you get home the next morning." Wanting to make her smile, I slid my phone her way. "Bentley sent me this."

She read the screen, his message telling me I could have the cabin for two weeks in October.

"Egan, that is wonderful! I requested vacation time, and since I rarely take any, my boss was fine with it."

"Then you, me, and the cabin."

She grinned. "Perfect."

I was at the hotel early the next morning. I scoped it out, familiarizing myself with the layout before I went to the hotel room. Roman Brock was a heavyset man in his early fifties. He was obviously used to getting what he wanted and had no problem expressing his wishes. He was constantly busy on the phone or directing orders to his PA. I stayed silent most of the time, observing. I stood behind him at every meeting, listening to him negotiate deals. He was very good at it, and I found it interesting, although he was difficult. His guards stood outside the office doors for all the meetings, which I found curious. Unable to help myself, I asked him why during a lag between calls. "Why do you have me in the room, not one of your own men?"

"They protect me. I do not like them to know my business. You have no involvement."

I didn't comment. It seemed to me that if you couldn't trust the people who protected you with business details, you shouldn't trust them with your life. But I kept my opinions to myself. I had a feeling not all his dealings were legal, but again, I kept my mouth shut. I didn't know much about the import/export business, but I understood a few key words when it came to illegal activities. I made a mental note to tell Leo that the next time Roman called, I wasn't available.

By the last meeting, I was tired. Roman was demanding and paranoid. Tense. I could feel his anxiety rolling off him. He contacted his wife several times, leaving the room to do so. For someone not expecting anything to happen, he was nervous. I had to check every room even after his own men did their sweeps. I had to follow him everywhere. He had his food tasted, luckily not by me. He had his own beverages brought to him. We had finally returned to his hotel, and once his room was swept three times, he ate a meal and rested while we took turns eating sandwiches, never leaving the door. The final meeting was in a private meeting room in the hotel late in the evening.

Grateful the day was almost over, I swept the room and assumed my position. Roman always sat with his back to a wall, facing the doorway. He was escorted into the room, offering me a terse nod. He sat down and snapped his fingers for coffee. I found his mannerisms annoying and degrading, but I kept my features neutral. My time with him was almost at an end. His chef poured the coffee and left the room. He met briefly with his PA, then sat with another man, speaking a language I didn't understand. By that point, I didn't really care, only wanting the day to be over.

His meeting ended, and he called for more coffee, once again snapping his fingers. After the cup was filled, he dismissed the chef and sipped his beverage.

For a moment, there was silence. Roman drained the coffee in one long drink then stood and turned to me. "You were an excellent addition today, Mr. Vulpe. I am sorry for my part in this, but I was given no choice."

I was confused by his words. "Part in what?"

He shook his head and walked out of the room. Before I could move, the door opened and someone else walked in.

Ivan.

For a moment, our gazes clashed. His triumphant, mine furious. I began to step forward, and he held up his hand. "I suggest you take a seat."

"I suggest you go fuck yourself."

He began to laugh. "I like your humor, Mr. Vulpe."

The door opened, and Alex and the man who had been with Ivan the first time walked in. They all sat at the table. I remained standing.

"Whatever this is, I am having no part of it."

I headed to the door, Ivan's voice stopping me. "You will not be able to leave until I say so. I have gone to a great deal of trouble and expense to get you here, and I will not be denied."

I opened the door, finding three men facing me. Their arms were folded in front of them, and they were all armed. Roman's guards had been armed as well, but I wasn't—at his request. I now understood why. Furious, I shut the door and returned to the table, sitting.

"You have ten minutes."

"I have as much time as I want," Ivan responded. "I paid for the whole day."

"What do you have on Roman that made him cooperate?"

"Information on the family he keeps so safely protected."

Internally, I swore. This whole day had been a setup. My gut had been right. It also made sense why Roman appeared so anxious as the day grew longer, and his constant calls to his wife.

"Why not just set up a single meeting? Why all day?"

Ivan smirked. "I enjoyed watching you act like a bodyguard. You're very thorough."

"I was paid to be. If, however, I had known it was paid by you, I would have refused."

"Then you understand why I had to leverage Mr. Brock's trip. Aside from his family's welfare, I knew he would hate to have some of his contacts refuse to deal with him."

I narrowed my eyes. *He had that sort of power? Who was he?*

"What is your name? It's not Jones."

He smiled. It was threatening in its intensity. "Ivan Petrov."

The name meant nothing, but once I could get in touch with Damien, it would.

The door opened, and a waiter wheeled in a cart. He set up a coffee service, complete with sandwiches, then left.

"Help yourself," Ivan said, pouring himself some coffee. Alex grabbed a sandwich, chewing fast, staying silent.

I shook my head. "I have no desire to eat with you."

Ivan shrugged, not put out.

"I want you to reconsider my offer. In fact, I'll add a bonus and more work."

"Not interested."

"You haven't heard my offer."

"How did you find me?"

"Your reputation precedes you."

"My reputation is not well-known."

He smirked. "It is to some."

He held out his hand, and Alex pulled a file from his bag. He slid it my way. I opened it up, shocked at the images and information it contained. Remnants of a past I didn't want to think of. I was no longer that man, existing on grief and anger. I had moved past it.

I pushed it back. "I am not that man anymore. I don't do jobs for hire."

"I suggest you reconsider."

"And once again, I suggest you fuck off."

He didn't react.

"There are a lot of explosives specialists. Go hire one of them."

He regarded me impassively, sipping his coffee as if we were having a friendly chat. "Not with your talent."

I was angry and tired of his games. "What is it you want done?"

He leaned in, the gleam in his eye malicious and intense.

"There is a situation. I need it eliminated. I need the *deadly ghost* to handle it."

That name from the past rocked me, but I kept my voice level. "Not good enough. What situation?"

"A storage facility. Highly protected. I need you to go in and plant a bomb in plain sight. Walk in with it, walk out without it. Detonate it immediately."

"What?"

"Everything and everyone in that building must disappear."

"You expect me to murder people?"

"I expect you to do exactly that. And you will."

My stomach turned. I had never killed innocent people. I saved them. "No, I will not. I don't kill blameless people."

"They aren't blameless to me."

"Your opinion on this doesn't matter. I refuse."

"Are you so certain of that answer, Mr. Vulpe?"

"Yes. Find yourself another gun for hire."

"Have you nothing to lose?"

Sofia's image flashed in front of me, but I kept my face neutral. "No."

His voice was soft. "Are you so certain of that?"

"Yes."

He crossed his legs, swinging his foot. "There are worse things that can happen to your gym aside from some water."

Sudden rage hit me, but I refused to let him see it. "So that was your handiwork?"

"I wanted your attention. You have more time on your hands now."

"Not for you."

"And no place to display your pretty little pictures."

I had to focus my attention on the wall over his shoulder. He had been responsible for that as well. Once again, my gut had been right.

"Do you not care if you hurt an innocent bystander? That you could have killed a lot of harmless people?" I asked through tight lips, already knowing the answer. He had no regard for human life.

He shrugged. "Alex was careful."

"Alex was sloppy," I snapped.

"That's why I need you."

I shook my head. It took every ounce of my strength not to lunge forward and wrap my hands around his neck and choke the life out of him. Except I knew Alex and the silent guard would kill me in seconds.

"I would hate to have to destroy that nice building where you make perfume."

I refused to let him see my distress. Angelica and Warren had done nothing to deserve that happening to them. The loss of their business would devastate them.

"Leave them out of this. I'm barely involved."

"Or…" he said, his voice low and flinty. Angry. "Your precious Elite."

"Again, it's just a building. You can blow up every place that I frequent, Ivan. It won't change my mind," I bluffed.

"Then I should kill you right now."

"Your situation would still exist," I pointed out. "As long as you think I might be of use, you won't kill me."

"So there is nothing you love enough to save from my anger?"

I stood, done with this. Before I was home, Angelica and Warren would be warned to vacate the building. Leo would be told to clear Elite. I would send anyone close to me away from the city. Sofia would be on the next plane to Damien, and then I was going to hunt down this man and his entire operation and eliminate them. For that reason, and that reason alone, I would become the deadly ghost again.

"You've taken away the things that mattered. I'm not changing my mind."

"Not even your home?"

I refused to show him a single glimmer of fear. "It's walls and a roof."

His mouth tightened. "You are stubborn."

"What I am is done. I am not for hire." I tapped the file on the table. "That man does not exist. Find someone else. Forget you ever met me. I plan to forget about you," I lied.

I was almost to the door when he spoke again.

"And what about your lovely doctor Sofia? Is she not worth it?"

I froze, turning around. He held out another file, and my feet headed back toward him before I could think about it. I opened the file. There was my Sofia. In my arms, dancing. Laughing. A picture of us at the cottage, taken from afar, obviously zoomed in. In my apartment, kissing her in the kitchen.

I sat down heavily.

The places I had felt safe with her. And the places I was sure we were not being watched.

They had been there. At the benefit. Somewhere close to my apartment. Spying on us at the cabin.

"Stay away from her."

"Ah," he said. "Too late."

I was on my feet, my fist connecting with his nose before anyone else could move. His head snapped back, the sound of bone meeting bone loud in the room. Blood spurted, and he tried to stem the flow with his hand.

No one moved. I lunged for the door, throwing it open. The hall was empty. I rushed down the corridor, dialing Sofia's number.

Behind me, Ivan's voice called out, "We'll be in touch. Soon."

CHAPTER FIFTEEN

Sofia

From the moment I walked into the ER, I was busy. I saw patient after patient, getting X-rays, scans, stitching cuts, setting broken bones. I swore it was a full moon since we were busier than normal. But it was just a bad night. We finally slowed down, and I was busy casting a young girl's arm when my phone vibrated in my pocket. I had to ignore it, frowning when it went off again and again. I finished the cast, pulling off my gloves and wiping some residue off my arm when Sally stuck her head in the door.

"Sofia, Egan is on the phone at the desk. The private number. He says it's urgent."

I lifted my eyebrows. He never called on that number, but given the number of times my phone had gone off, somehow I wasn't surprised. "I'll be right there."

She came in. "I can finish this. You go and see what's wrong. He sounds very upset."

I hurried down the hall, hoping nothing had

happened to Damien or Raven. I picked up the phone. "Egan?"

"Sofia," he replied, his voice panicked and rushed. "I need you to listen to me. Do exactly what I say. Do you understand?"

Something in his voice frightened me. "Yes."

"I don't have time to explain. Find a room. Somewhere you can lock the door. Go inside and don't come out until I get there. Do you hear me? Don't come out."

"Egan, what's—"

He interrupted me, his voice loud. "Sofia, just do it. *Now!* I'll be there soon."

He hung up, and I stared at the receiver.

I headed down the hall, unsure what to do. Patients were waiting. We were all busy. The rooms were all taken, gurneys and stretchers lining the halls. There were only a few places I could think of with a lock. One of the washrooms, the supply room, or the staff room. The supply room seemed the best place. It was at the end of the hall.

I glanced around, not seeing anyone looking, and using my pass, slipped in, the door locking behind me. It was dark, and I held up my phone, scanning the room. I leaned against the wall, unsure what was going on. Egan's voice had upset me, his unusual request scaring me. Outside, I could hear people walking, talking, issuing orders. I wondered how long it would be until I was missed.

I waited, my fear growing. My phone buzzed, and I looked at the message.

EGAN

Where are you?

Supply closet.

Go to the back stairs. I'll be there. Hurry, Sofia.

I opened the door, peering down the hall. Everyone was still busy, and I hurried down to the end, opening the door. It was dim in the stairwell, and I heard footsteps coming up toward me. No doubt, Egan had parked underground and was coming for me.

"I'm here, Egan," I called.

"Come," he called, his voice low and muffled.

I headed down, my feet suddenly stopping as I heard my name shouted behind me. It sounded like Egan's voice, but he was here in the stairwell with me.

Wasn't he?

"Egan?" I asked.

There was no warning. No time to move. A hand was suddenly clapped over my mouth and a rag pressed to my nose. I fought with everything in me, kicking at the man holding me, scratching at his arms. He cursed in a language I didn't understand, but he didn't lessen his hold. Lights danced in front of my eyes, and I began to black out.

I heard my name screamed again just as everything went dark.

Egan's face was the last thing that flashed across my mind before I was out.

EGAN

Some sporting event was happening and traffic was bumper-to-bumper, so I ran to the hospital, cutting down streets and through parking lots. I called and called Sofia's cell, finally getting hold of her through the private desk number. I barked orders at her, and once I was sure she would follow through with them, I called Leo, telling him what had happened.

"Call Damien," I instructed. "Tell him. Take your family and go away, Leo. Tonight. Call the Elite staff and tell them to stay away. Tell them all to be careful. I'll call Damien once I have Sofia safe."

I hung up and hurried to the ER. Sally was at the desk.

"Where is she?" I demanded.

She frowned, leaning forward. "I don't know what's going on, but I saw her go down the hall."

"Is there a room that locks there?"

"The supply room."

I rushed down the hall, horrified to find the door ajar and no sign of Sofia. I called her name loudly, heading toward the stairwell, some instinct driving me there. As soon as I opened the door, my heart sank. I could smell the chloroform lingering in the air. I rushed down the steps, bursting through the door into the parking lot, but it was silent. Either the car they took her in was gone, or they had gone up the stairs. I found nothing on the other floors, but when I returned to the main level, a glint caught my eye. Bending down, I picked up the small item that had captured my attention.

Sofia's staff pass. I stared at it, seeing small flecks of blood on the plastic.

They had her. I was too late.

I pulled my phone from my pocket, not caring about encryption, privacy, or anything else.

Damien answered on the first ring.

"Is she safe?"

"They took her," I said, my voice raspy and thick. "His name is Petrov. Ivan Petrov."

"I'm on my way."

He hung up.

I paced and cursed the floors of my apartment. I found her phone on the ground of the hospital parking lot. Saw the text I didn't send, but she thought I had, which was why she'd left the room. I hacked into the hospital security feed. They'd had a car waiting—a nondescript black sedan. I hacked into the traffic cams and followed the car until it disappeared down a side street where there were no cameras. I couldn't find it again, and I knew they probably switched cars. I called the number Ivan had left me, but it no longer worked. No doubt, it had been a burner cell they tossed once I called last time.

I had to wait for them to contact me.

Under the cloak of darkness, I slipped into the Elite

building, going to the server room. I found no trace of anything rigged to explode, and I spent hours using the computers there to dig into the name Ivan Petrov.

Two things became abundantly clear. He'd had work done, so his face was unrecognizable from the few pictures I could find. His hair color had been changed as well. The skillful hands of a plastic surgeon had made him able to hide in the open.

It didn't change his evil nature.

A lot of the files were encrypted. A lot of the prompts led to dead ends. Damien would be able to open them with his HJ connections. But what I was able to find made me ill. Murders, trafficking, drugs, arms. Anyone who crossed him ended up missing. Obviously dead.

And he had my Sofia. I had to tamp down my terror, focus on the end goal, which was to get her back alive.

Even if I died in the attempt. Damien would look after her.

I used the phone in the darkness of the Elite office to call Leo and make sure he was safe. I spoke with Warren, who assured me he and his wife would not return to the building that housed the perfume factory and were already at the airport. I checked on Mack, advising him to remain vigilant. I doubted they would go after him, but in case, I told him to get Cindy and take a trip on me. He could choose the destination, as long as they left immediately. He paused. "Is that necessary, Egan?"

"There are elements of my past that seem to be catching up to me. I have no idea how far this might go, but I would rather be safe than sorry. Please go away for a few days."

He was silent for a moment. "I always knew there was more to you than a gym owner. Okay. We'll pack now and be gone before the morning. I have a friend with a place where we can stay."

I scrubbed my face, relieved he had accepted my brief explanation. "Good."

Then I returned home, pacing, waiting. Anxious. I needed them to make contact. I needed Damien here to help me find her.

I sat on the bed, lifting Sofia's pillow, inhaling the scent of her. It filled my lungs, relaxing me for a moment. I could pretend she was in my arms, not at the mercy of a psychopath.

Worries and fears hit me one after another.

Where was she? Was she being mistreated? Had she been hurt?

The thought of her frightened and being manhandled or worse made me ill. I felt an ache in my chest, a helplessness I was trying to fight. I now understood how Damien and Julian had felt when their women had been taken.

I wanted to raze the city and burn it down to find her.

Instead, I had to wait for them.

Silently, I made a vow to myself and to Sofia. I would repay every bruise, every injury, and every moment of her fear tenfold. I would figure out how to beat this Ivan Petrov at his own game.

And I would get Sofia back.

Then I would take her to the island where I knew she would be safe.

My phone buzzed in my hand, and I sat up, shaking my head. I had fallen asleep holding Sofia's pillow, my exhaustion outweighing my anxiety. I glanced at the screen, seeing I had been asleep for two hours. I slid my thumb over the screen to a brief message.

In the workshop

Using the stairwell, I went to the basement. At the very back of the building was the place I used to plan, create, and build my bombs. It had been designed and built to my specifications. If something went wrong, the explosion was self-contained. If someone tried to bomb their way in, it would fail. It was so secret, only a handful of people knew it was there. I had never even told Sofia. The door was hidden, and there was a passage to an entry into the building no one knew about except the same few who knew about the room. It was located in a garage on the street behind the complex. Marcus had discovered it when he purchased the warehouse, then purchased that property as well and converted it. We made good use of it often. Anyone watching the building wouldn't see someone enter or suspect it was there. If Ivan had eyes on me, he would have no idea I had backup.

Using the code, I slipped in the door and was

greeted with a surprise. I expected Damien, but they were all there. Marcus, Julian, and Matteo. Their tired, concerned eyes met mine.

Damien stepped forward, pulling me in for a hug, slapping me on the back.

"I brought reinforcements."

I hugged them all, beyond grateful. "I wasn't expecting this."

Julian shook his head. "You helped me get Tally back. I owe you."

Marcus met my gaze. "You put yourself on the line for me over and over. Of course I'm here."

Matteo was his usual taciturn self. I had only worked with him rarely, but I knew he was lethal if he needed to be. We got along well. "We'll get her back."

Besides being blast-proof, my old lab was also bug-proof, would kill any tracking equipment, and had the ability to monitor the entire building, so I knew we could work in here and be safe.

"We're still secure in here—I think. I have no idea how they followed me. Tracked me," I said. "We have scanned everything."

Damien reached into his bag, removing a device I had never seen before. He passed it over me, a low hum emitting from it. He concentrated on my arm, then used a tiny machine that sucked up the skin, pulling what looked like a hair from it. He held it up.

"That's how. The most sophisticated device created. It can't be removed unless you have this machine. Water, soap, even fire can't harm it. Unless you have the technology, it's undetectable. I assume it was Ivan or

Alex. All they had to do was brush against your arm. The capabilities and distance it can span are incredible."

"All this time," I muttered.

"They didn't even have to be close. Those pictures of you at the cottage could have been taken from across the lake. The pictures at the gala, from the window across the street. It uses satellites and other technology."

"Jesus."

He nodded, putting it into a container. "I'm keeping it so I can study it. It's contained now, so the last fix they have on you is it. They'll think you haven't moved."

"Okay."

He scanned me again. "Nothing. You're safe now. So let's get to work."

"Have they made contact?" Damien asked, pulling a couple of laptops from his bag and setting them up.

"No. He wants me to suffer."

He nodded. "He likes to do that."

"I found some stuff on Ivan," I said.

"So did I. Let's get to work."

An hour later, we sat back. My anxiety was even higher. Ivan had no conscience. The men working for him, even less. Killing was like breathing to them.

Julian sat down, handing me a cup of coffee. "This group is lethal."

"What do they want?"

He sighed. "From what I have been able to piece together, there is an investigation going on. They've amassed a huge pile of evidence against this Petrov. Russia has turned its back on him. He has enemies everywhere. He's running out of places to hide."

Damien tapped the screen. "Hence the surgery."

"Whatever they have is in a safe house. It's all been done very quietly so as not to alert him."

"But he found out."

Julian took a sip of coffee and nodded. "Everything I'm telling you is classified. No one would ever admit to any of this. But the evidence is ready. He is about to become the number one wanted man on the planet. Him and his crew."

"And he wants me to blow up the building and murder everyone in there. Surely there are backups?"

Julian nodded. "Of course. But this is the kicker. Rumor is some of the witnesses are housed there as well. If they're gone, it's hearsay."

I shut my eyes, letting my head hang to my chest.

"I have to save her. Sofia is my priority."

"*Our* priority," Damien confirmed.

"And you will. We will." Matteo spoke up.

I lifted my head, meeting Marcus's gaze. His voice was firm when he spoke.

"We're going to figure this out, and then we're going to save Sofia and end this lowlife. Him and his people. Then you're retiring for good."

I nodded.

"Your house is ready," Matteo murmured.

I had already made up my mind.

"We'll take it."

CHAPTER SIXTEEN

Sofia

I woke up, my head throbbing and my body feeling as if it had been hit by a Mack truck. I slowly opened my eyes, the room around me dim. I was facing a wall, the surface damp and moldy. I could feel my arms behind my back, my wrists bound together. My feet were tied as well.

The sudden recollection of the stairwell, the rag over my mouth and nose, and the horrible feeling of knowing I had been tricked rushed back.

I had been kidnapped.

My breathing picked up as panic set in. I concentrated on regulating my breaths, recalling a conversation Damien had with me long ago.

"If you're ever taken, Sofia, ever in danger and knocked out, the first thing to do when you wake up is to listen. Try to ascertain where you are. Listen for voices, traffic, footsteps. Don't react. Don't panic. Let them think you're still out and try to grasp the situation. Find the weak spots. Figure out how to escape safely. Look around every chance you get to find a way out."

I had stared at him. "Is that likely to happen?"

"No. And if it did, I would find you. But I'm telling you anyway."

I didn't move. I shut my eyes again and listened. The building creaked and moaned. I could hear the wind outside and I thought maybe the sound of rain, but it was muffled, which meant I wasn't near a window or a roof. The floor under me was hard and unforgiving. Cold. In the distance, I could hear voices, sometimes louder than others, but I wasn't able to hear what they were saying. Those few louder words let me know it wasn't English they were speaking.

I thought of what Egan had told me. How worried he had been. He had been correct, and now they had me.

Which meant they had leverage over him.

A door opened, slamming into the wall. I was unable to help myself from jumping at the sudden sound. But I wasn't prepared when rough hands picked me up, dragging me across the floor, and crashing me into a chair.

"I know you're awake. Open your eyes."

I slowly lifted my lids, keeping my head down. The man wrapped a rope around my waist, securing me to the chair. He grabbed my chin and lifted my face. I was met with flat blue eyes. They were like ice, cold and unforgiving. His dark hair hung around his face, and he looked vicious. I had trouble focusing, and my eyes drifted shut again.

"Finally. Stupid idiot put too much chloroform on

the rag." He shook my shoulders roughly. "Stay awake or you'll be sorry."

Despite my fear, I drifted, suddenly waking as a hand slapped my face. I opened my eyes, meeting the dark gaze of another man. He smiled, the action making me shiver. He was even scarier than the first guy. His recently broken nose was red and swollen, out of place on the otherwise perfect lines of his face. Perfect, I surmised immediately, due to the skill of a surgeon, not the gift of nature.

"There you are. How are you feeling, Sofia?"

I narrowed my eyes. "As if you care."

He smiled again. "Ah, but I do." He brushed my hair off my face, and I jerked back, the movement causing my already aching head to hurt more.

"Don't touch me," I spat.

He stood straighter. "A fighter. Of course the deadly ghost would have a fighter as a lover." He stroked his lip. "How strong a fighter are you, Sofia?"

"Strong enough to survive you. You, however, won't survive Egan."

He laughed, the sound without humor. "You don't get it. Egan will do exactly what I want now. I took his gym, his gallery, and now his most prized possession. You. He'll do anything to get you back."

"I'm not a possession, asshole."

He laughed again and leaned down, testing the ropes that bound me. "You are going to send Egan a little message. Tell him to follow my instructions."

"No."

He lifted his head, narrowing his eyes. "Yes. Or he will suffer another loss."

I glared at him. His face was close, horrific in its anger. "I will take away everything he loves one by one until he does as I say. His friends, Elite, his business partners. His little perfume factory. His home. You. I will take and take until he is broken." He came closer. So close I could see the bloodshot veins that surrounded his pupils. "Then he will do what I tell him, and after that, the great Egan Vulpe will work for me. He will have nothing left. Not even his soul. He will belong to me."

I couldn't move my hands or my feet. I only had one weapon. I dropped my chin, using what little strength I had left, and I smashed my head into his face, catching his already injured nose. He howled at the sudden attack and the pain. I leaned back, admiring my handiwork. Blood flowed between the fingers of the hand covering his rebroken appendage. My head screamed in protest at the agony I caused it, but I didn't care. I braced myself as I saw the rage descend on his face. He reared back, slapping me, the explosion of pain across my cheek astounding. But I refused to show him my suffering. I grinned at him.

"Hope you have that surgeon on retainer. By the time I'm done with you and Egan finishes, you'll need a whole new face."

He removed his hand, the blood flowing freely down his face, dripping from his chin. He turned to leave the room. "You will be entertaining to have around. Enjoy your stay." He met my eyes, his even colder than they had been a few moments prior. "Shame this is where you will spend your last days on earth."

Then he walked out.

I had no idea how long I sat there. My head ached. I was thirsty. My body hurt. I was cold—so cold.

I let my head hang and kept my eyes shut, listening. I slowly moved my wrists and feet to try to loosen the rope. I gave up after a while when I felt the rough threads dig into my skin and the sting of the blood rushing to the surface. They were too tight to loosen.

I could hear the voices more clearly now, but they were speaking Russian. I tried to concentrate on the timbres of the voices and decided there were four, maybe five men. Other than the sounds of the wind and the creaking of the building, I couldn't hear anything else. Nothing to pinpoint where I might be. I lifted my head, trying to find a clue in the small room I was in, but there wasn't much to go on. Some rusted shelves, a high ceiling, and empty boxes. One corner of the room was missing floorboards, the damage obviously from the water that had seeped in over the years. I shivered as I wondered if the rest of the floor was stable. I tilted my head, peering at the empty boxes. One of them had a label, but I couldn't see what it said. I tried to stand and get closer, but my legs were too weak and my feet were numb. The ropes allowed them no movement. I knew I would fall and hit my face and maybe knock myself out.

The door opened, and two men walked in. From

Egan's description, I knew one of them was Alex. They set up a camera and a set of lights.

"I have to go to the bathroom."

They ignored me.

"Hey! I said I have to go!"

They exchanged glances, and Alex shrugged. "Then go."

"I am not peeing myself."

The man from earlier stepped into the room. Part of me felt great satisfaction in seeing his swollen, painful-looking nose. He tutted under his breath. "Escort the lady to the restroom, Alex. We must treat our guest with some respect."

I wanted to laugh at his words, but I kept my mouth shut. A moment later, the rope was cut from my feet, and I gasped as the feeling returned to my legs. They removed the rope at my waist and pulled me to my feet. I stumbled and wobbled around like a drunken sailor, holding in the whimpers as the painful pins and needles shot up my legs. Alex half dragged me to a small room that was grimy but necessary. I repressed my shudder.

"There," he grunted.

"My hands," I said quietly. "I need my hands."

He hesitated, then took a knife from his belt and cut through it. "You attack me or do anything stupid, I won't hesitate to hurt you."

I only nodded.

He left, shutting the door behind him. "You have five minutes."

I made the most of it. I emptied my bladder, splashed the cold water from the tap on my face, using my shirt to dry it. I looked around at the empty room. There was nothing to tell me where I was, not even a window. But from what I had seen in the short trip down the hall, it was a small, deserted warehouse.

Alex flung open the door, grabbing my arm. He dragged me back to the room, pushing me into the chair.

"May I have some water?" I asked. The water in the bathroom was rusty and smelled funny. The cold on my face helped wake me up, but I wasn't going to drink it.

He looked at the man I assumed was Ivan, who nodded. A moment later, a lukewarm bottle was shoved into my hand. I struggled to open it, then sipped at the contents, not wanting to drink too fast and throw up. I was also stalling for time. They had moved the chair, and I could see the label better on the discarded box. Sterling, it said. I had no idea what it was, but it was a clue.

Ivan stood in front of me. Far enough away I couldn't touch him, but close enough I could see the deadly intent in his eyes. "Tie her back up."

My hands were tied behind me again.

"We are going to talk to Egan now. You are going to tell him to do what I say."

"And if I don't?"

He turned his phone to me, showing me a picture. "He is in his apartment, waiting for me to contact him. The building is set to explode on my command. You tell him no, he is dead. You will be of no more use to me. So therefore, you, too, will be dead."

I broke out in a sweat, feeling the color draining from my face.

They had Egan's apartment building rigged? How could I warn him? How could I help him?

I began to shake, my emotions getting the better of me.

They turned on the lights, the glare hitting my eyes and making me wince.

"Let us begin," Ivan said.

CHAPTER SEVENTEEN

Egan

I downed another coffee, my head aching, my shoulders tight. Julian and Matteo were on one side of the room, Damien and I were side by side, running programs, searching for clues. Marcus made a pile of sandwiches, insisting I eat to keep up my strength. Then he joined Julian and Matteo.

I made a noise of distress as I found yet more of the crimes Ivan and his people had perpetrated. His entire crew needed to be eliminated from the face of the earth. Damien squeezed my shoulder in silent sympathy.

"I'm sorry," I murmured, meeting his eyes. "I failed her. I didn't protect her. I wanted to send her to you, but she insisted on staying. I should have listened to my gut."

"We didn't know who you were dealing with or what they were capable of, Egan. And I know Sofia. She is stubborn." He shook his head. "We had no idea she was on their radar."

"They played it well. And I was too confident. I still don't know what they want."

My phone rang, and I grabbed it. "I think it's him."

Damien tapped on his machine. "Okay. We'll stay quiet."

I answered. "Ivan."

His chuckle was loud. "How quickly you pick up this time."

"I want proof of life. Now."

He sighed and sent me a link, which I clicked. A video feed began, and I glanced at Damien, who nodded that he was trying to trace the call. Everyone was using their computers to run different software to track the call. I had to keep them on the line as long as possible.

My breath caught at the sight of Sofia tied to a chair. It was so like the dream I'd had, it was disconcerting. She glared at the camera, fierce and defiant.

"Sofia, *iubirea mea*."

Her expression softened. "Egan," she replied.

I scanned her for injuries, the bruises on her face making me angry. "Are you all right?"

"I'm fine."

Light glinted on her earrings, and I narrowed my gaze to them. "I hope your ear infection does not get worse."

She frowned, confused, then Ivan stepped beside her. "Enough chat. You will do what I want first."

He looked furious. His nose caught my attention. It looked terrible. Swollen, red, and painful, the wound fresher than I expected. As if it had been hit again. I glanced back at Sofia, wondering if somehow she was responsible for that. Pride filled my chest at the thought.

Sofia shook her head, the movement slight, but I saw it. She was telling me not to do anything. She had no idea what was going to happen.

"What is it you want?"

"I have a target for you. It requires a bomb and no survivors. Nothing must be left of the contents, the people, or the building. You have three days to plan and construct."

Damien made a rolling motion with his hand, telling me to keep going.

"Three days?" I snorted. "Obviously you know nothing about explosives. That takes weeks of planning."

"You have three days. Every day you delay past that, a body part will be removed from your love and sent to you."

Sofia's face paled, her eyes widening in fear. I tamped down the rage I was feeling, keeping my voice level. "You touch one hair on her head, add one more bruise to her face, and your end will be so painful you will be begging for death, Ivan."

He laughed, the sound ruthless and cold. "Such threats. I hold all the cards here. I have your woman. You want her alive, you will do what I say." He gripped her shoulder. "And you should tell her to behave."

She jerked away from him, glaring. "Touch me again, asshole, I'll do worse."

Her words confirmed my suspicions. She *had* hit him. My brave, feisty woman.

I dropped my head in pretend defeat to hide my smirk. Then I glanced up. "I need schematics. If you want a building gone and no survivors, I have to implode it. Bring it down on them, with a second bomb to finish the job. I need to know how to wire it. I need floor plans, pictures. A job like that requires planning or it won't work."

He grinned in triumph. "They will be sent."

"I will need hands. I will have to hire a crew. I cannot build it by myself."

"I will provide men. Alex will help."

"No. I need my men. Those who know my work," I lied. "Alex can help at the end, but I need experience, given your time frame."

Sofia shook her head wildly now. "No, Egan, no! You save the other people. You always save the most people you can!"

I met her eyes, knowing that was the doctor in her talking. I would normally agree with her under regular circumstances. But in this case, there was no choice, and the decision was easy to make.

"All that matters is you, Sofia."

"He's not going to let me go—you know that," she cried. "He will kill me anyway!"

It took everything in me not to assure her she'd be safe with me soon. I had to pretend. And if it came down to a real choice, I would still do it. She came above everyone else.

"I have no choice. I have to do this."

She became angry.

"Isn't that perfect," she spat. Then she spewed off

some words in Italian, all of them sounding angry.

"I have no choice," I repeated, sounding crushed. "I have to try."

She began to speak, but a gag was placed over her mouth, and the camera focused on Ivan.

"You will have blueprints and information within the hour. You have three days. Send your list to the email the blueprints come from. Materials will be delivered by this evening."

"You harm her, and you'll answer to me."

"She is safe as long as you do what I want."

The video feed ended.

I turned to Damien. "What did she say?"

He grinned. "Clues. The words she said were all clues. Five. Sterling. Paper. Hole."

"Five men?" I asked. "There's a hole in the room where she is?"

"Yes."

"Sterling? Paper?"

"That one, I'm not sure. But we'll figure it out."

"Did we get the location?"

Damien shook his head. "The signal was bounced all over the world. I will run some programs to see if I can figure it out."

"Her phone, purse, and pass all had trackers. All left behind. The one on her isn't sending a signal."

"Where is it?" Damien asked.

"In the earrings I gave her. It only works if the back is pressed in. It must have come loose."

"Ah, you dropped a hint as well. The ear infection."

"If she can get her hands loose and figures it out, maybe she can reactivate it."

"We'll find her. And we'll find the location of this building and get her out."

"Why Canada? Why is this evidence here?"

"Probably for security reasons. You know there are safe houses all over the world. How he discovered the evidence is here is a mystery. He's on the top of the wanted lists in many countries. His last known whereabouts was Europe. But with the surgery he had, he walks around like a free man. No doubt, he simply boarded a plane under his new identity and came here. He's been planning this for a while. Wipe out all the evidence and start a new reign of terror."

"I am going to end this."

Julian stood. "With our help and the backup of HJ."

"They know?"

"Yes. I spoke with my old boss."

"But we're all retired. Once you're out, you're out."

"This is an exception. Ivan's on their wanted list as well, now that he's stepped into this country. They usually leave other countries and their criminals to the proper law enforcements, but when one of their operatives is targeted, that changes things. And considering a group of their ex-operatives are joining forces, they're willing to open the vault. Unofficially, of course. We'll have everything we need. We'll get Sofia back safely and end this Ivan and his crew. Those are the expectations."

We all nodded. That was HJ's mandate.

Exterminate. Rid the world of the evil at its source. No judge, no jury, no trial.

He met my eyes. "You will have to give up your life here. Disappear."

"Not an issue. I will take Sofia to the island. We can find a new life together."

"Then let's get to work."

Damien sat down beside me. "I'm in HJ's system. I think I know what the evidence is."

"Major incriminating files, I imagine."

He shook his head. "People."

He showed me his computer. "Yuri Romanoff. Ivan's right hand for years. He was known as the dealer of death. His son Vlad, who followed in his father's footsteps. Sasha, Yuri's wife. Rumor is she loved bloodshed more than Yuri did. They turned on Ivan. They have all the goods on him. Turns out Vlad was excellent at keeping records. They carry the evidence with them, refusing to part with it."

"Family that kills together, stays together."

Damien smirked at my quip.

"Why the parting?"

"Money. Power. Who knows."

"How did they get away?"

"The plane they were in crashed. No survivors."

"I assume they were not on that plane?"

"Nope. They were spirited away. Ended up all over the place. Finally here. Ivan was about to be arrested when he disappeared and got himself a new face. They're under heavy guard. The evidence is on paper and in their heads. Destroy the paper and kill them, the case against Ivan is weaker. He'll disappear, and they won't find him."

I sat back. "Why not just take on a new persona, then?"

"Ivan and Yuri were like brothers. Yuri stole millions from him and disrespected him. Sold him out. Ivan is big on revenge. He wants him dead. Wants his whole family dead in retribution."

"He's putting his ego ahead of his freedom."

"Madmen often do."

We were both quiet. "Ivan's not wrong—Yuri and his family, they have to die too."

"Yes. But that's not our mandate. Taking out Ivan is. Getting Sofia back. We concentrate on that."

My phone buzzed, and I swiped it up as soon as Damien nodded. "Ivan."

A video began, and he glared into the camera. "I hope you are ready to begin."

"Why don't you just kill Yuri yourself?" I asked.

He shook his head, an evil smile on his face. "How busy you have been, Egan. I cannot get into the building. But the deadly ghost can. You can deliver the justice that the dealer of death deserves. Blowing him up like the plane he pretended to die in. Him and his whole lying, scheming family."

"How poetic for you," I snarled. "Coward. Not man enough to kill people yourself, so you have others do it."

"Tsk, tsk," he reprimanded me. Then he stepped out

of the way, and my heart went into my mouth. "Your materials will be delivered shortly. The shipment, however, is missing a few items. They were needed here."

Sofia was still sitting, but she was no longer bound. Her legs were drawn up to her chest, her arms wrapped around them. Around the room were a series of trip wires. In front of her on the floor sat a large box, no doubt containing more explosives. More wires ran from the top and bottom. Sofia was pale, her eyes watering. I could see the tremors, feel her terror. Once again, the images of my dream came back to me. Her in a room. Me unable to get to her.

I refused to let that dream come true.

"In case you have some idea of double-crossing me," Ivan said, the camera returning to him. "She will suffer. Alex doesn't have the expertise to blow up the building, so he is practicing on your girlfriend." He paused, his smile growing wider. "I hope he doesn't—how you say in this country—screw it up. Injure her so she suffers."

"You motherfucker!" I shouted.

The camera returned to Sofia. I struggled to get myself under control.

"It will be fine, my Sofia. I will do what they ask." I touched my ear, tapping it in what looked like a nervous gesture, but one I hoped she picked up on. "You will return to me safely."

She looked so terrified, I had to swallow. "I love you."

She buried her head in her arms, not responding. The feed went dead. I sat, unbelievable pain welling in my chest. Petrified for the woman I loved. Knowing what was at stake. For the first time ever, my failure could cost me everything.

My grandmother's warning came back to me.

This was my crossroads. I had to choose carefully. My plan to save Sofia had to be executed with absolute precision. Her life was in my hands. And without her, I had no life.

Damien's hands were clenched into fists on the table. Marcus and Julian both stood, coming behind us, but not speaking. It was Matteo who spoke up.

"Get rid of the picture in your head, Egan. Both of you. You can't let it mess with you. Sofia is alive. She is going to remain alive. We are going to make a plan, and you are going to get her back."

"I have to figure this out," I said between tight lips. "She is surrounded by explosives. The room is rigged. I saw the wiring on the floor. We go in, it kills her and us."

"No," Marcus said, standing with Matteo. "We're going to outsmart him. You are going to help us learn fast. I was mirroring your device. I captured all the images for you to study."

"Good. But I don't know where she is," I said, my fear overwhelming me. "I can't help her if I can't find her."

My words spurred Damien into action. "I'm going to fucking find her tonight. And Matteo is right. She's alive, and she's going to stay alive. I refuse to let her die or anything bad happen to you."

Julian came behind me, his voice low. "Have faith in

us, Egan, the way we trusted you. We will not let you lose her."

I shut my eyes, the tears gathered in them making it impossible for me to focus. Julian squeezed my shoulder, his tone sympathetic. "Tamp down your fear. Lock it away. We need your head clear. Sofia needs your head clear. She needs Egan, the Specialist. Not her lover. You have to remove your emotions for her."

"How do I do that?"

Matteo clapped my other shoulder. "You draw on your hate for Ivan. Get mad, Egan. Hold on to it. Let it settle in your bones and your head and remember what you have to do. Above all else, remember that. We're here for Sofia. Only she matters. We get her out, we kill Ivan and his cronies, and we all go to the island and fucking move on."

His words sank in. I met Damien's eyes. I saw his fear and worry. He saw mine. I huffed out a long breath and thought of Ivan. Of Sofia's fear and the promise I made to her. I released my anger, letting it build. I felt the rage fill me, cresting over my fear.

"Let's go. I need my woman back."

An hour later, my phone buzzed again. I went into the parking lot with Marcus and Julian and allowed the metal door to lift. Alex drove a truck in, smirking as he got out of the cab.

I was surprised he'd come alone, but he knew if I killed him, Ivan would hurt Sofia.

"Who are you friends?" he asked.

"Let me introduce my crew," I responded. "This is None-of-your-goddamn-business, and that's Wipe-that-smile-off-your-face-before-I-shoot-you. They aren't much for talking. They prefer to hit things I tell them I don't like." I paused. "They know I despise you."

He glared at me, opening the back of his truck. "Here are your materials."

Marcus and Julian moved the items carefully. None of it was explosive. I had all the really dangerous items already. As if I would trust Alex to even touch explosive material. I didn't need any of it, but if it kept one asshole busy, I was good with it. HJ would supply the real material needed.

"What are the espresso beans for?" Alex asked.

I had added that to the list just to amuse myself. "So the bomb smells good when it blows."

He frowned. "You are an asshole."

I stepped into his space. "And if you are responsible for so much as a scratch on that woman you've kidnapped, I will hunt you down to the ends of the earth and make you suffer." I squeezed his shoulder hard, making him flinch.

I also activated the invisible tracker on his hoodie.

"Now, fuck off."

"Don't try anything. She is rigged to blow," he taunted me. "You think I'm an idiot, but I took out your water pipes and that stupid gallery. I will enjoy watching her die if you cross Ivan."

I turned my head, counting to ten. It didn't work. In a move he didn't expect, I drew my fist back and hit him in the nose. Just like Ivan. The crunching of his bones was satisfying. His howl of pain was music to my ears.

"Get out. I don't want to see you again."

He held his nose, the blood spurting between his fingers. "You don't get to call the shots."

"When it comes to this, I do. Get the fuck out before I practice my skills on you. Toes hurt when they're blown off one by one."

He climbed into the truck, driving out too fast, his tires squealing when he hit the loose gravel outside. The garage door slowly closed behind him, and Marcus and Julian immediately covered everything that had been brought. We took it to a small room, locking it inside. If there were any listening devices in it, they wouldn't do them any good. I wouldn't use anything they sent either. I couldn't trust it.

We didn't speak until we were headed back to my old workroom.

"So, *None*," Julian began. "You gonna make us some food?"

"Sure, *Wipe*," Marcus said. "Need to keep the boss's strength up. Lots of noses left to break."

"Fuck off," I muttered, but I smiled, the levity of the moment much-needed.

Damien and Matteo looked up as we walked in. Damien waved me over.

"I think I found her."

CHAPTER EIGHTEEN

Sofia

The building was silent, the only sound was my rough breathing. I sat on the floor, my back against the wall, my head still aching. They had untied me and left me. I heard them lock the door, and for a while I heard other sounds, and I knew it had been rigged. There were wires. Explosives. Traps.

They left a couple of bottles of water. Tossed in some granola bars and set down a bucket before shutting the door, their laughter muffled but still reaching my ears. A red light blinked in the corner and I knew they were watching me, but I was sure I was alone in the building.

Earlier, before they had wired the place, I had crept carefully to the side of the room, staying away from the door, to where I saw the hole. The floorboards around it were weak and unstable. I had peered over the edge, realizing it did me no good. The floors underneath it were damaged and missing in places as well. If I fit through the hole, at best, I would break my legs, and at worst, die a slow death on the ground from my injuries after I fell down a couple of stories.

I wiped away the tears that seemed to flow constantly, tucking my hair behind my ear. I drifted my finger over my lobe, touching the earring there. Egan's gift. I frowned as I thought about his words. I didn't have an ear infection, so I didn't know what he meant. And he kept tapping his ear in an odd gesture when he talked to me. I wondered if somehow he could find me with these earrings.

I traced the earring, feeling nothing. I removed it, peering at it, but I saw nothing except the pretty stones. I did the same with the other one, noting how unsecure it was. The back had come away, hanging loosely on my ear. I was surprised it hadn't fallen off completely, given what I had endured. After looking at the gems and not seeing anything, I slid it back into place, making sure the backing was tight. I didn't want to lose them even if they didn't help Egan find me.

I tried not to think about the fact that I might die wearing them. I refused to. Egan would figure this out. I hadn't seen him, but somehow I knew Damien was there, which was why I had shouted out a few words in Italian, hoping he would understand. It had been my only shot—and I hadn't been able to warn Egan about the bomb Ivan told me was in the building. Ivan had slapped me again after demanding to know what I said, and I had lied as I looked him in the eye.

"I said you were a worthless piece of shit."

That earned me another slap. My face ached from the blows. I hoped Egan made him hurt when he killed him later. The doctor in me was shocked at the feelings of revenge. My oath meant nothing at the moment. I could suddenly understand Egan's calling. I wanted nothing more than this man and the people he used to die. The world would be a better place.

I wrapped my arms around my legs and rested my head on my hands. I shivered as the shadows grew darker, the room colder, and my hopes dimmer.

"Please, Egan," I whispered. "Find me."

EGAN

I bent over Damien's laptop. "What do you have?"

"There are a lot of businesses in the province with the name Sterling in them. Many of them closed in the past few years, but one stuck out. Just outside Toronto. A shipping company that was next to a printing business. Sterling Shipping. Sterling Printing."

"Sterling. Paper," I repeated. "Yes."

"Both businesses closed. Both are still standing, but one seems more logical." Damien showed me an image. "A small warehouse. Deserted."

"That works," I said, my heartbeat picking up.

"We need some heat imaging and visuals."

My phone beeped, and I grabbed it, staring at the screen. "My beautiful, smart woman," I breathed. "She figured it out. Her tracker is working."

We compared the logistics. "That's the building. We found her."

"Now we have to get her."

Marcus spoke. "Matteo and I will go in. Do some recon. We'll send you what we find so you can start making a plan. Send us the coordinates."

They left and Julian stood. "Tell me what you need."

"I need to know where this safe house is. I have the blueprints, but any identifying information is deleted. I know it must be in a fairly remote, safe location."

Julian stared at the blueprints. "They move Yuri frequently."

"Yes."

"Even HJ doesn't know the schedule, they keep it so tight. And they do it well. I think they pull a van into the garage as usual for shift changes and load him and his family in and take them away. They probably go to their headquarters, put them in another vehicle, and take them elsewhere. They keep up the appearance at the old safe house in case it's being watched for a while, then suddenly just stop. The witnesses are safely tucked away elsewhere, and no one is the wiser."

I pursed my lips. "One of his last demands was he wants to see Yuri before I detonate, so he knows he lost and Ivan won."

"If we arrange for the other agency to move Yuri, then get Ivan and his men into the safe house Ivan is aware of, we could take them down." He met my eyes. "Follow the HJ mandate."

"Trust me, I have zero problems killing Ivan."

"Yuri and his family will be eliminated, but not by us."

I shrugged. "Rid the world of all that scum."

Damien rubbed his head. "You're forgetting one thing. They want whatever evidence Yuri has and keeps with him, plus what is in his head. It implicates others. He or his son wears a briefcase chained to their bodies."

I shrugged. "Forget what's in his head. I'm sure what's in the briefcase will have names. The other agency can shoot them, cut off the briefcase, and dispose of them. I don't care. I only care about getting Sofia back and killing Ivan."

Julian stroked his chin. "You're probably right. I'll go make some calls. See what I can get rolling."

"How long until they get to the warehouse?" I asked, anxious.

"About forty-five minutes. You going to build some bombs?"

"No, I'm too distracted. What I will build can be done swiftly. I plan on a painful death for that group. The deadly ghost will make them wish they'd never heard of me. Whatever HJ does with the others is their business. My focus is Ivan."

"Okay. You can help me. I want to scan the area where the warehouse is—see what we're dealing with."

I sat down. "On it."

———

Marcus and Matteo returned, and we sat in the workroom. Julian joined us, his face giving nothing away.

"She's in there. There is one main heat source. I flew

the drone over it, but the windows were too dirty to get much of a look. But the room she is in has no windows."

"Are the doors wired?"

Matteo shook his head. "Marcus kept watch, and I patrolled the outside. No cameras or sensors on the building. There was a broken window I slipped in through on the main floor, but I didn't want to attract any attention. I saw a camera pointed toward the stairs. They are watching inside."

He and Marcus exchanged a look. "What?" I asked. "What aren't you telling me?"

Marcus put his hand on my shoulder. "Matteo saw a pile of broken boards and investigated. The second floor was badly damaged, so we had a clear view. He could see up to the third floor, right where we thought she would be, including the hole she mentioned. I sent up a small camera." He handed me his phone. "I had eyes on her."

I looked at the dim, grainy image. Sofia was leaning against a wall, her head down. She appeared to be sleeping, no doubt exhausted. My heart ached at the sight of her. She would be cold, scared, and alone. I needed to get to her.

"Did you get anything else?"

"Yes. I flew the drone inside, avoiding the cameras. I got a good view of the door that leads to her room. It's rigged, but I think you can disarm it. I also turned the camera and swept the room so you could see what you're dealing with. I'll send it all to your laptop."

Julian spoke. "Yuri and his family were moved a

short while ago. So, we can go with that plan, unless you've changed your mind."

Damien looked at me. "How do you want to play this, Egan?"

I rubbed my chin, my mind racing. I studied the pictures of the warehouse again then made a decision. I needed Sofia safe. I needed to end Ivan. In that order. A plan formed in my head. Dangerous. Possibly deadly. Ivan thought he had the upper hand, but he was wrong. He was working with a skeleton crew with little experience. The gaps in their planning would benefit us at the moment. Once Sofia was safe, I would deal with the fallout.

"Forget that plan. We know where she is. We go now. Get Sofia and make sure she is safe. Find Ivan. This ends tonight."

"How?" Damien asked. "What is the plan?"

"We're going to do what we did to get Raven out. Loop the feed, and I'll dismantle the explosives they have keeping her trapped. You'll take her away, make her safe. I'll unscramble the loop, so Ivan sees the place blow."

"And then?"

"Alex's tracker is active. I know where he is. I'm going there, and I will end them all."

"Not without backup."

"No, I go in alone."

"Not happening."

"I need Sofia safe. That is the most important thing."

Damien shook his head. "Getting you out safe is equally as important. My cousin needs you."

"I will not endanger any of you. This is my past catching up with me."

Marcus stepped forward. "Damien and I will back you up. Matteo and Julian can take Sofia to a safe place and guard her. Get her medical attention if needed. We will help you end Ivan, and we will all walk out of there." He met my eyes steadily. "That is how we work, Egan. As a team. We have one another's backs so we *all* walk away."

I began to protest, but Damien stood. "Marcus is right. You have laid your life on the line for each of us. We are returning the favor. Once you dismantle whatever is holding Sofia captive, we will get her out of there and move to step two—finishing Ivan."

I nodded, knowing I was outnumbered and realizing they were right. Together, we could do this.

"Let's go."

The warehouse sat deserted and dark. There was a slight drizzle coming down as one by one we slipped through the broken window. Matteo patrolled the outside, Damien in the van overseeing all the technical equipment we needed. Marcus and Julian followed me to the staircase, and we used one another as ladders, climbing up to the camera and attaching the equipment I needed to supply Damien with the feed. We waited patiently until his voice echoed in my ear.

"Go. I tapped into the feed in Sofia's location as well. Both are on a five-minute loop. I'll keep feeding it into the system. You're invisible."

"All is quiet out here," Matteo added.

We headed upstairs, our feet silent on the cement. Using the heat imaging, we found the room Sofia was in, and I studied the explosives and wires Alex had set up. His rudimentary style was obvious, but I was worried about the bomb that sat in front of Sofia and the wires that ran under the door and around the room. I needed to see what was in there, and I needed Sofia to help me. I was terrified his inexperience, combined with his overinflated ego, could lead to an unstable design.

I crouched down, getting as close to the door as I dared.

"Sofia," I called softly. "*Iubirea mea*, it's me. I'm here."

SOFIA

I was so cold, the shivers racking my body constant. I was terrified to move, not knowing what might set off the box in front of me. Or the explosives around the room. I stayed in one place, my head down, trying not to cry. Thinking about Damien. Egan. My life. Wondering if today was the last one I would have. If I would die in this room.

The light that filtered in under the door slowly faded, the blackness of the night swallowing it. As the darkness descended, so did my hope. Fear set in. I could hear the scurrying of animals in the walls.

What if they somehow set off the explosives? What if they startled me and I somehow activated something?

The longer I sat in the darkness, the more my fear soaked into my chest. Fear became terror.

I began to talk to myself. Whispering words of comfort. I thought about Egan. His warmth and smile. The way he surrounded me with his love—even when I hadn't returned it.

I listened to his voice in my head. The soothing cadence of his tone when he would hold me after we made love. The way he could calm me with his presence. How he touched me. Cared for me.

I knew now, without a doubt, how much I wanted a life with him. More than I wanted anything else. Even my career, which had been the one constant in my life.

I wanted it all with him. I wanted to marry him. Have children. Watch them grow. Bounce their babies on my knee and spoil them. Sit back and grow old with Egan, watching the way time would soften our bodies and gray our hair, but not change our love.

A future I could see but might never have.

I wiped at the tears in my eyes, tucking my legs closer as another wave of shivers racked my body. The waterworks didn't stop, and I gave in, letting them run down my face and sobbing into my hands.

"Please, Egan," I begged. "Please."

I cried until I was exhausted. Until I slipped into the darkness, joining it.

"Sofia," a voice called softly in my dream. "*Iubirea mea*, it's me. I'm here."

I lifted my head, the room still dark, my hopes dashing as I realized I was dreaming.

Until a noise made me glance toward the door and I saw the glimmer of light under it.

The voice spoke again.

"Sofia," it called. "Can you hear me? It's Egan."

"Egan?" I responded, my voice raspy, still unsure if I was hearing things.

"Yes. I'm here."

"Egan, there's a bomb! Don't come in here!"

"I know, my love. I'm going to get you out, but I need your help, okay?"

"Yes," I sobbed.

"Don't cry, my brave girl. Please. I need you."

I sat up straighter, wiping my eyes. "Tell me what to do."

"I am going to slip a light under the door so you can see. And a small camera. You will have to help me guide both of them safely to you."

"Okay."

I heard something, and then light filled the room. I blinked, and Egan waited until my eyes were used to it. He kept talking, encouraging me, and I heard another voice.

"Who is there?"

"Marcus and Julian. Damien is outside, and so is Matteo. You are safe now, Sofia. We will not leave you.

Be patient, and I'll have you out soon. Have your eyes adjusted?"

"Yes."

"Okay, I'm sending in the camera. You tell me how to get it to you."

I watched it, directing him, avoiding the wires and box sitting in front of me. When it was close enough, I gingerly reached over and picked up the thin wires and tiny devices.

"I have it. What now?"

Egan's voice was calm.

"Now you're going to help me dismantle the bomb."

CHAPTER NINETEEN

Egan

Hearing the fear in Sofia's voice caused my entire body to slow down. I focused on her and her alone. This was my one task. I calmed, my mind suddenly clear. There was nothing but the job. I was Egan Vulpe, the Specialist. Explosives expert. I had been taught by the best, and I had forgotten more about the art of bombs than Alex would ever learn.

I could defuse this inferior piece of garbage.

I spoke calmly. "Sofia, hold the camera and light over the box. I will direct you where I need them to go."

Her hands were trembling. From cold, fear, or both, I didn't know.

"I will have you free soon. Trust me, my love. I just need you to stay calm and focus with me, all right?"

"Y-yes."

"Turn the camera to your face."

She did, and I studied her in the dark and shadows. I could see the bruises on her skin, the terror in her eyes. "I have you now, and nothing is going to happen, except soon you will be in my arms. Know that above everything else."

"Okay." She drew in a breath that stuttered and caught. "I love you, *mio guerriero.*"

"You can say that to my face shortly. Now, turn the camera back to the box so I can render it useless. I need to hold you."

Her hand trembled as I directed her, studying the box. I had her hold the light and trace the wires back to the door. Knowing I was there, she was braver and able to stand and move a little. I narrowed my eyes as she let the light spread around the room. I traced the pathways, seeing his plan. Finding his flaws. Laughing at his ineptness. I was going to let his bomb blow, but only once I got Sofia out. He had made it overcomplicated, the box the last thing to blow. The delay he put on the sequence worked in my favor.

"Okay, *iubirea mea.* I have it."

Damien murmured in my ear. "Are you sure?"

"Positive," I assured him. "Get Matteo back to the van. Have the blankets ready."

"On it," Matteo said. "I'll be there fast."

I didn't answer, running my fingers over the wires and memorizing the sequence. Marcus and Julian had stood behind me, ready to follow any instructions.

"Sofia," I called. "I am going to start cutting wires. Once I'm ready, I need you to be prepared. I'm coming in and taking you out. We have to move quickly."

"I don't know if I can walk fast."

"You won't have to. I'll have you. When the light

begins to glow on the box, do not panic. I have you. All right?"

"Yes. I trust you."

"Okay, get ready."

I heard movement, and she spoke loudly. "I'm ready."

I turned to Marcus and Julian. "You kick the door as soon as I cut the wires. I'll get her. Be ready to run. We have three minutes."

Marcus nodded, looking grim. "We'll be right behind you."

"Damien, can you re-angle the camera in the room, make it look as if it shifted? Point it toward the floor?"

"So they don't know she's out. Got it." He was quiet for a moment. "Okay. Redirected."

"As soon as I have Sofia and we're down the steps, kill the loop. I want him to think the worst."

"Say the word, and I'll kill it."

I drew in a deep breath, holding the cutters to the wires. "On my mark. Three, two, one."

I snipped the wires and stepped back. Marcus lifted his foot, kicking in the door. I rushed in, grabbing Sofia, who was already trying to limp toward me. I lifted her into my arms and headed for the stairs. "Go!" I yelled.

I had no time to think. No time to comfort the shaking woman in my arms. We took the steps two at a time, Julian leading with a light and Marcus at my back. At the window, Julian went first, turning to let me hand him Sofia. I followed, pulling Marcus through. I got her back, and we ran as fast as we could, making it to the tree line before the explosion.

As I suspected, the bomb detonated, and the floor collapsed under it, sending the rotting, dry wood and ceilings down in a large mass of sparks and flames. The bomb wasn't strong enough to bring the warehouse down, but the fire it started would burn hot and fast, destroying it. It would have killed Sofia.

I pressed a kiss to her forehead, and we headed for the van. I climbed in the back, grabbing the blankets and wrapping them around her. She was sobbing, the events and emotion of what had occurred too much for her to handle. She gripped my neck, and I held her close as we began to drive away.

I met Marcus's eyes and nodded. "Step one accomplished."

He nodded grimly, knowing what we were still facing.

Sofia lifted her head. "Damien?" she asked, her voice raspy.

"Right here, Sofia," he assured her from the front. "We're all here, and you're safe."

Julian handed me a bottle of water, and I pressed it to her mouth. "Drink, Sofia."

She gulped it down, some of it running out of her mouth. I wiped it away. "It's all right now. I have you."

"Ivan said there was a bomb at the apartment—"

"No," I assured her. "He lied. Everything is going to be okay now. I have you," I repeated.

"Don't let go," she pleaded. "Don't ever let go."

"Never," I promised, shocked at the wetness in my eyes. I buried my face in her neck, holding her as tightly as I dared, not caring if my emotion was witnessed by my friends.

They, of all people, understood.

———

Julian directed us to a safe house, where a doctor was waiting. I refused to leave Sofia's side, and she clung to me adamantly, so the doctor examined her under my watchful eye. The others stayed outside or in the other room. Julian and Matteo were on the phone constantly, Damien was tracking Alex, and Marcus was busy in the kitchen, making everyone something to eat.

After the doctor finished, he smiled kindly at Sofia. "None of what I will tell you will come as a surprise. Nothing broken, but you have a lot of cuts and bruises. You're dehydrated, and your body has experienced a great deal of trauma. You need fluids, food, rest, and to warm up. The IV will help, but I would like you to eat as well." He studied her. "Once you're feeling better, perhaps talk to someone about your experience. It might help mentally."

She nodded. "I want a shower and clean clothes."

"I want you to rest," he countered.

"After," she said firmly. "And cap off the IV before you go."

He shook his head. "Doctors," he muttered. "Worst patients ever. Just keep up the fluids and rest, okay?"

I stepped forward. "I will help her and get her to bed as soon as possible."

He nodded, knowing when to give up the fight. "As soon as possible. She may be dizzy or disoriented."

"I understand."

"I'm right here," Sofia said, her tone snarky.

We ignored her.

He left, and I checked out the bathroom, grateful that Julian had made sure there were some clothes and toiletries here. Sofia was shaky, and I helped her into the shower, unsure what to do next.

"Are you coming in?" she asked, allowing me to see her vulnerability. "I need help."

I shed my clothes, stepping in behind her. I let the hot water run over us, feeling her body reacting to the heat and my closeness. Once she relaxed, I shampooed her hair and soaped her body, being as gentle as possible. She began to cry again, and I murmured soothing words as I cleansed her.

"You were incredibly brave, my love. I am very proud of you."

"I was so scared," she sobbed, turning to my chest and leaning into me.

I wrapped her close, letting her cry. "I'm so sorry. I failed you." I pressed a kiss to her head, her tears hurting my heart. "Please don't leave me, Sofia. I couldn't take it."

"I'm not leaving you, Egan. I want a life with you. I'm not waiting anymore. I want it to start right now."

Relief filled me.

"It will, *iubirea mea*. We will figure it out together."

"Is it over?" she whispered.

"Almost."

"Please let it go, Egan. Let's just go to the island. Forget him. Forget all this."

"I can't, Sofia. You know I can't."

"Even if I asked?"

I shut my eyes at the pleading tone in her voice. I knew she hated the thought of killing people. And she was terrified of losing me. "Please don't. I have to finish this."

"I won't survive it if you don't make it."

"I will. Nothing will happen to me. I promise."

"Will you come back to me?"

I pulled her closer. "Always."

She was trembling, her strength waning, and I finished, stepping from the shower and wrapping her in a towel before draping one around my waist. I helped her dry off and put on clean clothes. She insisted on seeing everyone, and I carried her to the small kitchen where they were all seated. She cried again hugging Damien, then thanked and hugged everyone else. Marcus ladled some soup into a bowl, insisting she eat. Then he put the pot on the table, making us all eat. It was thick and tasty, and I knew, given what lay ahead, I needed the nourishment. Sofia sat beside me, one hand gripping mine the entire time she ate. Her eyes fluttered more than once, and after she finished, I carried her to the sofa, wrapping a blanket around her. I restarted the IV, having added some medication to it upstairs before bringing it down here. It would help her rest.

"When?" she asked, the one word saying everything. I wanted her to rest, not to be worried and stressed, so I hedged.

"Once we have a plan."

She sighed, shutting her eyes. She was exhausted, and the medication was hitting her fast. She slipped into sleep quickly. I watched her for a few moments, then returned to the kitchen, sitting where I could see her. Before I went, I kissed her head, whispering my words of love to her.

"What's the plan?" Julian asked, knowing it would happen tonight. We couldn't risk Ivan finding out Sofia was alive or that I was on to him. He would disappear.

"Ivan will check in again. I want to ask him to let me talk to Alex so we know he's there. Once we confirm it, we go. You guard Sofia." I paused. "If I don't make it back, you take her to the island, Damien. Make her safe. Help her find her life again."

"Don't talk like that," he insisted.

"I want your promise." I met all their eyes. "I want it from all of you. We get caught in something, you save yourselves. Get back to your families. Leave me. If you don't agree, I'm going in alone. I need to know Sofia has all of you if I'm gone. Especially you, Damien."

They reluctantly agreed. I glanced at my watch. "He'll be calling soon. Be ready."

"I have everything you need in the van," Julian assured me. "Including the two bags you asked me to bring."

"Good."

"Do you have a plan?"

"Yes. I'm going to kill them all, walk away, and start my life with Sofia."

Damien glanced over at Sofia. "She won't like this."

"She won't know. I'll be back before she wakes up."

"You're not going to tell her?"

"No. It will upset her, and she'll worry herself sick while I'm gone. The painkillers will make her sleep, and when she wakes up, it'll be over. She won't have to think about it."

He shook his head. "You're playing with fire."

"No. I'm protecting her."

Before he could retort, my phone buzzed. Damien clicked some keys and nodded. "Stay calm," he advised.

"Ivan," I said tersely. "I want to talk to Sofia."

"She is sleeping. Don't worry, Egan." A grainy picture appeared on the screen. An old one that he assumed I would accept as real. "We are taking good care of your girl."

Liar. He thought she was dead and that I had no clue. He was going to pay for it soon enough.

"You hurt her, you'll be sorry."

"Do you have a plan?" he asked abruptly.

"Yes. I need to ask Alex a question, though."

"What is it?"

"Does he have experience with infrared technology?"

Ivan spoke fast in Russian, and I heard Alex's snort of disgust. "Yeah."

"He does."

"Fine. I'll need him tomorrow," I lied. Now that I knew he was there, we had the confirmation we needed.

"What is the plan? How will you get into the building?"

"I have connections."

"I knew you would. The deadly ghost always had connections."

I shut my eyes. I'd hated that name years ago, and I hated it even more now. "I'll tell you tomorrow."

"I want to know now."

"Too bad."

I hung up and stood. I studied Sofia, my heart aching at the thought of leaving her. I wanted to stay and hold her, be there when she woke up. Hold her if she needed to cry again. But I had to go. I needed to take care of this tonight and end it.

"Let's go."

Julian and Matteo stood as well. "We'll guard her with our lives."

"Remember your promise. Look after her if I don't come back."

Julian nodded. "We won't forget."

We approached the house with caution. Two stories, set back from the road and private, it was newer and obviously well-appointed. It was only about twenty minutes from the old warehouse, but the difference in the two buildings was night and day. Typical narcissistic, overindulgent behavior of a criminal. They always loved comfort and cared nothing for those around them—either their victims or their underlings. I could guarantee his men were sleeping on floors or sofas, while he commandeered the best room with every luxury he could ask. We used heat sourcing and found five bodies inside. Three on the main floor and two upstairs.

"Ivan and his sidekick, I'm sure," I muttered.

Marcus flew his high-powered drone around the house, careful not to get too close. It was stealthy and silent and gave us the information we needed. There were no cameras or security around the building, which surprised me, except Ivan thought he was invisible. His ego had overridden his intelligence, which often happened with criminals. They got sloppy.

Three men, including Alex, were in the living room, watching TV. Upstairs, the blinds were drawn in one room where we assumed Ivan was, and the scanner told us his sidekick was down the hall. I was certain none of them was remotely concerned that the building where Sofia had been held was gone, or the fact that she was supposedly dead.

"Did he think he would be able to fool me forever?" I muttered, my anger endless and burning.

"When you asked for proof, tomorrow he would show you another image they had captured. He would assume you were focused on the bombs and getting her back. Once you did your job, he'd kill you. He knew if Sofia was dead, he'd have no leverage over you."

"As if I would ever work for someone like him. Fear and intimidation. That is his mantra." I squeezed Marcus's shoulder. "I had the best. Real leadership. Friendship."

"Then let's end this. How do you want to play it?" Marcus asked after acknowledging my words with a wink.

My plans for a long, slow death for Ivan had changed. I wanted it over so I could get back to Sofia.

"We go in the back. I get Alex. You kill the others. Upstairs, Ivan is mine. I'm just going to walk in. Make sure he knows he lost and end him. I am not wasting time."

"Good. The house?"

"I have enough with me to blow it. I will attach it to the gas line. Eliminate every trace of them. Plus, I have a little extra something just for Ivan."

"Then let's go. Being this close to so much evil is making me nauseous," Damien muttered.

We skirted the house, and I shook my head. No lights on. No motion sensors. Ivan thought he was undetectable.

Big mistake.

The back door opened without so much as a squeak, the lock easily picked. The kitchen was a disaster, food, empty liquor bottles, and dirty dishes everywhere. Marcus shuddered beside me. "Pigs," he muttered.

The TV was blaring, and they all held glasses, their focus on the flickering screen, not their surroundings. They were drunk enough that they barely reacted to our presence, only glaring blearily at the guns in our hands. The silencers made the job easy, and two of them were dead before anyone could speak. Alex stood slowly, meeting my eyes, his baleful and belligerent. Rage, red and hot filled my body.

"Sit down."

"Fuck you."

I shot him in the knee, the excruciating pain evident

on his face. He fell into the chair, shocked and in agony. "I said sit."

Gripping at his knee, he glared at me. "Your girlfriend is dead," he taunted. "My bomb killed her."

"I told you not to touch her."

"I don't take orders from you," he hissed, trying to be stealthy as he slid his hand down the side of the chair.

His entire body arched as my bullet found its mark in his shoulder. Marcus leaned over, pulling the gun Alex had been going for from the chair, tossing it away. Alex bared his teeth, refusing to make a sound of pain. If it were anyone else, I would have respected that.

But I had no respect for him.

I shook my head. "You failed, you little piece of shit. I got her first."

He narrowed his eyes, his voice laced with agony. "How?"

I smirked. "Because I'm better than you are. You shouldn't have touched her, Alex. You shouldn't have frightened her. For that, I'm going to end you."

I felt only satisfaction when the bullet pierced his head and he crumpled down to the side, his eyes blank and staring. The look of shock on his face was almost comical.

I pointed my gun overhead, and Marcus nodded. We were silent on the stairs. Damien slipped into the room beside Ivan's, and I heard the muffled thump as his sidekick died.

That left Ivan.

Like a unit of death, we entered Ivan's room, the door swinging open, announcing our arrival.

He was waiting in the corner, his gun trained on us. There was a flicker of surprise on his face. Something had alerted him to our presence and he had been expecting me, but not Marcus and Damien backing me as well. Our eyes locked in soundless fury. He knew he'd lost. He knew he was going to die. Even if he managed to shoot, he was outnumbered, and one of our bullets would pierce his skin and kill him.

"You lied, Ivan."

He shrugged. "She must have done something. We did not detonate it."

"You never planned on keeping her alive. Or me," I added.

He waved his hand. "It does not matter. It is done. You are too late."

"No, I'm not."

"She is dead," he announced, his eyes narrowed, waiting for my reaction.

"She is asleep under guard. I have held her and cared for her already. She was my number one priority." I paused. "Killing you was my second."

He glanced over my shoulder, and I shook my head. "All dead, Ivan. All of them."

His brow furrowed as he processed the information. He tried bribery. "I could make you rich."

"I have enough money."

"Give you power you cannot comprehend. Make you the most feared man in the world. Luxuries beyond your imagination."

I barked out a laugh. "Yeah, I see how well you're doing. I have everything I need, including my soul. You, however, don't stand a chance. You'll be burning in hell before we're even back in the van."

Then, just to piss him off, I grinned. "Yuri and his family were moved. They're safe. Given full pardon, so they'll live free lives while you're in eternal hell. You failed, Ivan. And all your money, all your wealth, will go to people who need help. The people you hurt. Know that as you burn."

A tic started in his jaw, his already-frosty gaze becoming colder. His revenge had been stolen. He was being denied the satisfaction he felt due to him. He hated that more than anything.

"Drop your gun."

He bent as if to do so, then made the big mistake of attempting to take a shot. Damien's bullet snapped the gun from his hand as I stumbled backward from the impact as the bullet hit my flesh, the burn intense. His mark was way off and it only grazed me, but it ignited my hatred all over again. Ivan staggered backward, yelling out in pain. Damien held his stance. "If I hadn't promised you that he was yours, I would put a bullet between his eyes right fucking now," he growled at me.

Marcus examined me, and I shook him off. "It's a scratch."

He tore off the bottom of his shirt, wrapping it around the wound. "Sofia is going to have something to say about that."

"She's going to have a lot to say about all of this," I muttered. Ivan watched me, holding his hand, the blood seeping out fast. I refused to show him any of my pain. I kept my face stoic. He, on the other hand, shifted and moaned from his spot on the floor where he'd dropped to.

"What do you want?" Marcus asked.

"Pick him up off the floor. Don't bother being gentle," I instructed.

They did, and he whimpered like a little girl as they deposited him in the chair. He clutched his hand.

"Does that hurt?" I asked, my anger reaching an all-time high. Hatred burned in my veins as I stared at him. He'd touched Sofia. Kidnapped her. Slapped her. Threatened her life. He would pay for those transgressions before he died.

And neither Marcus nor Damien would stop me.

"Yes," he snapped.

Smiling, I pressed the gun to his thigh, the bullet burying deep into his skin and bone, the sound loud. Almost as loud as his scream. "That should take your mind off your hand."

He lunged, and I punched him, once again smashing his nose, the blood spurting. I slapped him, returning every single one he had landed on Sofia. Tears filled his eyes, and he began to beg. Plead for his life. He offered me his money, his information, his loyalty.

I laughed. I wanted nothing of his. I wanted to shoot off every toe and finger. One at a time. Riddle him with bullets so he would slowly bleed out. Then blow him up.

But I had to end this. I needed to get back to Sofia.

"Tie him to the chair while I'm gone, but leave the good hand free. Watch him." I hurried to the van and got the bags I had brought. Ignoring the dead bodies on the floor, I found the gas line into the house and attached the explosive device I had made. It was simple but effective. It would rupture the line, and the sparks would ignite an inferno. I added a few other explosives the fire would detonate. There would be nothing left of this structure.

Then I headed back upstairs and, as Damien and Marcus watched, set down the bag I'd been carrying. I indicated Ivan, and Damien came closer, his gun at the ready. I opened the second bag I had brought, then set four boxes at Ivan's feet.

I looked at his bloodied face, feeling nothing but satisfaction.

"I'm dying," he moaned.

I laughed. "Not yet. Damien didn't aim to kill, just to disarm you. My bullet will make you bleed for a long time. But right now, you're still alive and will be for a while."

I sat back on my heels.

"However, you *are* going to die shortly. The house will explode, reducing you and your comrades to nothing. But I'm going to give you a chance, Ivan. You can sit here and wait to die, or you can play my game. One of these boxes contains a bomb. One that will explode and send painful shrapnel into your body. The pain will be agonizing, and you will linger until the other bomb explodes. But the other three are harmless. Good odds, yeah? One in four. If you pull the right wire, you might even be able to escape. I'm leaving one hand untied." I tossed a set of car keys I had found downstairs to the floor. "Drag yourself out and run. You're good at that."

I could feel Damien's and Marcus's confusion behind me, unsure what I was doing.

"You'll be waiting so you can kill me with your bullet," Ivan spat.

I stood, shaking my head. "I don't care about you. Your new face is out there. Your men are dead, your plan failed. I'm leaving, and frankly, I don't give a shit anymore. You can die tonight, you can go free. You will die soon anyway. You have too many enemies looking for you. I took away what mattered to you the most. Your power. How you die is of no concern to me anymore. Your pain is for Sofia. You never touch what is mine. Ever."

I unfurled the wires, leaving them on the arm of the chair. He grabbed them, and I shook my head, laughing. "There is a delay. Pulling them now only seals your fate, not ours."

He let off a string of curse words, calling me every name in the book. I grinned, enjoying his anger.

"Sticks and stones, Ivan."

He glared, and I bent close. "You should have listened. You should have left me alone. I didn't care about your revenge. I didn't care about your reign of terror. But you brought it and your world to my doorstep. You threatened the one thing I love the most in the world. If you had really done your research on the deadly ghost, you would have realized the people I killed were just like you. I would never work for someone with no soul. It was always to stop the evil.

Never to add to it. And now, you're going to be on that list." I straightened. "Say hello to Alex when you get to hell."

I turned to head to the door, indicating Marcus and Damien should go in front of me. "Have fun choosing your death, Ivan."

We jogged down the steps, silent, and went out the way we came in.

I paused at the tree line, waiting.

Damien spoke. "Are you sure about this, Egan?"

"Wait," I instructed.

The sound of a small explosion and the screams that followed were music to my ears.

"I guess he chose the wrong wire," Marcus said dryly.

"That was probably his legs," I mused. "Ouch."

There was another explosion and more screaming. Damien looked at me. "You said one box. One bomb."

I smiled. As soon as you pulled one wire—any wire —it activated them all.

"I lied."

I detonated the main bomb from the van, the sound of the house exploding behind us the final checkbox for the night. We were silent for a while.

I passed a weary hand over my face.

"It is done. I need to go home to Sofia."

"Julian texted. She's awake. And angry."

That didn't surprise me. "I will make it up."

"Can you wait until I'm asleep? Seriously. She's my cousin," Damien lamented.

I chuckled. "Yeah."

Marcus turned to me. "How's the arm?"

I shrugged. "I've had worse." Sofia's words would probably dig deeper.

"It's over, Egan. HJ is looking after everything now. We're out. Done."

"Good."

"You ready to let it all go?"

"I never wanted back in, Marcus. Ivan forced my hand. I just want a life of peace."

"What's next?"

"A life with Sofia. Wherever she wants it to be. If she still wants it."

"You doubt that?" Damien asked. "She loves you."

"I broke every promise I made to her. If she can forgive me, we will go forward." I stared out the window. "If not, I will let her go."

The rest of the ride was made in silence.

We entered the house, my jacket hiding the wound on my arm. Julian and Matteo waited, sitting at the table. Sofia leaned against the counter, a cup of coffee in her hand. She was pale, her bruises showing up on her skin like shadows.

Julian stood as we walked in. "HJ has finished the job. The house is secure, and they have the documents needed. It will help sort everything out. We're done."

I nodded, my gaze never leaving Sofia's face.

Damien went over and hugged her, speaking quietly. I sat down, my legs suddenly too tired to hold me up anymore. Julian and Matteo left the room, pausing to exchange a look or tap me on my good shoulder. They knew I'd been shot but didn't say anything. Marcus grabbed a bottle of water and strode from the kitchen, pausing only to hug Sofia and say something softly. Damien crossed to where I was sitting.

"It'll be fine, Egan."

I met his gaze, seeing the sympathy in his eyes.

"Thank you," I said.

He nodded, knowing I meant for his quick action earlier. Thanks to his marksmanship, Ivan didn't cause a major injury. He paused then turned back to Sofia. "Egan's okay, Sofia, but he's been shot."

Her eyes widened. *"What?"*

I glared at him. "It's a scratch. He barely hit me."

She pushed off the counter. "You let him get shot, Damien? No one told me? I would have been ready!"

"I'm fine," I repeated, even though my arm ached like a bitch. "You should be resting, *iubirea mea.*" I narrowed my eyes at Damien. "And you should be leaving."

"You be quiet, Egan Vulpe. I'm so mad at you. Damien, bring me the medical kit."

He opened the cupboard, handing her the medical kit every safe house contained.

"Where?" she demanded, opening the kit on the table.

"My arm."

"Take off your jacket."

I did as she requested, still glaring at Damien. I had planned on telling her gently. Maybe tomorrow. I would have cleaned it myself. I had done it many times, and I knew it wasn't life-threatening. He grinned and winked at me, enjoying causing trouble.

"Egan was really awesome, Sofia. Kicking ass, taking names, all after being shot."

"Shut up, you *idiotule*," I snarled. "You're making it worse."

"Nope. My work is done." He left the room as Sofia leaned over me, muttering under her breath.

In moments, she had cleaned and dressed the wound, winding a thick white bandage over it. Something wet splashed on my arm, and I slipped my fingers under her chin, lifting her face. I was horrified to see the tears in her eyes, dripping down her cheeks. "Sofia," I murmured. "My love, everything is fine."

She let me pull her to my lap, and I cradled her close. "Do not cry. It hurts me when you cry."

"You left. You left without saying goodbye."

"I wanted you to rest after your ordeal. Not sit and worry."

"I woke up, and you were gone," she sobbed. "All I could think was you didn't give me the chance to say goodbye. To kiss you one last time. To tell you how proud I was of you. How much I loved you."

"I'm sorry. But it's over now."

"Ivan is dead?"

"Yes," I replied.

"And the rest of them?"

"All dead."

"When Julian said it was all handled, the other man and his family…" She trailed off.

"Dead," I replied flatly. "They were not good individuals, Sofia. They killed a lot of innocent people."

She nodded. "I know." She drew in a ragged breath. "So, it's over? You ended it?"

"Yes."

She let her head fall to my chest, breathing deeply. Silence descended, and I sighed. "Did I also end us, Sofia?"

She snapped up her head, meeting my eyes.

"Sofia?" I asked.

"Did you end *us*?" she repeated. "That's what you think?"

"I don't know what to think. You are angry."

"I'm not mad anymore. Not at you. I can't believe Damien let you get shot."

Suddenly, I understood. Her anger was relief. Relief that she could be angry and tell me because I had come home to her. Women's emotions were a mystery to me, but one I was happy to try to solve with her.

"I know," I huffed, trying to lighten the atmosphere. "Bastard."

That made her smile.

"I will be fine."

"Yes, you will. I will look after you."

I clasped her tight to my chest. "You still love me?"

She looked up, more tears coursing down her cheeks. "I will always love you, Egan. There is no end for us. Ever. *Mio guerriero*. Mine," she insisted.

I bent and kissed her sweet mouth. Tasted the salt of her tears. Felt her fear slowly ebbing from her hold.

With a sigh, I rested my chin on her head. "I need you, Sofia."

"You have me. But, Egan Vulpe, this is the last time I am treating you for a gunshot wound, do you understand me?"

"Yes, *iubirea mea.*"

"I mean it. No more guns."

"I can't make you that promise. If you are in danger, I will protect you by any means necessary."

Her face softened.

"But since I plan on a quiet, peaceful life, I think we are pretty safe from guns."

"Good."

"We're going to the island with them. You need to take a leave of absence."

"I already arranged it."

I stood, lifting her into my arms. "Good. Now, we're going to bed, and I'm going to hold you all night."

"Your arm—"

"Is fine. I have an excellent doctor."

She cupped my face. "And I have a great warrior."

I kissed her.

"Yes, you do."

EPILOGUE

Egan

I stood in the large room, the sunlight beaming in through the huge glass doors. The whitewashed walls and simple floors were perfect. Nothing to distract me.

I stepped onto the deck, looking at the vista. This side of the island was wilder, the ocean swirling endlessly. Rocks, sand, and birds surrounded us. The sounds of the wind and the waves were all I heard. I focused my gaze on the woman sitting on the rocks, staring out over the water. I walked toward her, bending to drop a kiss to her head, then sitting next to her.

"What are you thinking, my Sofia?"

"That I've never felt such peace."

From the moment we'd stepped onto the island, we both felt it. The warmth of the sun. The tranquility of the surroundings. The love and welcome of the people here. Former colleagues, now friends. Family. We spent a couple of days simply resting. Soaking up the sun, walking on the beach. Relaxing. Sofia slept constantly, falling asleep every time she sat down, her body catching up on the rest it needed after her ordeal. She felt safe and secure. Surrounded by people who would protect her. Surrounded by me as much as possible.

I slipped my arm around her, pulling her close. "You like it here?"

"I love it."

"What do you think of the house?"

She was quiet for a moment. "I think it changed everything I thought I wanted from life, Egan."

I squeezed her hip. "Then why do you sound so worried?"

She stared out over the water, and I let her gather her thoughts. The house was fabulous. Simple, open floor plan. Three bedrooms upstairs. The main floor consisted of the kitchen, dining and living space, plus the studio at the front and another room at the back. All with views that took my breath away. Inspired me.

"I see us here," she said simply.

"And?"

"It's not what I planned. I never imagined myself on an island. I've only ever lived in a city. Worked in the ER. The hustle and bustle surrounding me. But this"— she indicated the view—"this touches something deep within me."

"Sometimes what we want changes."

She slid off the rock and faced me, standing between my legs. "But what do you want, Egan? Matteo tells me there is a clinic and a hospital on the mainland. But you have your gym, your paintings, your perfume…" She trailed off, looking upset. Her eyes were anxious, and I felt her tension.

I cupped her face. "Will you go somewhere with me, *iubirea mea*?"

"Yes."

I took her hand, and we headed for the dock. I already had the keys to one of the boats in my pocket. I guided the boat out and headed to the mainland, the short ride exhilarating. I was nervous and excited, all at the same time. Yesterday, when Damien and I had been over, I had found a place I wanted to show Sofia. I was ready for this conversation and pleased it had come up so quickly.

We held hands as we strolled along the streets, the atmosphere so different to what we were used to. The air was fresh and crisp from the ocean. Most people traveled by foot, bicycle, or golf cart. There were some scooters. The few cars around used the main road and parked, the passengers walking around the small town. It hummed with its own energy. People smiled and said hello. The aromas were pungent. Spices, flowers, food.

I stopped in front of a corner building. Sofia looked at it, confused.

"Great windows," I explained. "For my gallery."

"Your gallery?"

"Tourists love memories, Sofia. A painting of the area? They would sell like hot pies."

She glanced at me, a smile tugging on her lips. "Cakes, Egan. Hot cakes."

I frowned. "That makes no sense. Hot pie is delicious. Hot cakes? Not so much."

She laughed, and I kissed the end of her nose, loving the sound. I continued.

"This is the perfect place to display them. I could add some local art as well." I paused. "Did you know Gianna started painting? She showed me some of her canvases. They are incredible. I could sell them for her. Let her have her own identity, yet she can remain private. She needs that."

I recalled the way her eyes lit up when I asked her. Saw the cautious hope. The smile she exchanged with her husband.

"Tally does beautiful charcoals. I saw some in their house."

"I know. I plan to talk to her as well."

She met my eyes. "Is that enough for you?" she asked.

I laughed because she knew me so well. I indicated the building across the street. "A gym right there would be great. Small, but top-notch machines, amazing staff. Day memberships available. Tourists who need to work off the extra calories. A place the guys can come sweat." I winked. "They are getting a bit soft. I need to tune them up again. Especially Marcus."

Sofia laughed.

"I could employ locals for both places. Warren and Angelica could come for a visit. I bet we could find florals and spices here to make a new exotic line. I can still fly to Canada and work on other fragrances with them on occasion. You can come with me if you want. We can still connect to our lives there."

"Sounds as if you have it all planned."

"I will stay busy until we have babies for me to care for," I said.

She blinked, startled.

"I am ready whenever you are, Sofia."

"I think you might be getting ahead of yourself."

I shrugged. "Just giving you all the information." I took her hand. "I have one more thing to show you."

We walked another block, and I stopped, indicating the large building. "The hospital and clinic."

The place bustled, the line for the clinic long. "They are short on qualified doctors, Sofia. You would make a huge difference here. And I would support you. Fully."

"This is so much to take in."

"I know. You think about it and decide what you want."

We walked around a bit more. Picked up some items from the market. We loaded up the boat and headed back to the island.

I moored the boat and held out my hand for Sofia to help her to the dock. She tilted her head, studying me. "What if I wanted one more thing, Egan?"

"Then you could have it."

"Would you marry me?"

It was my turn to blink. "Marry you?"

"Yes. I want to move here. Do everything you planned. Have your babies. As your wife."

I jumped onto the boat and pulled her into my arms. I kissed her, pouring all the love, joy, and passion she brought forth into that kiss.

"Yes, *iubirea mea*. Yes."

She smiled. "*Mio guerriero.*"

I started the boat again.

"What are you doing?"

"We're going for rings."

"Now?"

"Now. And going to find the local church and set a date. Tomorrow works for me."

She snuggled into my side. "I need a few days."

"Okay. Next week."

She laughed quietly. "Next week."

The sun setting cast a myriad of colors on the water and the sand. I had never seen such brilliance.

I had never known such happiness. All due to the woman standing in front of me.

My Sofia.

She wore a creamy-colored dress, the lace of it lovely against her sun-kissed skin. Her long hair was down, hanging in waves around her shoulders and drifting across the skin of her back. The earrings I had given her glinted in her ears. She wore the yellow diamond ring I had slid on to her finger, and soon the matching band would be added, marking her as completely taken.

Completely mine.

Our friends surrounded us, and the ceremony was simple and fast. I slid her band on her finger and held out my hand to receive the heavy, thick band she had picked for me. The weight felt right on my finger, and I swore never to remove it.

I vowed to love her until my dying breath and beyond. It was a vow I would keep.

My grandmother had visited me again last night. Her smile was wide, her time short.

She cupped my cheek, her voice so familiar and warm. "Live and be happy, micul meu leu. You deserve the rest from your former life. Your new blessings will be rich with love. Enjoy the blessing your bride will bestow upon you on your wedding day."

Then she was gone. I opened my eyes to the darkness, wearing a smile. I no longer fought the truth. She had been with me.

She would always be with me.

"I pronounce you husband and wife."

I smiled down at Sofia, cupping her face and kissing her. Our friends and family clapped and cheered.

Sofia was mine.

Finally mine.

I raised our clasped hands in victory.

It was as sweet as I'd hoped.

Damien clapped me on the shoulder. "Welcome to the family, cousin."

I laughed and hugged him. All around me there was laughter. Happiness. The tables groaned with food. Music played. It was a time of celebration and love. It had taken two weeks to arrange it all, but the day had been perfect.

"Thank you."

"I never thought you'd do it. I certainly never thought Sofia would be the one to propose."

I chuckled. "She surprised me as well. But she constantly does."

Everything was moving forward. I'd rented the buildings, ordered equipment. Started interviewing. I had even painted some canvases, ready to sell. Sofia had been to the hospital. Thanks to Matteo and Geo and the connections they had, she was offered a job right away. She sent in her notice to her boss in Canada, and we planned one trip back to close out our lives there. Then we would return and begin anew.

"You make her happy."

I met Damien's eyes. "She makes me complete."

Movement caught my eyes, and I saw Sofia headed toward the beach where we had exchanged our vows. Today had been incredible and emotional. I wondered if she was feeling overwhelmed.

I excused myself from Damien and followed her.

I found her on the beach, staring at the water. She sighed as I came up behind her, wrapping my arms around her. "I knew you'd come after me."

"Are you all right, my love?"

"I'm perfect."

I chuckled. "Yes, you are."

She leaned her head back on my chest, a catch in her voice when she spoke. "I love you, Egan."

"I love you, my wife," I murmured, loving being able to call her that. "Are you sure you are okay? You seem… distracted." I had noticed her well up more than once. She had been emotional since we'd arrived on the island, often crying, which was unlike her. Typically, she was so strong. Geo had assured me it was normal, given what had occurred, when I spoke with him.

"*She cries and sleeps a lot,*" *I confessed.* "*I am worried.*"

"*She is letting out the stress and worry,*" *he said.* "*Recovering from all the anxiety. I can arrange a counselor if she wants one. But give her a little time to adjust.*"

"I'm good. So many changes," she murmured, bringing me back to the present.

"I know. Good ones, though?" I asked.

"The best." She covered my hands with hers. "And I have another one to add to the list."

"Oh?" I asked. "A big one?"

She pressed my hand to her stomach. "Well, it's pretty little right now, but that is going to change."

It took me a minute before her words sank in. My body locked down, my mind going blank for an instant. I spun her in my arms. "Sofia?" I asked, my voice rough. "You—you are pregnant, *iubirea mea?* Now?"

"Yes. My birth control failed. I don't know—"

I cut her off, kissing her hard, then pulling her into my arms. "I don't care." I recalled my grandmother's words. "This is the best gift ever."

"You're happy?"

"Happy isn't a big enough word." I was also relieved. The crying and the sleeping made more sense. She was pregnant. With my child. *Copilul meu.* I was going to be a father.

I drew back, studying her face. "Are you happy, Sofia? I know children were in the future—"

She pressed a finger to my lips, cutting me off.

"Our future is now, Egan. We're building our life now. I am thrilled."

"And you are all right? The baby is okay? Were you…" I trailed off as a thought hit me. Sofia must have read my mind and seen the worry on my face because she was fast to reassure me.

"Yes, I was pregnant when I was taken. But the baby is fine. I am fine. I was crying for no reason again, and Raven asked me if there was a possibility that I was pregnant. I was stunned when I realized I was displaying so many symptoms and hadn't noticed. With all the women here, there were a few pregnancy tests around, and I took one. When it said it was positive, Missy and Raven took me to the doctor everyone has used."

I recalled her going to the mainland two days ago. She had said it was for wedding stuff, and I hadn't suspected anything.

"The doctor said everything looked good. You can come for the ultrasound."

"I will be there for everything."

Her eyes shone in the moonlight. "I know."

I dropped to my knees in the sand, spreading my hands over her stomach where our child grew. Still tiny, undetectable to my eye, but he or she was right under my hands. Safe and protected.

The way they would be their entire life.

I looked up at Sofia, tears filling my eyes and spilling down my cheeks. "Thank you, my love."

She cupped my face. "*Tati,*" she whispered.

My breath caught and I stood, holding Sofia close.

Today, I'd become two of the greatest words in the world.

Husband.

Daddy.

My former life faded away, and all that mattered was what I held in my arms.

My family.

My greatest gift.

———

Eighteen months later

SOFIA

I stepped off the boat, surprised not to see Egan there, waiting for me. He often came to greet me after another day at the clinic, unless he was busy in the kitchen. But with our daughter teething and fussy, I had a feeling she was keeping him occupied, instead of his recipes. I strolled the sand toward our home, enjoying the peacefulness. My life had changed, morphing into a reality I had never dreamed possible. I loved working in the clinic, the atmosphere like the family practice I'd always wanted. We were busy, my days flying by. I worked four days a week plus a Saturday once a month. The rest of the time, I spent with my family and our adopted clan. Someone was always around to talk to. Have coffee with. Laugh over the antics of the children. Sip wine and complain about stubborn, overprotective husbands.

It was a common theme here with all the men.

Our house came into view, and the reason for Egan's absence became apparent. My heart filled with emotion as I climbed the steps to the deck. Egan was asleep in the hammock, Luminița on his chest, her fist in her mouth, gnawing at her knuckles, even in sleep. His big, strong arm held her tight and safe, and she was content. I studied them for a moment, wondering how I got so lucky. Egan was an amazing husband. Protective, caring, supportive. So sexy it boggled my mind. Our passion hadn't diminished over the months we'd been together. It had grown, and we could barely keep our hands off each other.

He was a fabulous daddy, loving every part of being a father. Even changing diapers. He had kept his word and stayed home with her while I went to work. He went to the mainland once a week to oversee his businesses but mostly left them to be run by the people he hired and trusted. He did a lot of work on the computer, painted, and spent time with his favorite little person.

There was no danger anymore, nothing threatening us in any way. We lived a peaceful, quiet life that we both loved. The Specialist was gone, and in his place was Egan Vulpe—the man.

I loved coming home to them, sometimes finding Egan in the kitchen, Luminița in her bouncy chair, watching him as he cooked and talked to her. Or sang. She loved it when he sang. He made up songs about her. His little light. The name suited her so well because she was the light in our lives and had been from the moment we knew of her existence. When he suggested the name,

I loved it. When he told me it was his grandmother's name, I loved it even more. I knew how much he had adored her.

I took a picture of the two of them, wondering how the news I had to share would change our world. I ran a hand through Egan's hair, and he stirred, blinking in the sun.

"*Iubirea mea*. You are home," he mumbled. "My little light and I fell asleep once she finished cutting that nasty tooth."

"I love coming home and finding you together."

He shifted, lifting his arm. "Join us."

I kicked off my sandals and carefully snuggled in beside him. Luminița stayed asleep, her lips pursing as I tugged her hand from her mouth. "I'm glad that tooth is out."

"Me as well. Maybe we can get some sleep now."

"I'll take tonight's shift."

He pressed a kiss to my head. "No, Sofia. You need your rest now."

I looked up, meeting his warm eyes and wide smile. "You know?"

"I guessed. You've been tired again. And you cried when I made you *mici* last week. And again when I showed you my new painting."

"It was beautiful," I protested.

"It was the cat, and I painted it as a joke." He squeezed me closer. "Say it, my Sofia. I want to hear the words."

"I'm pregnant again."

He kissed me, his lips soft against mine. "Thank you, my love."

"I'm cutting down to three days a week."

"Good. By the time we have four *bebelusi*, you'll stay at home with us."

"Four?" I said weakly. "I thought two would be good."

"Two is good. Four is better. Lots of little legs running around. Lots of hands to hold and kisses to be had. So much love. We will fill our home with our love."

When he said it like that, four didn't sound so bad.

I rested my head on his chest. Under my ear, his heartbeat was strong and even. Constant.

Like his love.

Egan lowered his leg to the ground, rocking us gently. The sun surrounded us, the heat of it kissing my skin. The warmth of him soaked into me. He hummed quietly, lulling me into slumber. He shifted a little, keeping Luminița safe, but resting his hand on my stomach. Holding his family. A protective, loving bubble.

Yeah, I was the luckiest girl in the world.

A FINAL GLIMPSE INTO THE MEN OF HIDDEN JUSTICE...

MATTEO

The bright sun hit the spray, sending cascades of hues across the waves. The water swirled and touched the sand, the sounds muted. An arch of flowers was a splash of color against the blue sky, the scent hanging in the air.

All were beautiful.

But not as beautiful as the woman walking toward me.

Evie. My wife.

I smiled as I watched our daughter Aria frown in concentration as she scattered flowers, carefully spreading them evenly. Behind Aria, Maia walked patiently, holding her littlest brother's hand, keeping him steady and moving forward. He wobbled a lot, muttering in his little baby voice, excited and happy. The twins, Luca and Anthony, preceded their mother, each holding a pillow with special rings I had commissioned.

They would all pause behind Aria when she would hesitate, not looking pleased at the petal distribution.

She was a perfectionist.

Evie insisted she got that from me. I didn't argue.

I rarely did with my wife since I tended to lose. She was far too clever for me.

I thought back to the day I'd found Evie. Scared, beaten, and alone in that warehouse. A witness to my killing someone in cold blood. Terrified of me, yet somehow striking something so deeply protective and passionate within me that I reacted from my heart and not my head for the first time in my life. I didn't care about the consequences, what should happen, what I needed to do. All I cared about was taking that frightened, vulnerable woman home, making her safe, and making her mine. I wanted her to look at me with love, not fear.

Instantly it—*she*—became the most important thing in my life.

That was the best decision I ever made.

Today was a gift to her. One she never asked for, never said aloud she wanted, yet one I knew would please her beyond words.

I'd married her under duress, with her in a borrowed dress and no shoes. Covered in bruises and scared out of her mind. There was no cake, no pictures, and no sweet memories for her to think about.

I wanted to give all those to her.

Aria stopped, dipping her hand into the basket. She lifted out some petals, stopped, dropped some back in and turned to add them to the ones she'd already tossed.

Satisfied, she continued. My youngest son, Dante, spotted me and broke away from his sister, lurching and stumbling around Aria, and headed my way. I stepped forward, bending low to scoop him up and carry him back to the altar as we waited for the rest of my family to join me. He gurgled and patted my face, his words barely intelligible but his happiness evident.

Everyone seated looked amused. Evie smiled widely. Maia rolled her eyes—a habit she'd picked up from Evie. She'd hate the fact that her brother had broken protocol and raced down the aisle. She'd been practicing with him for days. The twins looked bored but stayed in place, which, in itself, was surprising. I had a feeling bribery might be involved. Cake or cookies usually worked with those two. I met Evie's eyes, and they held in love and shared entertainment of the antics.

I heard the constant click of the camera, capturing the emotions of the day, the expressions we shared, and the special moments. I hoped the photographer had gotten the whole thing with Dante. Evie would love it, and I wanted her to have it all.

If I could, I would give this woman the world.

Another, more recent memory stirred, and my heart beat a little faster.

"Evie," I murmured against her soft skin as I kissed her bare shoulder.

"Hmm?" she replied, tilting her head for better access.

"I want to give you something."

She opened one eye, mischievous and sweet. "You just did that, Matteo. Twice," she stated dryly.

I chuckled and spun her in my arms. She gazed up at me, the love and desire in her eyes what I had dreamed of seeing so long ago.

"I want to marry you."

"We are married."

"I want to do it right. I want to give you a pretty wedding. A fancy dress. Flowers. Pictures. A cake and music. You never got that."

"I've never complained."

"No, you haven't. And you never will. But I see the way your eyes linger on Marcus and Missy's wedding pictures. Julian's as well. I want you to have that."

"Where?" she asked, unable to keep the excitement from her voice.

"Here. Plan whatever you want. Let's renew our vows and hang some happy memories on our walls."

She flung her arms around my neck. "Yes!"

Today was her day.

As she drew close, the breath caught in my throat. Evie's dress was lace. The palest of pink. It hung off her shoulders and flowed around her legs as she walked in a profusion of frothy material. Her light brown hair had grown blonde and gold in the constant sun, and it hung in waves over her shoulders. She wore flowers and pearls in the silky strands. The flowers she carried were the same as on the archway she moved toward to join me. Flowers from the island we loved and shared. Our safe haven.

The girls wore matching dresses in a darker pink. Lacy, fluttery, and sweet. Just like them. They loved everything girly. The boys wore simple white shirts and shorts. I wore a lightweight suit and tie, which I planned to discard as soon as the ceremony was done. Considering I had worn a suit every day prior to coming to the island, now I found them constricting and uncomfortable.

Aria stopped in front of me. "All done, Daddy."

I bent and kissed her. "Excellent petal distribution, my angel."

I kissed Maia, setting Dante beside her. "You did well keeping him in a straight line that long," I assured her.

"He's impossible," she said, trying to sound upset, but her love for her baby brother was evident.

I smiled at the twins, high-fiving them. "Good job."

They grinned, and I knew my hunch on bribery was right.

Evie stepped close, and I held out my hand, smiling as she took it.

"You are beautiful today, my wife," I said.

"Just for you," she replied.

I tucked her arm in mine. "Ready to say I do again?"

"Always."

As a family, we turned to the man who would help us renew our vows. My former colleague and most trusted friend, Marcus, grinned at us, eager to use his new license and declare us husband, wife, and family.

He winked as he opened the tome in his hands.

"Dearly beloved..."

MARCUS

"You may now kiss the bride," I intoned. I grinned and clapped with everyone else as Matteo bent and kissed Evie, wrapping his arms around her tiny frame and holding her close. It was far too passionate for public viewing, but no one cared. The kids laughed, the adults cheered, and Matteo looked proud of himself as he drew back after ravishing his wife's mouth thoroughly. Evie's cheeks were pink, and she looked dazed for a moment before shaking her head and smiling up at Matteo. He cupped her cheek, bending and pressing a kiss to her forehead, the adoration on his face saying it all.

Evie had saved him. When I'd met Matteo, he was so deeply entrenched in his life at Hidden Justice that there was nothing else in it. His entire world was meting out revenge and going after the lowest of the low humanity contained. There was nothing in his life outside of that world. His meeting with Evie began in the bloodiest of ways and ended up being the catalyst in his life. She brought him peace. Love. A new direction. Their love had been a journey. One that, at times, was interesting and amusing to witness, and at others, touching and emotional.

I met Missy's eyes. She sat with our children, our daughter beside her and our son in her arms. She was smiling widely, loving the moment, no doubt thinking about our own nuptials. Like Matteo and Evie, our relationship had begun in the most unorthodox of ways, but it became the most important connection in our lives.

We had begun during the most terrifying moments of her life. I had rescued her from a cage, forming an instant bond with her that was never broken. Protectiveness had raged within me for the shattered woman in my embrace. The trust she had shown me was incredible. I helped her recover; she helped me live. Together, we defeated the man threatening our world and came here to this island to heal and find a new path.

She blossomed, the beauty and peace of this place drawing her out. I fell more deeply in love with her than I knew I was capable of. When she'd told me I was going to be a father, my life had been complete.

I returned to the present when Matteo swooped Evie up in his arms and strode down the petal-strewn aisle, his children running behind him, laughing. Dante, the littlest one, trailed in their wake, and everyone smiled as Maia stopped and held out her hand for him, lifting him onto her back and carrying him.

They did that, Matteo's family. Helped one another. We all did on the island since we were now all part of the same family.

Everyone stood, knowing the festivities would move to the large, canopied tent. A late-afternoon meal would be served, families would celebrate, then once all the children were off to bed, the adults would enjoy the dance floor and the music. The champagne Matteo had on ice. He and Evie were headed to the mainland after the party for two nights away alone. It was all the time he could convince her to be away from their children. I had a feeling it was all the time he was comfortable being gone from them either. He trusted us to care for them, but the deep, possessive instinct he carried inside insisted he be close to protect them.

I walked to my wife, bending to kiss her. Her warm green eyes shone with love, and I cupped the back of her neck, kissing her again. Her soft hair fell over my hand, the honey-red hue now brighter from the sun she was surrounded with daily.

"Daddy, did you and Mommy get married before?"

I kissed Missy once again, then turned to my daughter, Mariella, lifting her in my arms. "Yes. You look at the pictures, baby girl."

"How come we weren't there—like Maia, Aria, and the boys?"

I sat down, placing her on one knee and taking Michael from Missy, holding him close. He was a miracle to us. After many attempts and some heartbreaks, we were sure Mariella would be an only child. Michael was unexpected, unplanned, and so loved that my heart ached with it.

"Uncle Matteo and Auntie Evie were married before already, but they wanted to do it again," I explained.

"Why?"

I looked at Missy, who grinned and tapped Mariella's nose. "They didn't have a pretty wedding like today, so they did it again. Today was just for love."

Mariella sighed, the sound far too adult for my liking. "Just for love," she repeated. "How *romantic*. I'm going to do that."

Romantic? How the hell did she know that word? She was still a baby.

Then she jumped down and raced after the bridal party.

"Not until I'm at least sixty," I growled.

Missy laughed and stood, her pretty turquoise dress fluttering in the sun. "Brace yourself, Marcus. She has a boyfriend at school now. His name is Benny. She plans on marrying him when she is ten. She was taking a lot of mental notes today. She might ask you to perform the ceremony."

I gaped after my wife as she walked away. Who the hell was this Benny boy, and why was I only hearing about him today?

How could Missy be so calm?

"Not happening," I called after her, standing and catching up with her fast. I linked our hands, keeping Michael tucked against my chest. "No boys until she is sixteen, Missy. We agreed."

"You agreed," she replied. "But I'll let you remind her. That should be interesting. She likes Benny. He brings her apples."

I huffed out a long breath. Mariella had inherited Missy's stubborn streak and my temper. She hated being told what to do. Loathed being told what *not* to do. I would have to play this carefully. I'd get Julian to help me. He would understand, given Jujube and how crazy he was about her.

"I can give her apples."

"Not with a kiss on the cheek like he does," she replied. "It's so sweet. Raven says he's a good boy."

"I'm taking her to school on Monday," I replied.

Missy laughed and walked away.

Later that night, I held Missy close, swaying on the dance floor. Despite the difference in our sizes, she fit against me perfectly. We moved well together. I loved holding her. Feeling her softness pressed against my hard chest. Inhaling her light fragrance. The sensation of her fingers on my neck as she played with my hair. I wound my fingers into her long tresses, enjoying the weight and silkiness of the waves.

"You've calmed down?" she murmured, a trace of amusement in her voice.

"Somewhat. I'm still going to school with her Monday."

"You know how many little crushes and apple-bearing boys we're going to deal with for the next twenty years?" Missy mused. "You'll give yourself a heart attack."

"She's too young to know the word romantic and be planning her wedding," I grumped.

Missy laughed, tightening her hands on my neck.

"She'll never love any of them as much as she loves you," she assured me. "She thinks you hung the moon, Marcus." She lifted up on her toes and kissed me. "So do I."

I pulled her tight to my chest, not a whisper of air between us. I kissed her until she was breathless. Until I was aching with the need I felt for her. That hadn't diminished. It never would.

"Want to meet me on the beach and skinny-dip?" I whispered in her ear.

"And ditch the wedding?" she gasped quietly.

"For a while. Matteo's already dragged Evie away. God knows if they made it off the boat—he looked so wound up. Geo and Lila have corralled all the kids, and Gianna and Vince are helping them. We could sneak away, I could have my wicked way with you and make you smile."

"You always make me smile."

I put my lips close to her ear. "And come. I'll make you come—at least three times, Missy. My hands, my mouth, my cock. All of them."

I felt her shiver. Heard the soft whimper of desire escape her mouth. I loved her noises, and that one right there was one of my favorites. I maneuvered her to the edge of the dance floor and backed us into the shadows. I swooped her into my arms and headed for the cove. The water would be warm and the area deserted and private.

Perfect.

Julian caught my eye as I turned. He grinned and gave me a droll wink, wrapping his arm around Tally.

I winked back and headed to the beach.

———

JULIAN

I tried not to laugh at the sight of Marcus carrying Missy away. He was always trying to get her alone somewhere. The love he had for her burned bright in his eyes all the time, reaching inferno proportions on occasion. Only she could tamp down the flames to an acceptable level.

Given the heartache and torment they had suffered, we were all pleased to see them so strong and in love. The birth of a healthy son had helped to heal some of their pain.

I turned to Tally, pressing a kiss to her cheek. "Hey, pretty lady. Wanna dance?"

She laughed, stroking my face. "I always love to dance with you, my husband."

I stood, holding out my hand and smiling when she slid her palm against mine. I wrapped my arm around her waist, holding her close, enjoying the feeling of her.

"Marcus dragged Missy away?" she asked, sounding amused.

"Yep."

"Think they'll be back?"

"Probably. He has no shame, and there is still lots of food and booze."

"What a wonderful wedding," she sighed, leaning her head on my chest. "Matteo made every one of Evie's dreams come true."

"That's what he wanted."

"Were you there at the first one?"

"No. He called me the day after and came to see

me." I recalled the way he'd walked into the office and sat down, looking uncommonly nervous. Matteo was always sure of himself. It made him a great leader.

"So, I have some news," he stated.

"Let's hear it, then," I replied, signing some paperwork. I hated paperwork, and this job came with a ton of it.

"I got married last night."

My pen slipped on the paper, my signature looking like a child had written it.

"What?" I gaped at him. Those were the last words I expected to hear from his mouth.

"I got married." He explained what had occurred.

"You could have brought her to me," I said. "I would have made sure she was safe. Looked after."

"No." He looked fierce. "She's mine, and I have to look after her."

I sat back, shocked. "You have feelings for her, Matteo? Already?"

"There is something," he admitted. "I know I broke protocol, but I had to. I have to be the one to protect her."

I had nothing to say. No experience to draw on with a situation like this.

"I offer my congratulations, then. I hope you will be happy."

He nodded. "I think I will be. She is—" He held up his hands, a look of wonder on his face. "She is lovely and strong. Yet, vulnerable. She needs me."

"And you need her," I replied.

"Yes," he admitted. "I think I do."

"They need each other," Tally murmured, as I finished my story.

"The way we need each other."

She snuggled closer. "Yes."

I pressed a kiss to her head. "Are you happy here, Tally?"

She looked up, startled. "You have to ask, Julian? I love it here. I love our life. I love you."

"Is it enough?"

She stopped dancing, gazing up at me. "Is it enough?" she asked quietly. "I have you. Our children. A lovely home surrounded by friends. I get to do anything I want. Paint or draw. Hop to the mainland and shop. Sit in the sun. Laugh and enjoy the company of women I truly adore. I am encircled by beauty and nature all the time. I—*we*—have a wonderful life here, Julian. I am happy, fulfilled." She cupped my cheek. "Enveloped by love. How could it not be enough?"

"I wanted to make sure I was giving you your dreams, the way Matteo is for Evie. I don't want you to ever regret choosing me."

She shook her head. "Never. My dreams changed the day I knew about Jules. They have grown and changed again since we had Joseph. My dreams are in our children. Our life together. If you're asking if I am happy, then the answer is yes. Totally."

I crushed her to me, kissing her. "I love you, Tally."

She grinned up at me. "You want to sneak away to the other part of the beach?"

I kissed her until she was breathless. "No, I want you in our bed where I can take my time with you." I kissed her again. "In fact, I want a few days with you. How about a trip to Paris? You, me, some museums, good food and wine, and lots of sex."

Her expression was filled with delight. "Yes! I would love that. I've always wanted to go to Paris."

"Then dance with me, Tally, and think about your dreams. I'll make sure they come true."

She touched my lips. "They already have."

DAMIEN

I wasn't sure what Julian was discussing with Tally on the dance floor, but it looked pretty intense for a while. Then she flung her arms around his neck and appeared thrilled, so I relaxed. Beside me, Raven sighed.

"I wonder what that was about?" she asked.

"Had an HEA, whatever it was."

She smiled, and I leaned forward, kissing her cheek. "Did I tell you how beautiful you look today?"

"A few times."

A waltz started, and Egan was on his feet, pulling Sofia with him. We watched them twirl for a moment, and I had to smile. Sofia looked so happy. Content. There was a peace about her I had never seen before. Egan adored her, and it was evident she felt the same for him. I was thrilled to see how things had worked out for the two of them.

Raven followed my gaze. "They look great together."

"I know. You up for a spin?"

"My feet hurt."

"Baby giving you a hard time?"

She nodded, rubbing her swollen stomach. I loved her pregnant. When she'd carried our son, Benjamin, I had been fascinated watching the process. Helping when I could—rubbing her sore feet, aching back. Making sure every craving was satisfied. When she gave birth, I marveled at her strength. When she told me she was pregnant again, I was ecstatic. I loved being a dad. A husband. A family. I could hardly wait to welcome the new addition.

I bent and lifted her feet to my lap, slipping off her flat shoes and rubbing the arches.

She groaned in relief. "That feels so good."

I winked at her. "Keep up those little noises and I'll be stealing you away to the beach like Marcus."

She laughed. "None of you are very good at hiding your impulses."

I shrugged. "We had to for so long, it's nice to act on them. And Marcus was always a spur-of-the-moment guy."

Egan and Sofia joined us, both smiling.

Sofia instantly slipped into doctor mode. "Everything okay, Raven?"

Raven reassured her quickly. "Yes. Just sore feet. They're swollen from all the sitting today."

"Back hurt at all?"

"No. She's moving a lot today, though."

I smiled at Raven's words. We were having a girl this time. A little Raven for me to spoil. I was excited, and we'd even picked a name. Little Rose would be welcomed with a lot of love. It was Raven's choice, after her mother, and I loved the name. She was already Rosie in my heart, and I could hardly wait to meet her.

"You should put your feet up and rest."

"Soon. I'm enjoying the atmosphere."

Egan chuckled. "The crowd had dwindled."

I laughed with him. "It seems weddings bring out the romantic in all of us."

Just then, Marcus and Missy appeared, strolling toward the table, hand in hand. Missy's hair was messy, and Marcus's shirt was buttoned incorrectly, making me avert my eyes so I didn't laugh. He was trying to look casual and not guilty. He was failing at both.

They stopped by the table. "We're, ah, just gonna head home," Marcus informed us. "Missy is tired."

Egan refused to make it easy on him. "Your shirt, Marcus. You missed a button. Or two."

Marcus glanced down as Missy let out a little squeak. "You have twigs in your hair, Missy," Egan said dryly. "You two are bad at this."

Everyone began to laugh, and Marcus shrugged, taking Missy's hand and tugging her away. "Gotta keep my woman satisfied," he called over his shoulder.

Sofia shook her head. "Good God, you sound like the caveman here."

Egan smirked and ran his hand over his short beard. "I hear no complaints."

"Whatever," Sofia scoffed. "You are all the same. Overprotective, pound-my-chest, hear-me-roar cavemen. Every single one of you."

"Would you want us any other way?" Egan asked.

She smiled. "No."

He leaned forward and kissed her soundly. "Good."

I stood and scooped Raven into my arms. "On that note, we are headed home. I have feet to rub."

Raven's voice was low in my ear. "Maybe something else to do as well?" she whispered. I bit back my grin. My wife was constantly horny. I loved this part of her pregnancy.

I strode away, leaving the laughter behind me.

"Whatever you need, Raven. I'm your guy."

"Yes, you are."

Two days later

EGAN

The sun was bright as I sat in the gazebo. All around were the sounds of the island life. Children were playing, the waves hitting the shore, the breeze pushing the water fast against the sand. Conversations drifted in the air. All the women were working on some project in the other gazebo, their laughter loud. Boats dotted the horizon, dipping up and down on the waves. I sipped my coffee, feeling the sense of rightness being here brought out. Damien and Marcus were beside me, and I watched as Julian and Tally appeared on the beach. He kissed her, and then she headed toward the women and he joined us, pouring a cup of coffee and sitting down.

None of us said much until Damien spoke. "Here's Matteo."

The boat pulled up, and Matteo helped Evie to the dock. They strolled hand in hand down the sand, stopping as Evie indicated the direction of their house. Matteo leaned down, cupping her face and kissing her, smiling indulgently as she headed home, no doubt anxious to see the children. He turned our way, helping himself to a coffee and sitting down with a grin.

"How was the honeymoon?" Marcus asked, smiling widely.

"Far too amazing to share," Matteo replied. "And far too short." His eyes softened. "I can never have enough alone time with my wife."

"I hear you," I muttered. Being a father was incredible, but I loved being alone with Sofia. Spending hours making love to her, lying with her in my arms. I felt complete and whole.

Damien chuckled. "Your girls running you ragged, Egan? Can't keep up?"

I laughed with him. Luminiţa and Ana were my heart. Sofia was my nucleus. Everything I did was with them in mind. I loved being a homebody. Being with the girls. Running my businesses from afar and letting the people I hired do their jobs. I still painted, my canvases selling well. Gianna's work was loved, and the local artists we represented earned a good living from the small gallery. I had even convinced Tally to start drawing again. Her charcoals did well. It was a booming business, and I was pleased. On occasion, I went to see Warren and Angelica, or they came here and we developed a new fragrance. I enjoyed that process as well.

But being a daddy was my favorite.

I loved our life here. The peacefulness and tranquility that surrounded us. My love for Sofia had only deepened, growing and strengthening each passing moment. My favorite time of the day was evenings, when we would tuck our children into bed and be together. I loved talking to my wife, listening to her day, showing her a new painting or sketch. Secretly loving her demands that I hang her favorites in the house. My favorite was one I did of her and our children on the beach. That hung in my office, where I could gaze at it anytime I wanted.

Which was often. My family meant the world to me.

"It's Sofia I cannot keep up with," I admitted. "Especially right now." I met Damien's eyes, lifting my eyebrows.

"Holy shit," he said. "Again? She is pregnant again?"

I grinned. "What can I say? She cannot keep her hands off me."

The men all laughed, and there were backslaps and handshakes. I was thrilled. Sofia had been shocked, although she shouldn't have been. We really couldn't keep our hands off each other, and the babies happened easily for us. I would have my four little ones soon.

Then we would stop.

Maybe.

Five was a good number too. Six was an even half dozen. I could live with that.

I sat back and looked around the table. Four men, all of whom were once strangers. Now, they were friends.

Family. Add in the bonus of their wives and children, plus Geo and Lila, Vince and Gianna, Roza and Alex. So many people. So much love. We all lived our own lives, but we came together when it mattered.

I cleared my throat, stood, and raised my coffee mug. "This should be stronger and it should be in front of everyone, but thank you, Matteo. For building this community. For this life you have offered us—free from worry. A chance for something different."

He smiled and lifted his mug. But I wasn't finished.

"Marcus, you took a chance on me, and you became my friend. My mentor. The man who believed in me and helped me become Egan again. Thank you."

Marcus lifted his mug, waiting patiently, knowing I wasn't done. "Julian, you stepped in and helped me when I truly needed it to get my Sofia back. You became so much more than just a member of HJ. You became part of my family."

Julian joined in the toast as I turned to Damien. "You, my friend. You helped me track down the man who threatened my world. You stood by me when I needed it the most. You convinced Sofia to give me a chance. You are the godfather to my little light. You are my family."

He grinned and clapped my shoulder, lifting his mug.

I turned back to Matteo. "Thank you for giving me something I was missing. Sofia and I have our roots. This place is home. For that and you all, I will forever be grateful."

Matteo stood, and the rest joined us. "To family," he said.

"To friendship," Marcus added.

"To letting go of the past and embracing the future," Julian stated.

"To our wives and children, who make this life so special," Damien said.

I caught sight of Sofia walking toward us, her dark hair glinting in the sun. She wasn't showing yet, but soon, she would. And not long after, I would have another child to love. Another link in this chain we had created.

I raised my mug higher. "To love—for saving us all."

That was a sentiment we could all agree with.

Love.

Thank you so much for reading THE SPECIALIST. If you are so inclined, reviews are always welcome by me at your retailer.

This was an interesting journey from a small serial on Verve Romance to a five-book series. Thank you for loving these alpha protective, but melts for her heroes that you asked for more.

If you have just finished Egan's story in the world of Hidden Justice and want to go back to where it all began, pick up THE BOSS and journey as Matteo unexpectedly finds love.

Enjoy meeting other readers? Lots of fun, with upcoming book talk and giveaways! Check out Melanie Moreland's Minions on Facebook.

Join my newsletter for up-to-date news, sales, book announcements and excerpts (no spam). Click here to sign up Melanie Moreland's newsletter or visit https://bit.ly/MMorelandNewsletter

Visit my website www.melaniemoreland.com

Enjoy reading! Melanie

ACKNOWLEDGMENTS

As usual, a few thanks.

To Maria Mititelu and Andrea Ridolfo – thank you for the language checks. I appreciate your help and insight!

Lisa, I am going to get you a new batch of pens, but I am going with green. I like green. Red makes me ragey. I feel it is for the best. Love you.

Beth, thank you for your support and insights. You always make my words better.

Melissa, Trina, and Deb, thank you for your encouragement, laughter, and support.

Sisters Get Lit.erary Services, thank you for your eagle eyes and assistance. So appreciated!

Kim, our conversations usually consist of a lot of head nods and hmms... we communicate on a higher level. Don't tell Karen, okay? Our little secret.

Karen, you need to get Kim to talk more. She nods a lot. Get on that okay?

Seriously ladies, you are my rocks. My advisors. My friends. Love you.

Nina (Valentine PR). Thank you for your calm, your humor, and your guidance. I appreciate all you do.

To all the bloggers, readers, and my promo team. Thank you for everything you do. Shouting your love of books—of my work, posting, sharing—your recommendations keep my TBR list full, and the support you have shown me is deeply appreciated.

My reader group, Melanie's Minions—love you all.

MLM—for all you do I cannot say thank you enough. I wish I could hug you all. Maybe one day.

ALSO AVAILABLE FROM MORELAND BOOKS

Titles published under M. Moreland

Insta-Spark Collection

It Started with a Kiss

Christmas Sugar

An Instant Connection

An Unexpected Gift

Harvest of Love

An Unexpected Chance

Following Maggie (Coming Home series)

Titles published under Melanie Moreland

The Contract Series

The Contract (Contract #1)

The Baby Clause (Contract #2)

The Amendment (Contract #3)

The Addendum (Contract #4)

Vested Interest Series

BAM - The Beginning (Prequel)

Bentley (Vested Interest #1)

Aiden (Vested Interest #2)

Maddox (Vested Interest #3)

Reid (Vested Interest #4)

Van (Vested Interest #5)

Halton (Vested Interest #6)

Sandy (Vested Interest #7)

Vested Interest/ABC Crossover

A Merry Vested Wedding

ABC Corp Series

My Saving Grace (Vested Interest: ABC Corp #1)

Finding Ronan's Heart (Vested Interest: ABC Corp #2)

Loved By Liam (Vested Interest: ABC Corp #3)

Age of Ava (Vested Interest: ABC Corp #4)

Sunshine & Sammy (Vested Interest: ABC Corp #5)

Unscripted With Mila (Vested Interest: ABC Corp #6)

Men of Hidden Justice

The Boss

Second-In-Command

The Commander

The Watcher

The Specialist

Reynolds Restorations

Revved to the Maxx

Breaking The Speed Limit

Shifting Gears

Under The Radar

Full Throttle

Full 360

Mission Cove

The Summer of Us

Standalones

Into the Storm

Beneath the Scars

Over the Fence

The Image of You

Changing Roles

Happily Ever After Collection

Heart Strings

ABOUT THE AUTHOR

NYT/WSJ/USAT international bestselling author Melanie Moreland, lives a happy and content life in a quiet area of Ontario with her beloved husband of thirty-plus years and their rescue cat, Amber. Nothing means more to her than her friends and family, and she cherishes every moment spent with them.

While seriously addicted to coffee, and highly challenged with all things computer-related and technical, she relishes baking, cooking, and trying new recipes for people to sample. She loves to throw dinner parties, and enjoys traveling, here and abroad, but finds coming home is always the best part of any trip.

Melanie loves stories, especially paired with a good wine, and enjoys skydiving (free falling over a fleck of dust) extreme snowboarding (falling down stairs) and piloting her own helicopter (tripping over her own feet.) She's learned happily ever afters, even bumpy ones, are all in how you tell the story.

Melanie is represented by Flavia Viotti at Bookcase Literary Agency. For any questions regarding subsidiary or translation rights please contact her at flavia@ bookcaseagency.com

facebook.com/authormoreland

twitter.com/morelandmelanie

instagram.com/morelandmelanie

bookbub.com/authors//melanie-moreland